JUNKYARD ANGEL

NEON MADMAN

D1073834

JUNKYARD ANGEL

NEON MADMAN

Two Scott Mitchell Mysteries

JOHN HARVEY

MYSTERIOUSPRESS.COM

OPEN ROAD
INTEGRATED MEDIA
NEW YORK

Copyright © 2016 by John Harvey

Junkyard Angel © 1977 by John Harvey

Neon Madman © 1977 by John Harvey

Cover design by Julianna Lee

978-1-5040-3888-1

Published in 2016 by MysteriousPress.com/Open Road Integrated Media, Inc.
180 Maiden Lane
New York, NY 10038
www.mysteriouspress.com
www.openroadmedia.com

THE SCOTT MITCHELL MYSTERIES

An Introduction

Growing up in England in the immediate postwar years and into the 1950s was, in some respects, a drab experience. Conformity ruled. It was an atmosphere of "be polite and know your place." To a restless teenager, anything American seemed automatically exciting. Movies, music—everything. We didn't even know enough to tell the real thing from the fake.

The first hard-boiled crime novels I read were written by an Englishman pretending to be American: Stephen Daniel Frances, using the pseudonym Hank Janson, which was also the name of his hero. With titles like *Smart Girls Don't Talk* and *Sweetheart, Here's Your Grave*, the Janson books, dolled up in suitably tantalizing covers, made their way, hand to hand, around the school playground, falling open at any passage that, to our young minds, seemed sexy and daring. This was a Catholic boys' grammar school, after all, and any reference to parts of the body below the waist, other than foot or knee, was thought to merit, if not excommunication, at least three Our Fathers and a dozen Hail Marys.

From those heady beginnings, I moved on, via the public library, to another English writer, Peter Cheyney, and books like *Dames Don't Care* and *Dangerous Curves*—which, whether featuring FBI agent Lemmy Caution or British private eye Slim

Callaghan, were written in the same borrowed *faux* American pulp style. But it was Cheyney who prepared me for the real deal.

I can't remember exactly when I read my first Raymond Chandler, but it would have been in my late teens, still at the same school. Immediately, almost instinctively, I knew it was something special. Starting with *The Big Sleep*—we'd seen the movie with Bogart and Bacall—I read them all, found time to regret the fact there were no more, then started again. My friends did the same. When we weren't kicking a ball around, listening to jazz, or hopelessly chasing girls, we'd do our best to come up with first lines for the Philip Marlowe sequel we would someday write. The only one I can remember now is 'He was thirty-five and needed a shave.'

I would have to do better. The Scott Mitchell series was my attempt to do exactly that.

I'd been a full-time writer for all of eighteen months. Spurred on, to some extent, by tales of Chandler, Dashiell Hammett—another formative influence—and others, writing for the pulps at the rate of so many cents a word, I had given up my day job as an English and drama teacher to try my hand as a hack for hire. Biker books, war books, westerns: 128-page paperbacks at the rate of roughly one a month. One of the editors I got to know was Angus Wells, with whom I would later write several series of westerns, and it was he who gave my proposal for a new crime series the green light.

Scott Mitchell: the toughest private eye—and the best.

American pulp in a clearly English setting—that was the premise. A hero who was a more down-at-the-heels version of Philip Marlowe and Sam Spade. A style that owed a great deal to Chandler and a little, in places, to Mickey Spillane. Forty years earlier, I could have been Peter Cheyney selling his publisher the idea for Lemmy Caution.

Amphetamines and Pearls—the title borrowed from Bob Dylan—was duly published by Sphere Books in 1976. John Knight's gloriously pulpy cover design showing a seminaked stripper reflected in the curved blade of a large and dangerous-looking knife. 144 pages, 50,000 words, £500 advance against royalties. You do the math.

But, I hear you asking, is it any good?

Well, yes and no. Reading *Amphetamines and Pearls* and the other three books again after many years, there were sequences that left me pleasantly surprised and others that set my teeth on edge like chalk being dragged across a blackboard.

Chandler is a dangerous model: so tempting, so difficult to pull off. Once in a while, I managed a simile that works—"phrases peeled from his lips like dead skin" isn't too bad—but, otherwise, they tend to fall flat. What I hope will come across to readers, though, is how much I enjoyed riffing on the familiar tropes of the private-eye novel—much as I have done more recently in my Jack Kiley stories—and how much fun it was to pay homage to the books and movies with which I'd grown up and which had been a clear inspiration. Inspiration I would do nothing to disguise—quite the opposite, really.

As an example, quite early on, there's this:

What I needed now was a little honest routine. I remember reading in one of Chandler's Philip Marlowe novels that he began the day by making coffee in a set and practiced way, each morning the same. It also said somewhere that Marlowe liked to eat scrambled eggs for breakfast but as far as I can recall it didn't say how he did that.

What I did was this. I broke two eggs into a small saucepan, added a good-size chunk of butter, poured in a little off the top of a bottle of milk and finally ground in some sea salt and black pepper. Then I just stirred all of this over a medium heat, while I grilled some bacon to go with it.

They say that a sense of achievement is good for a man.

And later, this:

I didn't know whether she was playing at being Mary Astor on purpose, or whether she'd seen The Maltese Falcon so many times she said the words unconsciously.

But I had seen it too.

Intertextuality. Isn't that what they call that kind of thing? Metafiction, even?

Much of the success of the book depends on how the reader responds to its hero. In many respects, Scott Mitchell fits the formula: men are always pointing guns at him or sapping him from behind; women either want to slap his face or take him to bed or both. When it comes to handing out the rough stuff, he's no slouch. Anything but. He's the toughest and the best, after all. But, personally, I find him a little too down on himself and the world in general, too prone to self-pity. On the plus side, he does immediately recognize Thelonious Monk playing Duke Ellington, he knows the difference between Charlie Parker and Sonny Stitt, and he has a fondness for Bessie Smith.

The scenes in the novel that work best, for me at least, are those in which the attempts to sound and seem American are pulled back, letting the Englishness show through. That only makes sense: it's what I know, rather than what I only learned secondhand. And what I know, of course, London aside, is the city of Nottingham, destined to be the home of the twelve novels featuring Detective Inspector Charlie Resnick.

It had been so long since I last read *Amphetamines and Pearls* that I'd forgotten that's where quite a lot of the book is set. And in the chapter where Mitchell visits the city's new central police station, there's a description of urban police work that points the way pretty clearly towards the world Resnick would step into a dozen or so years later.

Men in uniform and out of it moved quietly around the building. Policemen doing their job with as much seeming efficiency as men who are worked too hard and paid too little can muster. From room to room they went, sifting the steadily gathering detritus of the city night: a group of drunken youths with colored scarves tied to their wrists and plastic-flowered pennants on their coats; the first few of the many prostitutes whose soiled bodies would spend the remainder of their working hours in custody; a couple of lads—not older than fifteen—who had been caught breaking into a tobacconist's shop and beating up the owner when he discovered them; a sad queen who had announced his desires a little too loudly and obviously in the public lavatories of the city center; and the car thieves, the junkies, the down-and-outs.

You couldn't work in the midst of all this without it getting to you. It didn't matter how clean the building was, how new. The corruption of man was old, old, old.

And down these mean streets . . . well, you know the rest.

—John Harvey
London, December 2015

JUNKYARD ANGEL

For Cérès: approximately

-1-

I looked at my watch: three minutes off nine o'clock. I yawned and stretched my legs out straight from the chair. I had been sitting there for a long time. Had been in that room for a long time. With a few short breaks to go and take a leak, I had been there for almost twelve hours. I checked my watch again: one minute off nine o'clock: twelve hours all but one minute.

The room was cold and steadily getting colder. There was a gas fire but the gas had been disconnected. I tried to huddle up further into my overcoat, but the coat wasn't having any. Maybe I had bad breath. Maybe I just stank of too many rooms like this, too many days and nights spent watching other rooms, spying on people I didn't know on behalf of more people I didn't know. Maybe . . . but what the hell! There were always a lot of maybes hanging around, some of them trying to fool you into thinking they were something more definite. Something that would stand. Something that would last.

But they weren't fooling me. Not any more. The world was a lot of little maybes, all running round looking for answers that didn't exist. And over it all presided the Great Maybe in the Sky.

Across the road, the tall wooden door was opening at its centre. A guy came out, looked quickly up and down the street, then hurried down the steps. He pulled his coat collar up around his ears. It had to be even colder out there.

The coat was in a kind of salt and pepper fleck and it hung too low to the ground to have been his. He had dark tightly curled hair and a youngish face that looked bleak in the dull orange pallor of the streetlights. He walked quickly along the pavement and out of sight.

I made a note in my notebook. A methodical man. Method in the face of so much maybe. It didn't solve anything but it kept me in touch with some strange illusion of reality that still bounced around somewhere at the back of my head. And it might mean something to whoever was paying me for my precious time.

Not that the notebook would tell anybody very much. Except that the same guy who had walked out had earlier, walked in. Much earlier. Mid-morning. Seven after eleven to be precise. It was in the book. The book didn't say that he had come up to the place with the same quick walk, had looked around anxiously at the top of the steps before going through the door. He looked like a guy who was worried, as if he was expecting someone to jump out at him, to be watching him.

Well, someone was. I was. Scott Mitchell: private investigator.

Very private. So much so that there were weeks when the phone failed to ring and the postman failed to call and I thought that I was the most private person on earth.

Then something would turn up that would make me realise that I was wanted after all. A nice cosy little job like this one.

I glanced down at the thermos on the floor, but I knew it was empty. I looked at the transistor radio I had brought along to help while away the pleasant hours; but I knew that if I turned it on then I would be reaching out a couple of minutes later to switch it off.

I thought about the bottle of Southern Comfort I had decided that I couldn't afford to buy.

I thought about . . . steady, Mitchell, that way madness lies!

I directed my mind back to the reason for my being there. As far as I understood even that.

*   *   *

It had been three days ago and I had been sitting in what I laughingly referred to as my office, indulging in some piece of activity with the spring of my biro. Anything to prevent total atrophy. Then the phone had started to ring. The sudden sound in that empty room made me jump and I dropped the pen on to the desk. It rang on and I sat there listening to it, thinking it had to be a wrong number and watching the various parts of the biro gently rolling towards the edge of the desk.

Finally, I reached out a hand and lifted the receiver towards me.

'Mitchell,' I said.

A man's voice at the other end said, 'Ah, Mr Mitchell, I thought you were out.'

'So did I.'

'Sorry?'

'Don't be.'

There was a pause. Now it was his turn to wonder if it was a wrong number.

'You are Scott Mitchell? The private detective?'

I looked down at myself to check. 'That's me,' I told him, 'but I thought there were more of us than one.'

'Sorry?' he said.

'Let's not go through that again. You want to talk to me?'

'That's why I phoned.'

'Fine. You want to tell me now or . . .'

'I'd prefer if we met.'

'So would I. Can you come to the office?'

'Couldn't we meet somewhere else? A pub or something?'

'I could force myself into a pub.'

'Do you know the Seven Dials?'

'Sure. It's near here.'

'That's why I suggested it.'

'Smart. You sure you need a detective, Mr . . .?'

'Blagden. Hugh Blagden. Yes, I'm sure. Will eleven thirty suit you?'

'Well, normally I don't drink until after lunch, but I guess I could make an exception.'

'Do that. I'll see you at eleven thirty sharp.'

And he rang off.

I spent five minutes or so searching the carpet for the spring from my biro. Finally, the only way I found it was by treading on it. Just the thing to inspire a detective with confidence. I went out of the office, locking both doors as I did so. You couldn't be too careful. I didn't want anybody wandering in and stealing my stale air as soon as my back was turned.

I made sure that I got to the pub early and took my beer over to a table facing the door. All part of my Wild Bill Hickok complex. And I wanted to be able to pick him out before he saw me. I managed it, but not by much.

He came through the door like a man who was used to walking through doors and having people jump to some kind of attention on the other side. I hitched myself back into my chair and sipped at my beer. He was around six foot and at least a stone heavier than he should have been. He was, wearing a brown suit in some kind of shiny material, three piece, the waistcoat straining slightly over his stomach.

He stood there and checked out the customers, then finally picked me out as the man most likely. As he walked over I was thinking that he might be okay: but I wouldn't have bought a used car from him.

'Mitchell?' he asked, leaning a little over the table.

I nodded and he asked me if I wanted a drink. I shook my head and he walked over to the bar, coming back with what looked to be a large gin and tonic.

So that was the way it was. I wondered casually who signed his expenses form.

He tried the gin, took a cigar case from his inside pocket, shook out a cigar, fingered a lighter from the right hand side pocket, lit the cigar, put the lighter and cigar case back where they belonged. He blew a couple of puffs of smoke across the table, then decided to look at me.

He didn't show much but he must have liked what he saw because a minute or so later he asked me if I would like a job.

'Sure,' I told him, 'who wouldn't? Times are hard and getting harder. Or so I read in the papers.'

'That's good,' he said.

'That things are getting tough?'

'No. That you read.'

'Nice.' I applauded him quietly with three slow claps of my hands. 'You don't need a detective. What you need is a straight man. Try the home for out-of-work comedians.'

He had another go at the gin. The hand holding the cigar rested along one leg. The cigar seemed to have gone out.

'Not the home for out-of-work detectives?' he asked.

'Meaning?'

'Meaning you don't look like a man who usually orders a small beer.'

I shrugged my shoulders and wondered who was investigating who. He was turning out to be smarter than my first impression of him had suggested; but I still wouldn't buy a car from him.

'What's the job?' I asked.

He realised the cigar was out and tried to light it. He gave up and pulled his chair in closer towards the table.

'I have an interest in a large block of flats. What agents call substantial and the previous owners used to call mansions with some chance of being taken seriously. It's going to be redeveloped, only . . .' Another drink, another pull on the dead cigar. 'Only one flat is still occupied. The people have a lease and they're not being receptive to any offers we've made. It's got to the point where they won't answer any letters we write and have refused to communicate with us in any way.'

He stopped. I was sitting there looking at him, not feeling any too keen on what I had heard so far. I put my empty glass back down on to the table.

'Sorry,' I said, shaking my head, 'it's not my kind of job.'

'What isn't?'

'Hiring myself out as muscle to force people out of their

property. There are plenty of others around who'll do that with pleasure.'

'You've jumped the gun, Mitchell. That wasn't what I was going to ask you to do.'

'Okay. Fire away.'

'As far as I can find out, the leaseholders are no longer in the flat themselves. But somebody else is. Now that may mean they're subletting. If they are, then they've broken the agreement in the lease and that puts us into a stronger position in getting them out.'

'Who's us?'

'Some associates and myself. Surely that doesn't matter?'

'What do you want me to do?'

'Watch the flat. Find out who goes in and comes out. Try to establish who's living there.'

'You could go and ask them yourself—you or one of your associates.'

'Uh-uh. There's one of those arrangements you have to speak into before they open the outside door. And they're not answering. They're certainly not letting me in. Of course, they have a perfectly legal right to refuse their permission.'

'Is that how you want it played?'

He raised his eyebrows a little, as though he had not really heard what I'd said.

'Legal?'

He shrugged his shoulders. 'The way you do your work is your affair, Mitchell. As long as nothing rebounds on to me. I simply want to find out who's living in the flat and what rights they have to be there. Nothing more.'

I tried to decide whether or not I believed him. There was no reason for not doing so. No reason, just a hunch. And something about that unlit cigar held between the fingers of his left hand.

We started to talk about unimportant little things like money.

Five minutes later he was gone, leaving me with a cash advance and a telephone number at which I should contact him as soon as I found out anything definite or after five days, whichever came first.

*   *   *

Sitting in that cold room, it seemed that the five days were going to win by a walkover. Apart from the guy in the salt and pepper coat, the flat was as busy as a suburban station at three in the morning. Of course, there was a back way in—if you didn't mind cutting across a garage forecourt, ducking along a low alley and jostling with a few empty dustbins.

But people living in a place that was rightfully theirs wouldn't stoop to any such thing. I mean, why should they? They weren't criminals or anything; they weren't even squatters; they were simply ordinary folk living an ordinary life and not wanting to be pushed around by some property speculator or other.

Well, good for them! If I had a drink, I'd have lifted it high and toasted them.

But I didn't have a drink. All I had was a notebook that was mainly full of blank pages, cold feet, and an aching back caused by sitting too long in the same position.

I didn't need to look at my watch to know that it was time I took a walk.

I didn't think there'd be much point in trying the front entrance, but I did anyway. I was right. There wasn't. Okay, I said to myself, if they want to play it coy . . .

It was dark in the alley and I kicked one of the bins and sent out a little clattering echo towards the rear door. I waited for a couple of minutes to make sure there was no reaction, then followed it. Of course, the door was locked and, of course, I was able to get it open without a sound. I hadn't been a professional all these years for nothing.

I shut the door behind me. I seemed to be in some kind of passageway which led into a larder. There was a light showing at the far end. I walked towards it. Carefully.

The light was in the kitchen and it swung shadeless above a

wooden table that was littered with mugs and plates which looked as though they had been simply used and left.

Perhaps the home help was sick.

The kettle was on a ledge in the corner of the room and the lead was plugged in. I touched its side gently; it was still hot.

Well, I thought, I could always call out and ask if there was anybody home. Then again, I could take a quiet look around and find out for myself.

There were two doors off to the right of the kitchen: bathroom and toilet. Both empty. There was a large square hall with coloured tiles across its floor. Enough to roof a normal-size house. In fact, any ten people could have camped out in that hallway without ever feeling cramped.

The door to the left of the hall was slightly ajar. There were two other doors leading off; they were both shut tight. On one of the walls was a large poster for an exhibition of work by Mark Boyle. Below it, a red bicycle rested against the paintwork. It was a lady's model and looked as though it had had a lot of use. No one was using it at the moment. The rear tyre was flat with the air of a tyre that has been flat for a very long time. I thought I knew how it felt.

I went through the door that wasn't closed. The guy with the curly hair was sitting cross-legged on the floor at the far end of the room. He was sitting on a large purple cushion with a mug on the carpet in front of him. He wasn't wearing his overcoat, but I recognised him anyway.

He looked up at me with a startled expression. His mouth opened as if he was going to say something, but he must have changed his mind. The mouth stayed open so that he looked like one of the fish in the tank under the window. I started to go over towards him.

A second before what ever hit me hit me I sensed it was coming. You always can. It might be the sudden proximity of another person, the sound or the warmth of their breath, the smell of their sweat, the swish of a solid object being swung through the air. It might be some sixth sense, some conditioned reflex brought on by being hit from behind more times than can be healthy for one man.

Not that I thought about the possibilities at the time. I didn't think about anything for very long. I tried to swing round, knowing all the while that I would never make it. I didn't.

I had this final glimpse of the curly haired guy's mouth open even wider, his eyes staring past my shoulder; then someone drove a small but efficient train into the back of my head and I lost interest in anything else in the world.

I wasn't even aware of falling to the floor.

But I had. I woke up on it some time later. There was a pain in my arm and another in my right ankle. The arm hurt because I had been lying awkwardly on it; I couldn't work out what was wrong with my ankle. I could have twisted it on the way down, or whoever slugged me might have been feeling vindictive.

It didn't look as though he'd stayed around to discuss it with me. Nor had my fast-walking, coffee-drinking friend. It was just me and fishes. The least I could do was go and exchange a friendly word or two. I pushed myself up off the ground and was suddenly conscious of what felt like a hole in the back of my skull.

I put my fingers round there gingerly and was relieved to find that they didn't sink in several inches. Rather, it was the opposite. There was a bump there that would have made a maternal duck want to sit on it and hatch it out. That and some dried blood which had stuck to my hair.

The fish didn't regard me very sympathetically. They didn't regard me at all. Simply went on with their own fishy business. I reached down and shook a little food out of the cardboard container alongside the tank. It floated on the water and they ignored that too. There was something about the way they refused to get involved which struck me as admirable. For fish.

I checked my wallet. There had been seven five pound notes; they had been going to see me through some time ahead; they were missing.

I didn't like it. I didn't like losing the money and especially I didn't like being slugged and rolled like some sucker. If it got around it could be bad for business. Supposing that I had a business it could be bad for.

I shook my head to clear it but only succeeded in making things worse. I rubbed my eyes with my fingers and when they were open again I noticed the photograph.

It was standing on top of a chest of drawers behind the door, propped against the wall. A large black and white picture of a girl. I stood a while and stared at her; there was something about the way she stared back that I liked. The eyes said, I'm me and I don't care who knows it; I'm me and you can either love me or hate me, take me or leave me.

I thought I knew which I would do if I got the chance. I wondered how many others already had. I went and looked at the photo more closely.

The girl was lying along a bed, propped up on one arm. Her head was towards the camera. She was wearing a black leather jacket, which was marked enough to suggest that it wasn't her own, a short skirt and a pair of black leather boots. Her face was pale yet open; her eyes were dark; her hair was a medium browny shade and cut so that it followed the shape of her head.

She looked as though she could be very young. Like the song says, not a minute over seventeen.

Very young and very sexy.

I didn't want to leave her there with the fish, but there wasn't any point in making love to a photograph. Even I knew that. I'd tried it once or twice before.

Besides it was time I looked in the other rooms. This time I'd make sure I peeped behind the doors first.

Not that that was necessary. The first room I went into was empty, even of furniture. Just a few books propped against the wall on the far edge of the carpet. The second room had a lot more in it.

There was a table which might have been oak, a circular job with one of those massive central legs that splay out in all directions. There were four chairs set around it and an empty fruit bowl at its centre. In front of a white-surrounded fireplace there were two deep, old-fashioned armchairs covered in a floral print. High on a shelf on the far wall, incongruously, was a large television. The wall to my right was taken up with bookshelves and books. The books were nearly all leather bound and some of them were nearly as fat as they were high. They looked very dusty. Directly opposite the doorway there was one of those settees with one curved end against which ladies used to drape themselves decorously.

Only this lady was looking anything but decorous. Her dress had managed to get itself hitched up to the top of her thighs and her tights were exposed to the v where they joined. You could see the dark bush of hair underneath; she didn't seem to be wearing any pants. There was a wide ladder running down the inside of her right leg.

From where I was standing I could only see the left side of her face and what I could see I didn't like at all. Not that she wasn't pretty. She could have been; you couldn't tell. Not any more.

Somebody had given her a working over which made the tap on the back of my own head seem like a love bite from a passing gnat.

The flesh on that side was swollen out to twice its normal size and was a strange mixture of purple and dark brown. At the centre of this uneven ball of bruising, the skin had peeled back as though a bird had bitten down into it, mistaking it for an over-ripe fruit.

Above this, there was another swelling around the left eye, which was almost completely enclosed. From close-up I could see that the eye itself was still open. Half of it appeared to be covered by a bright red membrane. The other half stared up at me vacantly.

I looked at what I could of the far side of the face. It was un-touched, beautiful even. I had thought she would be the girl in the photograph but she wasn't. I was pleased, without knowing exactly why.

Except that I didn't want her to be dead. Dead like the girl who was stretched out beneath me. I wanted to pull the dress back down but I didn't. I wanted to find out what had killed her, but I didn't do anything about that either; apart from make one or two guesses.

I could do without being mixed up in a murder. At least, on what I was getting for this job. Murder came higher.

I went out of the room and shut the door behind me. The telephone in the kitchen didn't work; it had been thoughtfully disconnected. I checked my pockets for change. One call would need to be paid for, the other wouldn't.

I left the house the way I had gone in; making it seem that the door had never been locked. Then I found the nearest phone box. For a change it wasn't vandalised. After a short discussion with myself as to which call to make first, I lifted the receiver and got through to the police. They told me to wait where I was. I assured them that I would.

While I was waiting I tried the second number. The one Blagden had given me. I thought a dead body and a sapping counted as something to report.

Only I didn't like the tone the telephone was adopting. It made me feel sick low in my stomach. The operator was polite but definite: number unobtainable.

If I'd made that call first, maybe I would never have phoned the cops at all. But I had and now all I could sensibly do was wait. The fact that the proof of my reason for being in the flat, in the first place seemed to have disappeared wasn't anything to worry about. Was it?

-2-

They soon arrived and began a whole lot of measuring and dusting, taking of photographs and drawing of white lines. After a few curt questions they allowed me to stand in the corner and watch. I was the naughty boy who'd flicked an ink pellet at the teacher and been found out. In case I decided to make a break for the playground or run home and fetch my big brother, these two guys stood on either side of me looking at me as though I was someone's regurgitated lunch.

The clicking and scribbling had been going on for ten minutes or so when the guy in charge finally showed up. He had the air of a man who has just been dragged out of bed at the wrong time and for the wrong reason.

It wasn't that late and I wondered whose bed he had pulled from. It didn't need another look to tell me that I wasn't going to ask him.

He was around fifty and wore the expression of a cop who didn't particularly like what he did and so did it all the harder. I guessed that was what had made him chief inspector: but no more. His face was turning to flab low on the cheeks and around the chin; wherever he'd been that evening, he'd been careful to shave before he went. Hoods of skin tended to mask his eyes, so that the pupils looked duller than perhaps they were.

His blue overcoat made him appear bulky, even allowing for his being over six foot. I didn't think I would like to cross him, but it was already too late for thoughts like that.

He only turned his head in my direction once, when this other plainclothes man gave him a quick run-down on who I was. I couldn't tell what he thought. Not then. Later I would and it wouldn't be across a crowded room.

There was an air of suppressed excitement in the police station: maybe they didn't get too many murders. In their part of London it was mostly bomb scares at the air terminal and the odd Australian who forgot to put a match to the gas fire as he sat in his bedsit dreaming of Bondi Beach.

The uniformed man who took me down to the interview room even smiled. He must have known what I was in for.

There was another one standing in the ritual position, against the wall directly behind my chair, so that I would know he was there without being able to see him. I sat a while and waited. The chair opposite me was vacant. Possibly he was busy; possibly he wanted to make me jumpy. I leaned my elbows on the table and let a few things run through my brain.

The startled expression on the face of the curly-haired guy who had been sitting on the floor; the empty eye of the girl on the settee; the girl in the leather jacket, her face open to the world. I was wondering what the world had done to it when he came in and pushed the chair back from the table with a dull grating sound.

He stared down at me for long enough to have imprinted my face on his mind for a long, long time. Then he sat down. He took out a packet of cigarettes and lit up; he didn't offer me one.

The smoke hung lazily in the still room.

Cut off from all of the activity and expectation outside, that room was like a place out of time. A lot of things could happen there. A lot of things already had.

I sensed the man behind me shifting his weight from one foot to another.

'You're Mitchell.'

It wasn't a question, so I just sat there. A mistake. His right hand was flung out across the table and slapped me hard along my right cheek. He was wearing a heavy ring and I could feel that it had cut the skin on the edge of my cheekbone.

'Don't play dumb and don't play smart. If I ask something I want an answer. Understand?'

I must have been a bit slow in nodding. He caught me this time with the open flat of the hand. The sound rose up towards the ceiling then fell back, killed by the deadness of the room.

He fished in his pocket and brought out the wallet I had handed into the sergeant at the desk. From it he took my card and my licence. He placed them on the table between us and looked at them with a sneer. The same sneer he had on his face when he asked me if I'd been working long.

I told him how long.

He asked me how much longer I expected to go on working.

I shrugged my shoulders and said that I didn't know.

His eyes suggested that he did.

'What were you doing in the flat, Mitchell?'

He asked the question as though he wasn't prepared to believe a word I said and I told him the same way. I could have been reciting 'Goldilocks and the Three Bears.' Only this Goldilocks hadn't been asleep, she'd been dead and there hadn't been any sign of the porridge. What was more, the other two bears had split fast and left Papa Bear with the body.

It didn't look good. It didn't sound good. The guy behind me didn't like it either. He changed feet again. Nothing about the face in front of me changed.

'I know it doesn't sound much,' I said, 'but the truth seldom does.'

His sneer returned. 'Skip the philosophy, Mitchell. Besides, you've been grafting in the gutter so long that you wouldn't recognise a piece of truth if it spat in your eye.'

'If it wasn't true, then why would I have called you in the first place? Why would I have hung around for your men to arrive?'

'You called us originally because you panicked. You stuck around because you realised that you were so deep in the shit you couldn't get out without falling head first in it and suffocating. You're a cheap hoodlum who thinks that a couple of words like private investigator after your name give you the right to take the law into your own hands. You broke into the flat illegally and found the girl there. You tried to get something out of her. It might have been information and it might have been sex. Who knows? It doesn't much matter. What does matter is that she wasn't giving you what you wanted so you beat up on her and you beat up too hard. Then you thought up this cock and bull story and tried to save your hide by trying it out on us.'

He looked across the table at me like he was looking at a piece of rotten meat someone had brought in from the abattoir we call the world.

I thought it was time to level with him. 'You're talking crap! I'm not the one who's up to the ears in shit, that's you! Up to the ears and beyond. You've been doing your job in your own stupid way so long that the shit's oozing out of your ears and eyes and pouring from your mouth each time you open it to speak! If you checked up on the couple of names I gave you, then you'll know that whatever else I might do, there's no way I'm going to throw a panic. I'm a professional, too. As much as you are. The only difference is that there are times when my eyes actually open and I can see things through them. What's more, I'm not into slapping people around the head. That seems to be more in your line. Come to think of it, where were you earlier this evening, chief inspector?

'Oh, and one more thing, she didn't die from the beating up. She died from something else.'

He hadn't tried to say anything; he hadn't interrupted. He had sat there and taken it, his face growing a stronger shade of purple as he listened. Now that I had finished he didn't do anything either. Not immediately.

Then his eyes went past mine to the uniformed man standing at the back of the room. They motioned him towards the door. I heard it shut hollowly behind him. Watched the man in front of me stand up.

He walked round behind me. Stood there. The muscles at the back of my neck tensed for a blow that didn't come. Not yet.

When he did speak his voice was low, controlled. I wondered how much effort that control took.

He said, 'How do you know the beating didn't kill her?'

I said, 'I don't. It just didn't feel right.'

He stood there, not saying anything. His presence bore down on me.

'What did kill her?' I asked.

I thought he wasn't going to answer, but then he said, 'Somebody injected an overdose of something, probably morphine, into her system.'

I thought about it for a while, then said, 'Or she did it herself by mistake.'

I couldn't see him shake his head, but I thought he might have. 'She was a regular user, from the marks on her. She would have known what she was doing.'

'On purpose then?'

'Suicide? No note, no explanation. How many cases do you know of people who've killed themselves right after being smashed around the face the way she was?'

He was right. I didn't. He didn't. Two professionals together. But he was still standing behind me. The muscles in my neck were still tense, waiting.

'Get up.'

I got up.

'Turn round.'

I turned round.

'All that stuff you gave me a few minutes ago. You know there's no way you're going to get away with that, don't you.'

I knew. I told him so.

Still he did nothing. Just looked, his face very close to mine. I could smell something on his breath that might have been brandy and I wondered again where he had been earlier. Not that I supposed it really mattered. It was just that I had a naturally curious mind.

Something to do with my line of work.

'Are you charging me with anything?'

His eyes told me he wasn't.

'All right if I go then?'

He said, 'Get out!' through his teeth. But he still didn't move out of the way; even without his top coat he was broad. I couldn't figure out why he hadn't hit me again.

He said, 'There's no hurry for me, Mitchell. I can haul you in any time I want you. And want you I do. But I'll wait until the right time, when you can't wriggle out. Then I'm going to throw everything possible at you and you'll wish that licence of yours was somebody else's confetti.'

I turned my back on him again and picked up the licence and my card. Something plopped on to the table alongside my hand. My wallet. I put the things back inside it and slipped the wallet into my inside pocket.

I didn't like the way it felt light; I was still annoyed about getting taken for the money. I knew that I was going to try to get it back.

I faced him again. 'There's nothing else?'

There wasn't anything else. I stepped around him and walked to the door. When I opened it to leave and looked back he was still standing close to the desk, looking over at the blank wall: a man with things on his mind.

But then, who didn't?

The car crawled along the kerb as though it was aiming to pick up a girl walking home alone and late. It was a dark Ford and there were three men in it. One in the front, two at the back. It had caught up with me by the time I reached the Natural

History Museum. It was unmarked, but I thought I could guess where it had come from; who had sent it. It wasn't looking for girls.

There didn't seem to be anything else to do, so I carried on walking. I didn't even have enough money for a cab. I thought of waiting for the car to catch me up and asking them for a lift.

After all, they could follow me better if I was inside there with them. But I didn't want to be in there with them. I didn't want to be with them at all.

I had the usual kind of choice: none.

I walked on. The car followed slowly, fifty yards behind. At least there was no danger of feeling lonely.

I had a flat, but that was too far away so I thought I'd go back to my office near Covent Garden and spend the rest of the night there on the sofa. I could use a good sleep. There were a lot of things I wanted to do in the morning.

Like see if I could track down Mr Hugh Blagden.

Like taking a look for the guy in the pepper and salt overcoat.

Like calling Tom Gilmour at West End Central and asking him a few questions about a West London cop with preoccupations.

Like . . .

I realised that the sound that had accompanied me for so long had disappeared. I looked round and the car squatted close to the kerb, stationary.

They couldn't have run out of petrol. Perhaps they'd simply lost interest. Then again, they might have realised where I was going. I turned a corner and when next I looked back there was nothing but a grey and white cat stalking the empty street.

The office was up a couple of flights of stairs with a landing in the middle. It was dark but I didn't bother with the light. Why should I? I'd been up them enough times before. Knew the number of steps, the number of paces along the lino-covered floor to the outer office door.

I unlocked it and stepped inside. Still I didn't reach for a light switch. The second door now. Inside, I nearly locked it behind me but what was the point? I didn't want the door kicked in. I couldn't afford to pay for a new one.

This time I did flick on the light. Just for a moment. There were one or two things I wanted to do, one or two things I wanted to stash away where even the most prying eyes might not find them. Things like my Smith and Wesson .38. I didn't want them getting the wrong ideas about me.

I put out the light and went over to the window. I was in time to see the dipped headlights ease along the street, then halt, then cut off. I went over to my desk and sat in my chair. It was quiet enough to be able to hear their footsteps all the way up the stairs, even through the two closed doors. If you listened very hard.

I was listening very hard.

One of them stopped half-way up; the other two kept on coming.

Then they were in the room. Big men. Hard, anonymous men. Night visitors. They had nothing against me; I had nothing against them. The finger had been pointed. They had a job to do. I hoped they were good. I hoped they wouldn't be careless or messy.

I stood up. One of them switched on the light. I looked at them: the faces, the trilby hats, the suits. I had seen them a hundred times before: I had never seen them in my life.

A hand switched out the light. They came towards me. I moved out from behind my desk to meet them.

I knew I couldn't just stand there. Even this game had rules. I feinted towards the one on the right and threw a punch at his partner. It caught him on the jaw and sent him staggering back across the office carpet. At roughly the same time a fist landed hard against my ribs and another went in lower down at the centre of my stomach. My head folded forwards on to the bones of his knuckles.

I shook my head and tried to step out of reach. All I did was step into the arms of the guy I had punched. And he wasn't asking me to dance. Not this time.

He grabbed both arms and held them fast, then brought me sharply backwards so that his upraised knee struck me in the small of the back. I shouted out something which was cut off by a fist full in the face.

I think one of them said something at this point, but I couldn't be too sure. One of them held me while the other one hit me, mostly about the body now. No longer hastily, but with a lot of deliberation.

I had shut my eyes but when they opened involuntarily for a second I saw the figure of the third man standing in the middle of the outer office, watching through the open door. Not a face, an identity; merely a shape.

The one who was holding me got tired of it and they changed round. Pretty soon, it didn't matter which of them was hitting me. Just as long as they stopped.

They did. Suddenly there was no one holding me and I was vaguely aware of the floor coming up to meet me for the second time that night. Then nothing . . .

When I came to there was something lying close to me that seemed to be in pain. Something that hurt. A body. It was several minutes before I realised that it was my own. I didn't want it. To hell with it!

I lay there a while longer but it didn't crawl away. It got so that I didn't think it would. I picked it up carefully off the carpet. It tried to fall down again so I leant it against the side of the desk for a few minutes.

My eyes blinked back the daylight from the window. My watch had stopped. My throat felt thick and my tongue tasted like yesterday's news.

They had gone through the filing cabinet, the cupboard, the drawers of the desk. Papers were strewn across the room; two empty Southern Comfort bottles stood side by side close to the door. I didn't know what they had been looking for. Perhaps they hadn't known either. Perhaps there hadn't been anything to look for. Perhaps it was just the natural course of events: you knocked a guy about on his own premises and then you searched them.

It was the way of the world.

At last I thought my body and I could make it back together again, so we moved away from the desk and stood on our own two feet.

It was a lonely thing to do.

I reached over to the phone and dialled the time. It was seventeen minutes after ten precisely. At the third stroke.

I started to pick up the papers from the floor, but each time I bent down if felt as though someone inside my head was trying to knock his way out with a heavy duty chisel. So I decided to leave the mess where it was and go out and buy myself a cup of coffee. Better, three cups of coffee. There was this coffee shop down the road where they made really good coffee.

As I passed the mirror I'd put in the outer office so that my clients could tidy themselves up while they were queuing up to see me, I caught sight of someone who bore a passing resemblance to somebody I used to know.

I looked again. If I went into the coffee shop looking like that they'd probably call the cops.

I went back into the other room and cleaned myself up at the small sink in the corner. After several minutes I decided that it wasn't going to make any difference but I needed the coffee enough to take the risk.

The stairs took a long time to get down and by the time I was out on to the pavement, my ankle was aching again. The least of my troubles, I concentrated on it like mad until Tricia had poured me my coffee and I was sitting down staring at its dark brown surface.

−3−

The place was small and friendly enough without getting intrusive. Upstairs they sold health food and down where I was sitting they had things like chick peas and lentil soup. And cheesecake. And Brazilian Plantation coffee.

The tables were scrubbed and varnished pine, with rush mats and dark wooden bowls of soft brown sugar. The first cup of coffee tasted good, the second even better. I was half-way through this when three young girls came in.

They were smartly dressed and nicely made up and they couldn't have been any older than fourteen. I wondered idly why they weren't at school.

They sat down at the table next to mine without noticing that I was there. One of them went up to the counter and ordered three portions of cheesecake and three coffees. When she got it back to the table they started to talk in low voices about how much it had cost and how much they had left. They began to push coins across the table from one to the other.

I went and got my third coffee. On my way back I noticed the girl in the middle. Her hair was long and fair and she had a face that was perfect. I watched her again when I sat down. When she opened her mouth to speak she showed a flawless set of white teeth and tongue that was pink and pointed. She was eating blue-berry cheesecake.

She dropped a coin on to the floor and it rolled near my feet. I could have reached down and picked it up. I didn't.

Her friend got up and bent down for it. I sat a while longer, sipping my coffee and watching the girl as she put the cheesecake into her mouth with her fork.

She still didn't know I was there. None of them did. I put my empty cup back in my saucer and walked up the stairs. Half-way up I remembered that my ankle hurt.

Back in the office I tried to raise Gilmour but the cop on duty said that he was out. I looked in the phone book for Hugh Blagden. There were thirteen Blagdens in the book, none of them with the initial letter H. I tried the numbers anyway.

One was a fishmonger and poulterer, one a chemists' merchants; another was a spinster lady of somewhat advancing years who thought I was the young man from the book department at Harrods. The rest were either out or so far away from being any use as to be impossible.

I dropped the book to the floor and tried West End Central again. Tom had that minute got back into the building. After a couple more minutes he was at the other end of the line.

'Hello, Scott, what's up?'

'Have you read the papers?'

'Not yet. Should I?'

I told him he should and waited while the rustling of pages sounded down the line from his desk.

After a while he said, 'You mean the dead girl in Earls Court?'

'That's the one.'

'How are you mixed up in that?'

'I found her.'

'They haven't given you a name check.'

'You're surprised?'

He wasn't. He asked me what had happened. I told him. It sounded even sillier this time.

'Who did you have to pull that one on?'

'A heavy guy with a face that's getting flabby and a lot on his mind.'

'Hankin?'

'I guess so.'

Tom whistled down the phone.

'You know him?' I asked.

'By reputation. I've seen him a few times, passed the odd word. Nothing much.'

'Would he be the kind of guy who would send a nice little visiting party out to tuck me in for the night?'

'He might. That would depend if you gave him cause.'

I let that one ride. I said, 'He seemed very preoccupied. Any ideas about that?'

A slight pause, then, 'Could be he's snowed under with work. Could be trouble at home. Anything. Perhaps he didn't need another case dumped on him. Especially not a murder.'

'Maybe.'

'Does it matter?'

'I don't know. It might. Probably not, though.'

'You've no idea where this character who hired you might be?'

'None at all.'

'Then you'd better find him. You might end up needing him.'

'And just how do you suggest I go about doing that?'

'Why ask me? You're the detective.'

'So are you.'

'Sure. But I don't want to find anybody called Blagden.'

'Thanks, Tom. You're a great help.'

He laughed pleasantly down the line. 'That's okay, Scott. Anytime. Anytime at all.'

And he hung up. Fast.

I took a slow walk down to the Seven Dials and asked the barman some questions about the man in the brown suit I had met there several days before. He didn't remember seeing him; he didn't even remember seeing me. He told me I looked as though I could use a drink but not in such a way as I thought he was offering to buy me one. I left the pub and took a tube down to Earls Court.

I got into the room opposite the flat I had been watching and picked up the few things I had left behind. From the window I could see a uniformed cop standing guard on the front steps and I didn't need to walk round the back to know there would be another one round there.

A few buildings further along there was an estate agent's board advertising flats to let. Across it had been posted diagonally the words, 'One Remaining.' I made a note of the address and left clutching my thermos and transistor. I would pay them a visit but not until later, when I had been able to do something about my appearance.

Some sticking plaster and a suit that was recently back from the cleaners made me look more presentable. After all if I was going to make enquiries about property then I had to create the right sort of impression. I would be getting close to life's real nitty gritty: property was what it was mostly about . . . wasn't it?

I found a hat that was big enough to cover the bump on the back of my head and set off for Knightsbridge. I wasn't going to waste my time with any old two bit estate agent. Not me. I was after the big time.

From the minute I entered the place I could tell that I was going to get it. The carpet was several feet thick and when I stood in it my shoes disappeared from sight. Behind a glass desk, a brunette with tied-back hair and rimless glasses was talking into the telephone. She was dressed like something out of *Vogue* and she had all the warmth of cut-glass. If you liked cold things she was very beautiful. I didn't think that I did, but I stood there staring at her anyway, up to my ankles in deepest acrilan. Wide-eyed and legless.

To the right of her desk there were two doors with discreet little nameplates on them. I could see from where I was that neither name was Blagden. But what's in a name?

There were two canvas and chrome easy chairs and a round glass table with a handful of magazines on it. They didn't look like the kind of thing I usually read. Possibly that was part of my trouble.

She had put the phone down and was looking at me. Something about her expression suggested that she thought I had stepped into the wrong place by accident. I wondered where she thought I should have been.

Eventually she accepted the fact that I wasn't going to turn right around and walk out again. She asked, 'What can I do for you?' in a voice which sent a shiver along my spine and released several ice crystals into the atmosphere.

I tried a smile. Just a little one. For one thing I didn't want to overwhelm her—not all at once—and for another I didn't want to risk the plasters on my face working loose.

I said: 'I'm looking for a flat.'

I might as well have said I was looking for a rare edition of a book about early Eastern religions.

'A flat?' I prompted her.

'Sorry, we don't have any.'

'You don't have any flats?'

'We don't have any flats.'

'You are an estate agents?'

Her lips formed a tight line across her face. Then she said, 'Of course, we are. What did you think?'

'I thought you might have changed over to the deep freeze business. They tell me it's all the rage. Did you know you could buy boxes of five hundred fish fingers at the most alarming discount?'

I couldn't understand it. She didn't seem interested. The phone on her desk rang and she picked it up on the first note.

'No,' she said. 'No, I can't. No, I'm busy. There's someone in the office. Yes, all right. I'll call you back. Good-bye.'

By the time she had replaced the receiver she was looking slightly flushed. Only a trace of reddening around the cheeks but I didn't think it did her any harm at all.

'He'll understand,' I said, quietly sympathetic.

'What business is that of yours?' she snapped.

'It isn't.'

'Then what is?'

'I told you, I'm looking for a flat.'

'And I thought I told you that we don't have any.'

I took my notebook from my pocket and read her off the address I had seen advertised.

'That's already been taken.'

'But the sign said one was left.'

'Well, I'm sorry, but it's gone. We should have changed the notice.'

'As long as you're sorry. But you must have some other things you could offer?'

She shook her head.

'You do handle a lot of property in that area?'

She shook her head the other way.

'I noticed a large place across the road from there. Wentworth Mansions. They all seemed to be empty. Is that one of your properties?'

She flushed again. 'Yes. That is, no. I . . . I'm not sure.'

'You're not sure?'

'Not exactly. You would have to talk to Mr Cooper about that.'

I tried a step towards one of the doors. 'Mr Cooper. Is this his office?'

She was half-way up out of her seat. 'I'm afraid Mr Cooper is out at present.'

'And Mr Barnard?' I asked, reading the name off the other door.

'He's out as well.'

I turned and faced her quickly. How about Mr Blagden?'

She stared back at me, but if she was covering up she did it very well. 'Sorry,' she said, 'we don't have anyone of that name working here.'

'My mistake.'

'Yes, wasn't it.'

She was sitting down again and back in control. The area of carpet between us seemed just as wide.

'I'm sorry to have troubled you,' I said.

She didn't assure me that it was all right; she didn't smile. She got up from her chair and walked all the way round the desk and over to the door.

She stood by it looking at me and I thought for one moment she was going to turn the open sign to closed and pull down the blind. But she didn't even take off her glasses. She opened the door and held it open while I walked through and out on to the pavement.

Oh, well, I thought, she probably hadn't even seen the movie and if she had she wouldn't have liked the part.

I was on my way back to the underground station, when I glanced up and there he was. Sitting in the downstairs front seat of a double-decker bus. The curly hair, the overcoat—I couldn't miss them; even the nervous look on his face.

I ran across the road, causing a taxi to swerve round me as I did so. The driver's words of good fortune followed my erratic chase along the edge of the pavement, one foot, sometimes two, taking to the gutter as I attempted to keep out of people's way without slowing down.

Thirty yards in front of me there was a bus stop with a small queue; the bus was pulling in towards it. I tried to increase my speed but my chest was starting to tighten and burn and my ankle felt as though it was going to give out on me altogether.

I finally made it with three large left-footed hops which took me on to the edge of the platform. Anxiously I looked along the bus; he was still there. Whatever else I did now, I couldn't risk letting him see me.

I paid the conductor and went upstairs, sitting at the back so that I could see the platform below through the circular mirror. I would have to get down quickly, that was all there was to it.

I sat there and got as much of my breath back as I could, hoping that he wouldn't move too soon. He didn't. I paid two lots of extra fare before he stirred.

I hovered on the stairs and watched him get off and look around in his usual worried manner. He finally went to cross the road behind the bus and I watched him go, then jumped off as it was gathering speed. It was okay; there was a large privet hedge to break my staggering fall and I had managed to land on my good leg. Things were starting to look up.

I let him get a good way ahead of me, without risking losing him if he took a sudden turning. But he seemed content to walk easily now, confident of where he was going.

As we went from side road to side road the houses got smaller, more cramped together. Some were painted in new, garish colours, purples and yellows; others had paintwork and plaster flaking off them like a disease. It was outside one of these that he eventually stopped.

He did his, usual little look round but I was ready for it and had ducked back out of sight. He knocked a couple of times on the front door and after a few moments it opened. There was a brief conversation and he went inside.

I waited a while, then crossed the road and walked by on the opposite side.

What looked like an old blanket had been draped across the window of the downstairs room and the bottom pane of glass had been broken. Cardboard was propped uneasily behind it. There was net curtaining at one of the upstairs windows, nothing at the other.

I walked on to the cross roads, then switched sides again. The garden at the back ran on to the garden of the house behind; there was no proper rear exit.

I went back and waited within sight of the front door. I didn't know how long he would be, but if he'd gone for what I thought, then it wouldn't be too long.

It wasn't.

A little over half an hour later he came out. The door opened just enough to let him through and no more. I couldn't see anything or anyone else.

I let him get a good start and began to tail him back to wherever he was going. It was tedious and boring, but it might be necessary. Besides, I was used to it. Much of my job consisted of the same dull routine. Only interrupted by the odd blow to the back of the head, the boot in the guts.

Still you carried on, following up leads that seldom went where you expected them to. You kept chasing them down and somehow, somewhere you found yourself with something useful. Not often. But it did happen. And it was better than standing still.

We caught a bus back towards the centre of town; my mind on him, his mind on who knows what.

He got off the bus and on to a tube and I watched him through the windows of the communicating doors. His eyes closed, he sat with his head back against the woodwork at the top of the seat. After a couple of stops, he lifted his head and looked at the map of stations opposite. Satisfied, he put his head back and closed his eyes again. His right hand went into his overcoat pocket and stayed there. As though he had something he wanted to keep safe.

I held on to the strap and watched over him, as though watching a sleeping child.

We got off the train at Camden Town and I followed him up the escalator. At the top he went through his hesitation routine, took a few paces to the right, checked, went to the left, then left again to the row of telephones. I stood at the bookstall and shielded my face with a newspaper while he dialled a number.

The girl's death was already off the front page and I turned over to find it near the foot of page five. There was nothing new. Except, of course, that the police were confident of making an early arrest. Chief Inspector Hankin was anxious to talk to a man named Trevor Warren, who was believed to have been staying at the flat where the girl's body had been found. He was in his twenties, with dark curly hair and a pale complexion.

He pushed his coin into the slot and started talking. After a while, he stopped talking and listened. He listened for several minutes. Without saying anything else he hung up.

When he came out of the phone booth and crossed the station forecourt towards the far exit, Trevor Warren seemed a very worried looking young man.

-4-

I followed him as he turned left and jogged across the busy road, overcoat flapping loosely around the bottoms of his legs. He hurried along the pavement, head down, hands in pockets. Every now and then he would stop an instant and shoot his head round nervously, like a bird.

I guessed that whoever he had spoken to on the phone had told him that the police were looking for him. He was probably seeing dark blue uniforms in every other doorway and behind every curtain.

What he didn't see was me: I could follow my own mother into the john and still she wouldn't know.

We passed the Catholic church, the bakery and then the railway station. He stopped to buy a paper; stood on the island in the middle of the road, thumbing through it. He found the column he was looking for. I watched him read it. I watched him carefully.

His skin couldn't have gone any paler, but his eyes seemed to widen then set up a feverish blinking; his head began a series of tiny shakes from side to side, the curly hair bobbing to a spastic rhythm of its own.

He tried to fold the paper. There was no way that he was going to make it. It took on a life of its own, the pages curving out of his hands at will. Finally, he pulled his fingers away from it and let it fall slowly, crazily to the ground.

The wind peeled off page after page and moved them across the road, wrapping them round car wheels as they went.

He stood there and looked after it, helplessly. The hands began to shake now. He jammed them deep into the pockets of his coat. Closed his eyes. Swayed slightly.

I stood in the shelter of a shop doorway and watched him going to pieces. It was getting cold. I wished he would do something, move somewhere else.

Then he did. He turned and walked down the steps of the Gents that was underneath the road island. I wasn't immediately sure what to do, but I decided that I'd wait for him to come back up. For a while anyway.

He must have found a lot to do down there. Perhaps they had a good standard of graffiti. I wouldn't know. I was just waiting in the doorway of a dry cleaner's, getting progressively colder and more fed up with hanging around.

Ten minutes. That was long enough for any man. For any man who had looked as though he was in a hurry to get somewhere. For any man who had something in his overcoat pocket that he had made a long journey to collect.

I crossed over to the island and stood at the top of the steps. I couldn't see anything and I couldn't hear anything either. I started to walk down the stairs. Half-way down I heard a cistern begin to flush and then one of the door bolts being pulled back. I hurried back to the top and over to my cleaner's. The amount of time I'd spent in their doorway, they could have given me the full works right down to my pants.

I turned my head away as he got to the top of the steps and looked around. Even at a half glance I could tell that he was feeling better. The twitching had stopped and his eyes were steady in his white face. Something had done him a lot of good. For now.

He carried on his way and I waited the usual time before picking him up again. This time it wasn't far. He turned into a block of small flats and went into the first of four entrances. I hoped he would wait for the lift.

He did. I matched its speed on the stairs and was ready when it stopped on the fourth floor, flattened back against the wall on the flight below.

There were two doors on each floor and he rang the bell at the one I couldn't see. I edged up higher. There didn't appear to be any answer. I wondered what he would do, whether there was supposed to have been someone there to let him in. But it didn't make any difference. When it was obvious that no one was coming, he fished in his pocket for a key and unlocked the door.

Which meant that he was almost certainly now in the flat by himself.

Which meant that it might be a good time to go visiting. There were some questions I wanted to ask and I figured that I had waited long enough to ask them. It seemed that the only person Trevor Warren was going to lead me to was Trevor Warren.

And if I could find him, then so could the cops. I'd rather he answered my questions than theirs. I didn't know if he would see it the same way, but I thought it was a good time to find out.

I went over to the door and rang the bell. Of course, there was a good chance that he wouldn't answer the door. Not with the nervous disposition he seemed to have: But some of the nerves had been calmed, and, besides, he could have been expecting someone.

Whatever the reason, he opened the door.

Not far, but far enough for me to push my big foot inside so that he couldn't slam it shut in my face. If he didn't like my face. He stared at it; recognised it. No, he didn't like it.

Well, it was a point of view. Lots of people haven't liked it. From time to time they'd tried ways to change it. Usually none too subtle at that. The subtle ones had been those who had tried to change what was behind it. Instead of the bunched fist, the soft kiss that sought to suck out your brain.

Warren was still trying to shut the door on it. I didn't think I was going to let him. I rocked myself back a little then crashed my shoulder hard against the door.

He went backwards across the tiny hallway as though he'd had a sudden electric shock. He was still sliding down the wall when I was inside with the door shut behind me and my hand on the lapels of his jacket,

'Hello, Trevor,' I said. 'Nice of you to remember me.'

I helped him through the fiat into the room on the left that looked as though it was going to be the living room. It was. There was a moquette settee in the centre and the springs were starting to sag. When I dropped him down on it, he hardly bounced at all.

'What . . . what . . . ?'

It was the best he could do. At the moment. He was going to need a little help and it was going to be my kind, not his.

I stared down into those frightened eyes: all the terror that be had been feeling earlier had returned. They were wide, wide and dark. There was a fear reflected in them that I was certain was more than a fear of me, more than a fear of the cops, more than anything I had yet worked out.

I didn't like it.

I didn't like it but that didn't matter.

I said: 'We've got to have a little talk, Trevor.'

He gulped in some air and stared back up at me. Then the blinking started again.

I got nearer to him and put out my right hand towards his face. He flinched and his eyes clenched tight shut. But I didn't hit him. I took his jaw in my hand and held it, firmly but gently. His skin under my hand was smooth, smooth and cold. Like a child.

'You know the police are looking for you?'

He nodded. Only fractionally, but it was enough.

'They won't be gentle with you Trevor. You see these plasters on my face? They paid me a visit. They wanted to ask me some questions. Now, you wouldn't like that, Trevor, would you? You wouldn't like that at all.

He shook his head. The smooth skin slid back and forth underneath my fingers.

'How . . . how did you know . . . ?'

Again the question didn't finish; I finished it for him: 'Where you were?'

The eyes said yes, that was it.

'I followed you, Trevor. This afternoon, I followed you.'

'No!'

He tried to pull his face away but my fingers gripped the bone of his jaw, gripped it and pushed up against his gums.

'Yes, Trevor, I know where you went. I've got a good idea what you went there for. The police might like to know as well. I might have to tell them. Unless you tell me what I want to know first.'

I relaxed my grip and he closed those dark eyes and sat further back on the settee. His arms were by his sides, hands clenched tight.

He looked up. 'What do you want to know?'

'I want to know about the flat that you were living in. Who else was living there? Who the girl was who was dead when I arrived? Who killed her? Who the girl is who was in the photograph? Who the man is who calls himself Hugh Blagden? I want to know a lot of things.'

He thought about that for a minute or two while I watched him, then he said, 'What will you do then? Will you help me to get away?'

I didn't answer. I didn't feel like lying.

He knew that I wouldn't help him. He started to shake again. He pushed himself forwards and when he spoke again his voice was louder, more shrill.

'You'll use me,' he said. 'Use me like everyone else tries to and then let the police have me. Well, I won't play that game any more. I won't!'

And then he surprised me. He launched himself at me, head first into my stomach. The charge caught me off balance and I went back towards the wall, tripping over a small coffee table as I did so. He swung a punch that missed me by several feet, then ran for the door.

He almost made it. His hand was on the chrome handle when I grabbed him, with my left arm tight around his neck. My other hand chopped down on the fingers that were closing on the handle. He shouted out and I hit him again, this time in the kidneys. I felt him go limp against my arm and swung him round.

I threw him at the settee. He didn't bounce this time either. Just flopped there like a bundle of old clothes.

I went back over to him. He was breathing heavily and trying to massage his side where I had punched him. A trail of mucus was slowly running down from his nose, curving over his upper lip like the path of a wayward snail.

I said, 'That was very silly, Trevor. I thought we were getting along fine.'

He glanced up at me for a second, then looked down at his feet again. I didn't want him thinking about his feet, I wanted him thinking about the other night. And fast. Something told me it wouldn't do to hang around too long.

I said, 'Trevor!' and when he looked up I hit him. Not too hard. Enough to jerk his face sideways and stop him getting lost in his own thoughts.

I wiped the wet from his face off against my trouser leg.

'Now, Trevor, are you going to be a good boy and tell me what I want to know?'

He raised his head slowly, frightened of being struck again. But I didn't need that any more; neither did he. He said it so quietly that I could hardly hear him, but he said, 'Yes.'

I relaxed my muscles.

And then I heard the door open behind me. I don't know who I was expecting to see standing there, but it wasn't anybody that I had ever seen before. I did recognise what was in his hand: it was a Smith and Wesson .38. I didn't like the look of it. Not at all. Especially the way it was pointing: straight at my stomach.

From behind I heard Warren standing up, saying something which might have been, 'Don't.' I wasn't thinking about that. I was concentrating on the man in the doorway: the eyes: the finger on the trigger. He was going to use it.

He knew that.

I knew that.

I was too far away to hope that I could jump at the gun before he could fire. Not a chance that way. Not a chance. I jumped.

I was somewhere in mid-air, arms outstretched, when the gun went off. I must have got pretty close because the sound filled my ears to the point where they should have punctured and the heat of the blast seemed to scorch my cheek.

Then I was aware that something solid had slammed into me. Hard.

In a second that was split down the middle like cracked glass I had two thoughts: one that I was dying; the other was a sudden vision of her, whom I thought I would never think of again—sitting in a window wearing a white night dress, corn-fields beyond.

Nothing.

Both thoughts, in their separate ways, were lies.

The gun may have been aimed at me when it came round the door, but I was not its target. Why should I be? I didn't know anything. Trevor Warren had known a great deal. It had brimmed out of his eyes.

His knowledge had frightened him: it had killed him.

I sat on the carpet and looked across the room at his body. The bullet had flung him past the end of the settee into the corner of the room. He was lying on his back, legs thrust upwards at odd angles against the stained oak drinks cabinet. I got up, gingerly, and walked over to take a closer look.

Whoever the guy was with the gun he had known his business. He had missed the centre of the forehead by no more than a couple of millimetres. The face looked more like a death mask than ever. There wasn't even a trace of blood upon it. I knew that would be at the back, where the slug had made its exit, taking with it a lot of brain and not a little bone.

I could have lifted his head forwards by the hair and made sure. I didn't want to.

I wanted to get out. Now. The cut at the front of my head where I dived into the edge of the door had started to bleed again. I would have a bump there big enough to balance the one at the back. I felt like Punch, after a particularly bad night with Judy. Any Judy.

And no way was I going to call the cops this time. I could imagine Hankin's reaction if I told him I'd come up with a second stiff in a couple of days. He'd have me inside so fast it would be yesterday.

I went round wiping my prints off everything I might have touched. After I'd touched a few more things for luck. But my luck was out. Again. Nothing there would point me in any direction I wanted to go.

I shut the outside door behind me and went.

−5−

The girl in my dream was beautiful: in dreams they usually are. She was standing close, close enough for me to feel the tips of her nipples against my bare chest. One minute I looked at her and she was a wonderful milky white colour; the next she was shiny black. It didn't bother me. My lusts admitted no prejudice.

A mouth came up to kiss me. I met it and the tongue pushed against mine, thick and strong. My hands slid up her body seeking the points of her breasts. Diamonds in my hands.

We stopped kissing and she moved away. Black with close-curled afro hair. She became he. Back again. Then white again. A face I remembered but I couldn't be sure from where. I placed my hands around it lovingly; with the index finger of my right hand I began to stroke her forehead. The end of the finger sank through the skin, deep, deep, in over the knuckle. I tried to release it. The face moved up towards mine, mouth closing on mine, the softness of the insides of her lips.

I pulled my mouth away, pushed against her head with my left hand trying to free my finger. Finally it slid from the hole. I thought that the skin would close over behind it, but it didn't. It remained, a deep hole drilled between dark eyebrows.

As I stared at it, a purplish goo started to ooze out and run thickly down her face. It crossed her slightly parted lips and I saw the little pink tongue slide out and lick it. Not once: several times.

I closed my eyes and kept them shut tight: even when I realised that the phone was ringing.

I reached out and mumbled something into it that sounded vaguely like my name. Whoever it was at the other end sounded surprised when I said that I was in bed, trying to sleep. Apparently it was half past eleven in the morning. I wasn't impressed.

I told him to hang on. I dropped the phone on the bed and opened my eyes for the first time. The digital clock on the cupboard told me that he was right. I rubbed my eyes with the backs of my hands, careful to avoid the cuts and bruises that were making my face look more like an ice hockey rink every day.

I got out of bed and went into the kitchen. Found a carton of orange juice in the fridge and poured some into a wine glass. I took a couple of sips there and then carried the rest back into the bedroom. I sat on the edge of the bed and had another drink. At last I felt able to communicate with another human being, even if only on a very superficial level.

'Hello,' I said into the phone, 'this is Scott Mitchell. Who are you?'

He said, 'George Anthony,' in a way that suggested that maybe I ought to recognise the name.

I didn't. I said so.

'You don't know my work, then?'

'Sorry. What kind of work do you do?'

'I'm a writer. Poetry, mostly.'

I'd read a poem once. It hadn't been one of his. On a better morning I might have apologised for that, too. But it wasn't a good morning.

'What can I do for you, Mr Anthony?'

'Find a lady for me.'

'Any particular one?'

'Very particular.'

'They mostly are.'

'Not like this one.'

'That's what all you guys say.'

'What kind of guy is that?'

'The kind that phones me up and drags me out of bed to find the very special lady he couldn't keep hold of himself. I can never understand it.'

'What?'

'If she was that special why did he let her go?'

There was no answer from the other end of the phone. Possibly he was clean out of words. Then again, he could have been scribbling a quick sonnet on the cover of the telephone directory.

'You sound a hard man, Mitchell,' he finally said.

'Sure. That's me. Hard as they come. So where are you?'

'In Hampstead,' he said. I needn't really have asked.

'You've got transport?'

'Yes,' he said.

We were living in an affluent consumer society; even poets had cars nowadays.

'You'd better come round here.'

'All right.'

I gave him the address and checked that he knew how to get there. Then I put down the phone and drained the glass of its orange juice.

After ten minutes in the bathroom I climbed into some clothes and made it back to the kitchen. I put some coffee beans into the grinder and set it going while I switched on the grill. When the coffee was ground, I filled the kettle with water and set it to boil. I sliced two pieces of toast for the grill, then put butter, a couple of eggs, the top of a pint of milk and some salt and pepper into a small pan ready for scrambled eggs. As I was stirring this mixture slowly around with a wooden spoon, the kettle started to whistle. I shook the coffee into a red enamel pot and filled it with boiling water. Now it was time to put the toast on and finish off the eggs.

I enjoyed doing all that: it was the kind of thing that I could handle with ease. Maybe I should hand in my licence before

Hankin took it away from me and look for a job as a breakfast chef. That way I wouldn't overextend my talents and I wouldn't make so many dumb remarks down the phone to people I didn't even know.

Why did he let her go? If I knew anything at all, it was rarely a case of letting go. If the lady was really as special as he had said then he probably did what any other guy would do in the circumstances.

He did everything he could to get her and then when he had her, he treated her so damn badly that he drove her away again,

Well, I thought, that's life and this is scrambled eggs on toast and never the two shall meet.

I was finishing my second cup of coffee when the doorbell rang. I went to the door to let him in. I'd never spoken to a real live poet before.

He was medium height, around five seven or eight, and he walked with something of a stoop. All those hours bending over a hot manuscript. His hair had started to fall out at the front and on top, so that he was left with a greying fringe around the sides and a fluffy line stranded somewhere across the centre of his scalp. He was probably in his early forties.

He shook my hand with a grip that should have been firmer than it was and waited politely until I ushered him into the room and asked him to sit down. He accepted a cup of coffee without milk or sugar and sat there with both hands round it, looking at me expectantly.

It was as though he thought I had found her already.

I let him drink his coffee.

Then I started to ask all the usual questions. A couple were enough to get him going. It usually is. They can't stand the pain of what's happening to them and they'll talk about it at the drop of anybody's hat. They don't restrict the outpourings of their tortured souls to friends, tried and true. They'll let it all out to bus conductresses, milkmen, the girl who delivers the newspapers and the guy who calls at the door with a set of encyclopaedias. Even private detectives.

I sat back and got myself ready for a long wait. A fresh cup of coffee in one hand and I could listen for hours: especially to a professional like George Anthony.

He didn't look at me all of the time he was talking. Just stared at a spot a foot or so in front of him on the floor. That, and fiddled continually with the ring on his left hand. It was circular, about the size of a penny and twice as thick. The centre seemed to be some kind of grey stone, maybe even slate. The surround was in tarnished chrome, but it looked as though it had been remounted on a new silver band.

All the while he spoke about her, he toyed with this ring, rubbing the central finger of his right hand round and round its smooth surface.

'Her name is Anna. Anna Vaughan. She . . . we lived together for a year. Almost exactly. A year all but four days. Of course, I'd known her for longer than that. About three years longer.

'The first time I saw her was at a poetry reading I did in Nottingham. I still don't know what she was doing there. I don't think she'd been there before and I'm sure she hasn't been there since.

'I remember that she sat on the floor in the corner of the room, her head resting against some kind of cupboard that had been left there. While she was listening her face changed. She became more and more like a child. I half-expected her to slip her thumb into her mouth. I wasn't even sure if she was listening to what was being read. She gave no sign of understanding or enjoyment. She never looked up at the platform.

'Yet all of my attention that evening was focused upon her. When I read my poems I read them to her, for her.

'When it was all over, the organisers took us off to the pub and she was there again, different as she could possibly be. She was sitting at a table at the far end of the bar surrounded by a lot of other young people. There was no doubt as to who was the centre of attention. She seemed to be drinking a lot and her voice got progressively louder as the evening went on.

'Finally it was time for me to catch my train back to London. I had just settled into my seat when I caught sight of this figure running along the platform. Of course, it was her.

'I jumped up and opened the door and helped her on to the train as it was pulling out. All she had with her was a paper carrier bag stuffed full with I don't know what. She was wearing a fur coat she'd bought in an Oxfam Shop. She sat down opposite me in the carriage and within ten minutes she was sound asleep.

'I sat there and watched her. Her face moved a lot as she slept and once or twice she called out names, odd words, nothing that I could really distinguish. We were almost in London before she woke up.

'When we left the station she was holding on to my arm. I was staying in a friend's flat in Hammersmith. She didn't let go of me until we were inside. It was very late; early morning really. She . . . she took off her clothes, straight away, there in front of me. Her body was like a young girl's. Perhaps it was. All the time I knew her, she never told me how old she was.

'She stood there for a minute, like that, naked, then went into the bedroom and lay down on top of the bed. I followed her into the room and she closed her eyes and parted her legs slightly. I remember kneeling down beside her and kissing the flat of her stomach, just once, and saying: 'That's not what I want, you know.' But it was. I wanted her more than anyone I'd ever seen.

'We made love until it was fully light and the street outside was busy with the sounds of people going to work. I've never known anything like it. She . . . she knew everything, wanted to do everything; things that I'd thought could only exist in people's fantasies, we did there in that bed that first night.

'Later I got up and she asked me if I would go out and buy her some cigarettes. When I got back she had gone. I didn't see her for over a month. Then, there she was again, sitting on the floor at a poetry reading—at the ICA this time—looking as vulnerable as she had the first time. After that she was around more often; sometimes she would come and stay with me for days at a time, others she would kiss me on the cheek and disappear from sight.

'Then, about a year ago, I was offered this job in Devon. Running a kind of writer's centre down there, poetry courses and things like that. It sounded ideal: time to write, interesting people to meet and a chance to get into the country. I jumped at it. One evening I met Anna in a pub in Soho; she was almost falling down drunk. I got her back to my place and tried to sober her up. In the morning I asked her to come to Devon with me. To my astonishment she said yes.

'Of course, I never thought she would actually come. But she did. I was so happy, proud. Just to be with her was enough for me. I fooled myself into thinking it was enough for her. She seemed to enjoy it, revel in it. The fresh air gave her a colour I'd never seen before; she really seemed to be a new person. Happier, more stable. She said the farmhouse where we lived was the most beautiful place she had ever known. She was always saying that. She said it the last time just two days before she left.'

George Anthony looked up at me for the first time since he had started talking; but he didn't stop playing with his ring. I didn't know what to say. He had lived with a girl he loved for a whole year before she walked out on him and he thought he was the most miserable person on earth. I thought he had been very, very lucky.

I didn't think I'd tell him that. Not now. Later maybe, but not now.

Instead I said, 'And you don't know where she's gone?'

'I haven't any idea. Except that I imagine she's come back to London.'

'Which is why you're here?'

'Of course. I've been looking for her. Everywhere I could think of. There wasn't any sign.'

'Her friends?'

He shook his head. 'I didn't really know her friends. They weren't . . .'

'Poets?' I suggested.

He almost grinned. 'Something like that,' he said.

'How much idea did you have that she might leave?'

He gestured with empty, wide hands. 'None. None at all. That was the worst thing. I didn't know anything was wrong. I thought she was really happy living there, with me. I . . . I . . . no, it just paralysed me. I couldn't do anything, think of anything.'

'How long ago did she leave?'

'A little over three weeks.'

'And when did you come to try and find her?'

'Three days ago.'

'You took your time.'

'I told you, I was numbed. I couldn't think about anything at all: apart from the fact that she had gone.'

'But I expect you managed to write a few poems about it,' I said.

'What does that mean?'

'Nothing. I thought emotional stress was one of the things that made for the genuine article. You know, kick a composer in the crutch and a whole symphony comes pouring out.'

'I don't think that's very funny.'

'Neither do I, but for what it's worth, it wasn't meant to be.'

I got up and emptied the coffee pot. I could use some more even if he couldn't.

As it happened he could, so we sat around for a while longer and discussed the difficulties of making a living as a poet. He made it sound almost as bad as being a private investigator. Perhaps he ought to try thrillers; they might sell a little better.

'So,' I said at last, 'what do you want me to do?'

'To bring her back to you? No deal. From what you've told me about her, there's only one way she's going to go back to a guy and that's on her own two feet.'

'No,' he said, 'that's not what I want. All I want to know is where she is and if she's all right. I want her to know that I'm there and . . .'

'Sure, sure . . .' I brushed the rest away. There was just so much of that stuff that I could stand. Then it began to cloy in my throat like candy floss.

'What makes you think she might not be all right?' I asked.

His eyes told me there was something, but I didn't think he was about to tell me. I wanted him to tell me.

I said: 'If you want me to work for you I can only do it if you don't hold out on me. So tell me what you know.'

'Eight days ago she telephoned. It was after two in the morning and she was drunk. Again. She didn't seem to be making very much sense. All I could make out was that she wanted some money. A lot of money.'

'Did she say what for?'

'No. Only that she needed it badly. She must be in some kind of trouble.'

'Any idea what kind?'

'No.'

'What did you say about the money?'

'What money? She knows I don't have money. Not spare. To give to people just like that.'

'Not even when they're supposed to mean as much to you as she does?'

He looked at me with a mixture of anger and helplessness. His hand was shaking and his cup spilled a little coffee down on to the carpet. We watched the spots darken.

I said, 'She gave you no idea what the money was for or how you were supposed to get it to her.'

His eyes were looking tired. 'I told you, she wasn't making that kind of sense. She could even have been making the whole thing up.'

'But obviously you don't think so.'

'Why obviously?'

'Because you're hiring me.'

He gave me a list, neatly written out, of places she used to go to: pubs, clubs, the odd restaurant with an even odder name. She must have been a vegetarian—when she wasn't being an alcoholic.

'These are the places you went to yourself?'

He nodded. Then added, 'There is one other possibility, only . . . only I didn't do anything about it myself. She used to stay, live, call it what you like, with this musician, Gerry Locke. I think he plays the saxophone. She spoke about a lot of men from time to time, but he was the one she mentioned most.'

'Most girls have a thing about saxophonists,' I told him.

'Why's that?'

'I'm not sure. Unless it's all that triple tonguing they have to practice.'

He didn't look as though he thought that was funny. And this time it was meant to be.

Oh, well, lose a few here, lose a few there. It all adds up.

I took his empty cup away from him and carried it into the kitchen along with my own. When I came back he was holding out two envelopes.

'Here,' he said. 'One of these has got some money in it. The other has photographs of Anna.'

Christ! I thought. He's even more methodical than I am! And I'd always thought poets were scruffy buggers who couldn't even find a sharp pencil when inspiration struck.

I took the envelope with the money first. Opened it and counted the contents. It would do. For a while. Then I reached out for the other.

As I did so it hit me. You know, that sudden wave of coldness that starts in your arms or along the backs of your thighs and sweeps right through you. A warning. A fear. An omen.

By the time my fingers had closed around the brown manilla I was sure they, would stick to it forever. Somehow I got the thing open. The first photo was enough.

'You know her,' he said. 'You've seen her before.'

'No,' I lied.

'But . . .'

'She's just a beautiful girl.'

And I walked towards the door, hoping that he'd follow. He did.

I said: 'Where can I get in touch with you? Will you still be in London?'

He shook his head. 'I've got to go back to Devon. There's another course about to start up. Here . . .' He reached inside his coat and pulled out a printed leaflet. 'The address and telephone number are on there. You'll get in touch as soon as you . . .'

'If I . . .'

I opened the door and watched him as he walked down towards his car. It was a green Citroen Deux Cheveux. One of those things that look like an empty can on wheels. Just right for a poet.

I shut the door and looked at the rest of the photos. She wasn't wearing the leather jacket, or the boots, but there was no missing who she was.

Whoever she was.

–6–

I thought it was time I went to the office: if only to get the moths out of the mail box.

It seemed that I had thoughtful friends. Someone had beaten me to it. Only they hadn't kept themselves to the mail box. They'd given the place the kind of going over that was guaranteed to leave every speck of dust looking shiny and new.

The search Hankin's boys had made the other night looked like amateur night at the Co-op Hall.

I admired the way they'd picked the locks instead of breaking the doors down. Not only professionals, delicate as well. Men with a well-developed sense of property.

Mine.

I wondered how good they really were. There were two places I had specially arranged. I had used them when my last lot of visitors had been on their way. It would take someone really experienced, really dedicated to find them.

That was what I was up against. They'd found them all right.

From the way the photographs were arranged I could tell that they'd been looked at, but they hadn't meant anything so they'd been left. I didn't want to look at them again, but I did anyway.

Nothing seemed to have changed. They hadn't even started going brown with age. I slipped them back into the folder.

Photographs! Poets should come to me with photographs!

I got up and looked at my second stash. They'd found this one too. They'd been more interested in what they'd turned up. The Smith and Wesson .38 had gone, along with a box of ammo.

Why had they taken it?

Guns weren't hard to come by if you knew the right people and these guys obviously would. So why . . . ?

My mind went back to the sound of the opening door in the flat in Camden Town; the revolver tight in the man's hand. I found that I was touching the line of the cut down. my forehead.

Then the phone rang. The sound echoed oddly in the empty office. Strange, I'd never noticed that before. I walked over and picked up the receiver. I didn't have time to say my name. Whoever was calling knew who I was.

'Listen, Mitchell. Listen good.'

What did he think I was doing? I was fascinated. Even my grammar wasn't that bad.

'You're poking your nose into all the wrong places. You're disturbing all the wrong people. Do yourself a favour. Leave it all alone. Forget it. Pretend it's all been a bad dream. Otherwise you're liable to get yourself blown away. Like your friend, Warren.'

I didn't say anything. He seemed to have everything covered pretty thoroughly.

'You hear me, Mitchell?'

I told him that I'd heard him.

'Okay. See you do what we say. If you know what's good for you.'

And he went away as if by magic. My Fairy Godmother. Or should that be Godfather. Whoever it was, they seemed to be making me an offer I couldn't refuse.

That's what I should do. Forget it all. Erase the last couple of days, and pretend that they hadn't happened at all. But now I had George Anthony's money in my pocket and a job to do. If that job brought me up against people who didn't fight shy of a little first degree murder then who was I to complain?

I'd taken on the job: taken the fee. Now I had to get on with it. If I knew what was good for me!

Oh, I knew all right. Lying back in a nice deep armchair, a glass of Southern Comfort in one hand and an almost full bottle close by on the table, Roy Eldridge and Dizzy Gillespie playing something like 'I Can't Get Started' over the stereo. That was good for me. Or sitting down to a large rare steak, with jacket potatoes dripping with chives in cream, mushrooms and a side salad. That was good, too. Holding late night conversations with the few old friends I thought I still had—somewhere; holding a girl close on a crowded floor, indulging in a little slow dancing; holding the tips of her fingers loosely inside my own as we lay, eyes closed, in the sunlight.

Yes, I knew what was good for me.

Sometimes I thought that was most of my trouble.

I left the office and walked down the stairs and out into the street. A few desultory flakes of snow were falling from out of a wide sky the colour of sour cream. They touched the pavement and disappeared.

I crossed the road, and set off for Soho. I almost got past the coffee shop without going in. Almost was pretty good for me.

Tricia looked as slim as she usually did behind her black and white striped apron. She was stirring a large pan of soup when I went in and the steam had clouded her glasses. She took them off and wiped them clean on the apron before pouring me my coffee. I thought I'd have a piece of flan and some salad. She fixed it for me, shaking her head at the strand of dark hair which kept falling across her face.

I thanked her and paid her and she smiled back and thanked me back and I went over and sat down.

See. Life can be straightforward and simple. When it's taking its lunch break.

I was turning into Gerrard Street when I first noticed him. Standing in the doorway of a shop doing his best to look as though he wasn't there.

It wasn't a dry cleaner's and he wasn't me. He wasn't that good and from the shape of his raincoat he didn't know what a cleaner's was for. I hesitated about letting him know that I'd tumbled him.

Finally, I thought I'd let him tag along for a while. He wasn't going to follow me anywhere I didn't want to be seen. Not yet he wasn't.

Jazz clubs in the afternoon are strange places. Like swimming pools when all the water's been drained out. I stepped past the desk at the front and into the club itself. Chairs stacked on tables; neat piles of dirt and cigarette ends arranged at the ends of rows; a set of drums and a less than grand piano up on the stand; a row of stained beer mats and empty ash trays along the bar. And a single glass. Also empty.

I sat down at one of the tables and prepared to wait.

Outside in the street, I guessed that my new friend was preparing to wait as well.

He had longer to wait than I did.

Twenty minutes or so later, Mike Burns came wandering in, sax case in hand. I wondered idly if he went to bed with it. There had been one or two people in the past I could have asked, but not any more.

Mike didn't even recognise me at first. Then he did and his face spread into a broad smile. He sort of shuffled towards me, fatter in the face than when I had last seen him. Business must be at least partway good.

He was wearing a crombie overcoat that looked as though all the instalments on it had been paid and a neat leather hat that wasn't quite big enough for his head.

He must have bought it in leaner times.

'Scott!' he said, grasping me by the hand. 'How are you? Haven't seen you in ages!'

I shook his hand and he pulled another chair off the table and joined me.

'You're not looking too good, buddy. Which particular lamp post did that?'

'Skip it,' I told him. 'It wasn't any one lamp post in particular. They've started going in for random attacks.'

He looked at me with his head on one side, as though he was trying to work out the extent of the damage.

'So, Mick, things are going well, yea?'

He shrugged his shoulders and raised his hands in mock indifference.

'You make a little here, lose a little there. You know how it is, Scottie.'

I could guess. At least on that reckoning, he was fifty percent up on me.

'You get to blow any now, Scott?' he asked.

I shook my head a little sadly. 'No, Mick, I couldn't beat four-time in the middle of a pipe and drum band. Not any more.'

'You're kidding!'

He took hold of my hands and held them upwards, examining my wrists.

'Couldn't play, nothing. The muscles you've still got in these wrists you could play all night. Give it a little time to get back the feel of things and you'd be up there on that stand any time you wanted.'

He let go of my hands and gave me a wink.

'Hey, Scottie,' he said, 'you remember how we started? The times we had?'

Jesus! I remembered. His face hadn't been fat then; skinny, sallow. I never knew where he got the breath from to blow horn. But blow he had: scales, exercises, tunes. Early Brubeck stuff with me trying to keep a rhythm going using a pair of brushes on the back of an old suitcase. Then, when his old man got fed up with the noise and I had got myself a full kit, we hired this room over a pub in Kentish Town on Sunday mornings.

Well, times had sure changed.

He had his own jazz club and I had.

'Mick, I'm looking for a guy. I thought you might be able to help me.'

'Shoot. I'll do what I can. Anything for an old pal, you know that.'

'Right. It's Gerry Locke. Know anything about him?'

Mick pulled a face. 'Not too much. He's a generation after us. Missed the band thing and came up with a lot of small modern combos. Time was when he was reckoned to be one of the men most likely. But he got a need for bread that jazz by itself couldn't feed.'

'How d'you mean?'

Mick shrugged. 'He got hold of the same little habits that a lot of us got into after the bop thing. The difference was that his habit wasn't so little and it got hold of him.'

'I see. Same old story.'

'I'm afraid so. Someone else who thought that if you lived the way Bird did, took the things he took, then you ended up playing like him. Whereas the only thing you did was likely end up dying like him.'

'Locke didn't do that?'

'Not yet he didn't. Not unless it's been pretty recent.'

'So what's he doing?'

'Sessions, mostly. And doing pretty well at it. Look on the sleeve of any dozen albums made in this country and you'll find Gerry's handled the horn solos on more than half of them.'

'Any idea where he lives?'

Mick shook his head.

'Or where I can find out?'

'That I might be able to help with. Know the drum shop in Golden Square?'

I nodded. I should do. I'd spent my first week's wages there putting down the deposit on a new snare drum.

'There's an old guy who works there. Crippled fellow with a hump on his shoulder. Best drum tuner ever lived. See him. Tell him I sent you down. He knows where every musician in the smoke hangs out. If he can't help you, nobody can.'

I stood up and held out my hand. Mick took it warmly.

'Stop by one evening, Scottie. Sit in, even. We could have a ball.'

I walked towards the door.

'Sure, Mick,' I said. 'Sure. I'll do that.'

I gave him a wave and he waved back. We both knew that I was lying.

When I got back out on to the street I couldn't see him straight away. But after I'd gone thirty yards I picked him up, pretending to be interested in some flabby-looking nudes outside a strip club.

Who knows? Maybe he was. Somebody had to be and sure as hell it wasn't me. Though there was Sandy, who'd been a stripper and a good one. But she hadn't been flabby. There hadn't been an ounce of surplus flesh on her body.

Not even when she'd given up. There'd just been scars then. Drawn with an open razor down the length of her. After that she hadn't stripped again.

Not for money. Not for me. Not after that.

She'd taken the razoring for me: that had been enough.

When I got to the drum shop he was still tagging along behind; he watched me from the other side of the square. This time he was doing his best to be enthralled by the jackets of the paperbacks in the Granada office windows.

I soon found my dwarfed percussion expert and when I told him I'd come from Mick Burns he couldn't do enough for me. I was lucky to get out of the place without a new Premier kit at a twenty-five percent discount. Finally I had to tell him that I was a bankrupt and couldn't sign cheques.

But I did come out with Gerry Locke's address.

Which meant that I wanted to lose chummy across the square. If I knew musicians' working hours, the limbo between waking and going out on a gig was a good time to find them hanging around. Of course, he might be in the studio, in which case I would have a little time to wait.

I walked down into Berwick Street, taking my time, looking on the record stall to see what there was in the way of old 45s. There he was, buying apples a few barrows higher up. He certainly looked scruffy and he didn't look as though he'd be up to much in a fight, but with the shape of that raincoat it was difficult to tell what muscles lurked underneath it.

I thought I might find out. I went back on my tracks as far as the cinema on the corner. It was showing the usual cheap porno rubbish. Some epic called, 'Groupie Superior'. The stills outside suggested that it was about a convent full of nubile schoolgirls, lesbian nuns and randy gardeners.

A real education for somebody.

I joined the queue of one and got ready to pay over my eighty pieces of silver. I hoped that the guy in the dirty old rain-coat was going to follow me. At least he would look the part. I felt conspicuous in having nothing that I could drape across my lap.

I sat on the end of a row and kept half an eye on the screen, half on the curtain across the entrance. After a couple of min-utes he came in, waited while his eyes adjusted to the light suf-ficiently to work out where I was, then took a seat several rows behind me.

We both settled down to watch the movie.

After five minutes of shots of girls pretending to play tennis and spending all of their time bending forwards as far as they could go in their little tennis dresses, I decided I'd had about as much as I could take.

From the amount of heavy breathing that was going on around me, I wasn't the only one.

I got up and walked towards the Gents. The thing was, it also led to the exit. He was going to have to follow me in case I was going to use the latter.

He did. I was waiting for him round the back of the first door. I hadn't gone out, but he was going to. Cold. I hoped.

The thing was, he wasn't quite as easy as I'd thought. Or else I was getting stale. He took the first punch all right, letting himself be knocked back against the wall alongside the door to the Gents itself. Then he kicked out at me as I went for him. Not direct enough to strike home, but it made me jump back away from him. He pushed into the john and slammed the door in my face.

Now that just wasn't friendly.

I opened it with the sole of my shoe and went in fast, allowing it to close behind me. He was standing alongside the urinals and with his back to the grubby wash basin.

He had a nasty look in his eye and an even nastier looking knife in his hand. He was waiting for me to make another move and the knife was being held steady enough to suggest that he wasn't worried.

I should have learnt by now that it doesn't pay to underestimate people. Except yourself.

But I couldn't wait all afternoon. At any minute someone was going to want to come in and for a more natural reason than ours.

Although in a place like that you never can tell.

I feinted with my right hand, then swivelled my left shoulder. That should fool him! He didn't budge. The knife didn't waver. Why the hell was he looking so bloody confident!

Unless . . .

Unless I was even stupider than I'd thought possible . . .

Unless I was being followed by two of them and they'd set it up that smart. One who would make himself obvious enough to let me drop my guard, so that I wouldn't notice the second one.

Then if the first one lost me, the other could take over. Or if he got into trouble there would be someone around to help him. Which was what he was keeping me at bay for. A cute little threesome. There was even a cubicle each if we needed it.

Another look in his eyes told me that I was right.

He was expecting help to come through that door right enough. I was expecting it. The only thing was, the guy coming through wouldn't know exactly what to expect.

It wasn't a very big space and I was able to jump to the other side of the door as he came in. My hands yanked the woodwork away from him. But only for a second. Then I let him have it back. Right in the face.

He didn't like that. He said so.

The fellow with the knife didn't like it. He said so too.

Suddenly everyone was getting very talkative. A regular party.

I thought I'd join in. The second guy was leaning back against the door frame and he wasn't looking any too friendly. He opened his mouth to call me a very rude name and spat out one of his teeth and a spurt or two of blood in the process. Well, it served him right for being so bad-mannered.

Though he had a right to complain. His mouth sure looked a mess. I took another poke at it with my right. My fist crunched into him hard and I thought I heard something cracking behind his pulped lips.

I hoped he had a good dentist.

The guy in the raincoat didn't think much of me either. He called me something even nastier and lunged at me with the knife. I managed to side-step it and chopped down on his arm as hard as I could. He must have been made of steel.

All I succeeded in doing was hurting the edge of my hand; his arm stayed where it was. He swung it round towards my stomach and I jumped back into the centre of the urinals; the knife missed my gut by a good six inches and a good deal of cold water splashed up inside the back of my trouser legs.

I was going to get out of there.

I hoisted myself up by pressing down on the white porcelain sides that divided the stands and swung myself back slightly. Then I levered my legs forwards. My feet swung together and this time my aim was good. They caught him high on the chest, not far below his neck. He went backwards like something out of a catapult.

Somewhere on the way he collided with his friend and bounced off in another direction, ending up against the exit door rail.

Meanwhile, the one without the teeth was trying to get back into the action. Some guys never learn!

He didn't trouble with finesse. Just rushed at me as though he was a bull and I was the proverbial shopful of china. One of his arms wrapped itself around my side and the other tried to do the same. I didn't think I'd let it.

I grabbed hold of it below the elbow with both hands and

brought up my knee at the same time. Then I slammed the outside of the arm downwards and didn't let go. Not even when I did it a second time and he screamed right up high in the top of his head.

I let go of his arm and gave him the old one-two: one to the stomach, two to the jaw. He went back against the door frame one more time.

The raincoat merchant had decided that he wasn't going to use the exit door after all. He was determined to use his knife instead. I thought this time he might succeed.

Persistence deserves its rewards.

I waited until he was good and close and watched his right arm go back. Waited longer. Waited for the forwards lunge, the length of sharpened steel cutting the air between us.

And then there was something else between us.

I grabbed the guy away from the door and pulled him across in front of me. Fast. Fast enough. The scream was high again, tempered with anger and surprise. I let him fall. The knife must have fallen with him. I didn't see it again.

Only a pair of startled eyes, staring down at the body that was curling into itself on the floor and making little gurgling sounds.

At that point the door from the cinema opened. A man took half a step forwards; stopped short; looked quickly from one to the other of us; retreated rapidly.

He might rush off and tell the manager. He might go back to his seat and pretend that it had never happened. I didn't want to wait and see which it would be.

Neither did the now worried looking guy over by the exit doors. He had them part way open when I dived on him and brought him down to earth. There were lots of things I might have liked to have done to him, including asking him a few questions about who had set him and his buddy on to me. There wasn't time. I stood over him and he gazed up at me with a look almost of pleading in his eyes.

Oh, yes, I thought. And then I put the toe of my shoe hard into his right temple, immediately in front of the ear.

I didn't know what expression he was wearing after that. I didn't bother to look. I was on my way down the alley and heading in the direction of Piccadilly tube station.

Although he didn't know it yet, I had a heavy date with a sax player.

-7-

The front door was at the top of a flight of stone steps and it looked as though it was open. It was. There was an electric light on in the long hallway and some kind of gas fire which flickered and burped.

Gerry Locke was home.

The notes of a slow blues rolled and tumbled down the stairs. I stood a while and listened. Yes: he was good. I waited to see if he was about to finish. But the choruses continued, twelve bars on top of twelve.

I began to walk up the stairs.

At the top of the first flight there was a long landing with another door at the end. This one was closed.

I opened it.

Locke was sitting on the edge of a single bed with a sagging mattress. Blankets and sheets were pushed up against the wall behind him. It looked as if the first thing he did when he woke each day was to swing his legs over the side and reach for his horn before his feet had touched the floor.

He must have heard me come in, but he didn't look up. I shut the door behind me. He didn't react to that either. The sounds that came from the bell of his sax were fuller in that enclosed place. They swallowed up the air. I felt stranded. He carried on with his blues.

I wondered who they were for.

I went over and stood in front of him. Still he didn't stop. I put my hand round the neck of the horn and pulled. He stopped. In mid-note. For some seconds his fingers continued to work over the keys. Then he slowly looked up at me.

His nose was broad and it had been broken at least a couple of times. That nose dominated his whole face. Somewhere behind it a couple of eyes were tired and trying to sleep between hoods of sallow skin. His mouth was slightly open; a child whose dummy has been suddenly snatched away and who doesn't know why.

Finally he spoke: 'You didn't like it?'

'I liked it.'

'So . . . ?'

'So I've got other things to do than listen to you running through them old changes.'

'Like . . . ?'

'Like Anna Vaughan.'

He continued looking up into my face, then pursed his lips and let out a low whistle.

'How about that?'

'How about what?'

'All of a sudden all of you cats are mighty keen on meeting up with Lady Anna.'

'She's a lady?'

He grinned, 'Right down to her cute little butt.'

'And who else has been looking for her?'

'Don't you know, man?'

'If I knew I wouldn't be hanging out in here breathing in all this foul air waiting for you to make with a sensible answer.'

His expression changed. 'You saying I stink or something?'

'Not something; I'm saying you stink—period.'

His face broke into a broad grin, then an open laugh. 'Well, ain't you the cat's doodads!'

I was beginning to get the feeling that we could just go on all afternoon. I thought I'd try and hurry things along a little. I put on my fierce look—the one that suggested that I ate saxophone players for lunch.

'So who else has been asking for her? You heard the question first time.'

The voice was hard and he didn't like it.

'More of you pigs !' he snarled.

'I ain't no cop,' I told him.

'Then you must be the next best thing. Why else you poking round here trying to find out where she is?'

'Maybe we're just friends.'

He laughed aloud again, his huge nose bobbing up and down in the centre of his face. I had an almost irresistible, urge to hit it. I fought hard and controlled it—for now.

'What's wrong with that?'

'Anna don't mess with no straights. I know her, baby; I know her of old.'

He gave me a wink but it wasn't friendly; merely said that he knew a hell of a lot that I didn't.

And which I didn't seem to be getting close to finding out. But if he wasn't going to be hastled into it, then there were other ways.

George Anthony's cash was already making me feel as if I was walking with a list to one side. I wasn't used to toting that much bread for that long. I thought I'd off-load a little.

I took out my wallet and sprinkled some notes on the bed. Locke looked down at them with something approaching disgust.

'Look, pig! You don't think I'm going to sell Anna out, do you? Not for a few lousy pennies!'

I couldn't be sure what I'd insulted: his integrity or his business sense. I added some more to the pile; then more still. It was going to be okay. I could tell from the way the muscles in his face relaxed.

'What you want to know?'

'Where she is?'

He shrugged his shoulders. 'That I don't know. Not for definite. She hasn't been around for months.'

I reached down my hand on to the bed and grabbed up the money.

'What's that for?!'

'You're lying!'

In the far corner of the room a fly had somehow materialised and was buzzing around in a half-dazed fashion. The stench of his bed was getting to my throat and I didn't think I could hang around too long without throwing up.

He was concentrating on the notes in my right hand.

'All right,' he said.

We both watched as the notes fell back to the blanket.

'She was here four nights ago. Asking for bread. She wouldn't say what for. Not that it could be too many things with Anna. Anyway, I didn't have anything on me. Not the kind she wanted. I tried to get her to stay. Said I'd go round with her the next day and we'd see what we could turn up together. But she wouldn't have any. She split most as soon as she got here. She looked pretty bad.'

'Beaten up?'

'Not yet. But she was waiting. For that or worse. Man, I tell you I've seen that chick in some pretty bad scenes, but I've never seen her as down as that night.'

He shook his head in disbelief.

'And did she say where she was? How you could get in touch with her?'

Locke shook his head slowly from side to side and said, 'Nothing, man. Only . . .'

'Only, what?'

'She did say that she was working.'

'Where?'

'Shit, man, some straight gig I just couldn't figure. Some air line office up West. Piccadilly somewhere, I think she said.'

'You can't remember the name?'

'Uh-uh.'

'Which leaves one more thing. Who else was round here asking the same kind of questions?'

He looked at me questioningly. 'You really don't know?'

'I could make a few guesses. But why guess when I've just paid for the answer?'

'Right. It was a cop. A big guy. Hard. Nasty.'

'Name?'

'He didn't say.'

'Rank?'

'He didn't say that either.'

'How did you know he was a cop? Didn't he show a warrant card or something?'

Locke grunted and coughed up phlegm deep in the back of his throat. I guessed that was all he was going to say about that one.

'There was one thing I noticed about him,' he went on after whatever was shifting around behind his mouth had settled. 'He had this heavy ring on his right hand. Chunky, sort of.'

Well, I thought, this was getting to be quite a case for rings. And I remembered this one only too well. Maybe Locke did too. Although I couldn't see the marks on his face.

I started to walk away; my eyes were beginning to smart. The fly was still batting away against the wall, unaware that there was no way he was going to win.

'One thing, man,' Locke said.

'What?'

'Lady Anna. What you aiming to do if you find her?'

It was my turn to shrug my shoulders. 'I don't know. Help her, I guess.'

His head dipped and when it came up again he was laughing all over his face. And loud.

'What's so funny?'

'Man, she's got you hooked the way she always does and you ain't even seen her yet.'

I opened the door and carried on walking. Half-way down the stairs I heard the sound of the sax following me. Fine. There's nothing like a little exit music.

Except that he was playing *I Can't Get Started*.

I was thinking about what Gerry Locke had said, that I was hooked by Anna Vaughan without ever having met her. Yet I had seen that photograph; and I had listened while George Anthony talked about her. You can learn a lot about a woman from the way a guy talks about her—especially if he's a poet.

I was also walking up the stairs from Piccadilly underground. Right into the back of a West Indian who was standing there rapping to a friend about the latest Rastafarian news. I apologised and carried on up the other side. I didn't mind being called a piece of white shit by someone who was probably called Earl and came from somewhere in Willesden. In his place I'd be thinking the same.

The air line buildings that I knew were down in Lower Regent Street as well as in Piccadilly itself. I thought I'd try the Piccadilly ones first. Which brought me to Hatchards bookshop.

It was time I went into a bookshop again. I tried the paperbacks downstairs. A guy with a lot of tight hair and an earring told me that I might find something by George Anthony up in the literature department.

He was right.

The book was tall and thin and was standing in line next to a lot more books by some guy called Auden. I pulled it down from the shelf. There was his picture inside the front cover. It had been taken when he had more hair, but he had been greying even then. He looked distinguished in a soulful kind of way. Leaning against an iron bridge with a river behind. I turned into the book and ran my finger down the list of contents to see if anything caught my eye.

My eye caught on one title: *Aubade for Anna*. I didn't have any idea what an aubade was, but I found the page anyway. Hell, I even read the thing!

I think of yellow roses
& stillness

grass moves in waves
shuddering my heart
to sudden movement

under warm spray
memory sings
the heads of grass
tremble

the poppies call
bodies fold against the green

turn

across the valley
a motor grazes silence

poppies bleed
into grass

perhaps there never was
a yellow rose
perhaps
my heart has never stilled.

I almost liked it, though I didn't begin to know why. I almost read it a second time. But I didn't. Not then. I took the book down to the woman at the till and paid over a little more of George Anthony's money. He'd get a little of it back in royalties and I could always put it down on expenses as research.

I thought it was time I went and looked at the real thing.

I found her in the first office in Lower Regent Street. The front was a couple of acres of plate glass window. Inside, set at an angle, there were four dark wood desks with four well-groomed females sitting in a neat row, one to a desk. Anna was the third one.

Even there, even in that huge goldfish bowl of a place, something about her stood out. Sure, all four girls were beautiful, but she had a presence that the others lacked.

She.

Anna.

I looked at the clock on the wall and figured out that she should be finishing in about twenty minutes. I could have stayed there just staring at her, waiting for her to look out and smile and mouth through the space between us the words, 'Come fly me!'

Instead I retreated to the other side of the road and stuck an evening paper up between us. I held it there or thereabouts until she came out. Then I folded it quickly, tucked it under my arm, and prepared to follow her through the rush hour crowds.

But it wasn't going to be the hastle I had feared.

She obviously wasn't in any kind of hurry and she didn't make it difficult to keep her in sight. If she was still worried then she was doing an excellent job of not showing it. And if she didn't want people to know where she was, then she was going about that in a strange way, too.

She went down the subway and through the long queues waiting for tube tickets, then surfaced again at the other side of the Circus. She spent some time looking in the window of a shop in Shaftesbury Avenue that obviously specialised in the more colourful and brief kinds of ladies' underwear.

I was sort of disappointed when she didn't go in and buy something, but walked on by instead.

After a couple of right and left turns she went into an Italian place in Old Compton Street. She sat over against the wall and immediately fished into the tapestry bag she was carrying and pulled out a pack of cigarettes. I watched her slip one between her lips and light it with a gas lighter. She dropped the cigarettes down on the table and went back to her bag. This time she took out a paperback and opened it about two-thirds of the way through. When the waiter came and stood by her table, she didn't notice him at all. Not until he leaned towards her and started speaking. Then she looked up, slightly startled, and smiled.

He went away happy.

I decided that she was going to be there for some time and that I might as well watch her from the warm.

The place was divided into two by a stucco wall which had painted tiles showing views of Italian fishing villages stuck along it. There was also a large gap in the wall through which the waiters could shout at one another . . . and through which I could see Anna. So I sat on the far wall and watched her, still pretending to read my paper.

It was a hell of a time before the waiter even noticed me and when he went away with my order for one cappuccino he wasn't smiling.

Anna wasn't either. She sat there turning the pages at quite a rate and smoking non-stop, though she didn't actually light the new one up with the butt of the old; she used her lighter each time. She also drank four cups of coffee, which was pretty good going even by my standards.

I was lagging behind by a score of one coffee, a whole lot of cigarettes, and as for reading matter . . . I'd ditched the paper and was actually sitting there trying to read a book of poetry.

What a great scene it would make for a movie! Big, lough private eye sits in restaurant reading poetry. If my friends could see me now!

I'd managed to get that far in my life on just one poem and suddenly in the space of less than an hour that total was sent rocketing into double figures.

I wasn't sure if my mind would ever live it down.

And then she moved. All that time she hadn't looked at her watch once, but for some reason that I wasn't able to work out she laid the book down on the table, checked the time on her wrist, put the book and the pack of cigarettes and lighter back into her bag, lifted the bill from the table, got up and walked over to the counter to pay.

I followed her out into the street. She seemed to be heading for Leicester Square tube station. She was. She put a coin into the machine and bought a ticket. I did the same. The crowds were not as bad by this time and it was easy for me to keep tabs on her.

Then it occurred to me. One of those obvious thoughts that always hit you too late. Like remembering you didn't clip on your safety belt when your face is half-way through the windscreen.

Of course she was making it easy. Of course she was taking her time. She was expecting to be followed. Encouraging it.

It was the second time that day I'd got so far ahead of myself that I hadn't been able to see where I was going—or who was going along with me.

I wondered who was taking who for which ride.

Anna was taking the Northern line in a southwards direction. I sat opposite her at the far end of the carriage and tried to work out if there was anybody else there doing what I was doing. I didn't spot anyone doing anything obvious like pretending to read his paper while actually staring at her. Maybe guys only did things like that in books. Apart from me.

But then I was brought up on the wrong books, except that in my case they were movies.

While I was doing all this thinking and looking, Anna was unconcernedly reading the last few pages of her novel. I could see that the cover was green and black, but I wasn't close enough to be able to read the author's name or the title.

At Waterloo she got up and walked on to the platform. So did I. So did a lot of other people. I still couldn't figure out which was the one I should have been taking an extra special interest in, or if he was there at all. Supposing it was a he.

I followed Anna to the escalator and then along the passage-way that led towards the Festival Hall and all of those other arty buildings along the South Bank. She went over a couple of bridges with a right degree bend in the middle, then under a covered way which had posters for concerts along its walls and an old man sitting in the wet at the far end blowing tunelessly into a mouth organ and looking hopefully at everyone who went through.

She hesitated, dipped into her bag for her purse, threw some coins down into the greasy cap that was in front of the man's legs. Sorry, leg. One of the coins bounced out and rolled round on the ground in ever decreasing circles. Finally it wobbled on to its side and was still.

He lifted his eyes from the coin and looked up at me: I looked away.

She climbed some more steps and went through the glass doors into the Festival Hall itself. I had this sudden horrible thought of having to sit through a couple of concertos and the odd overture. All that culture in one evening!

But she went down to the cafeteria on the ground floor and stood in line for yet more coffee. I was beginning to think we might get on really well. At least we had one thing in common.

She sat on a kind of double tier which ran along by the window. The window looked out over the river. There were buildings lit up and every now and then a boat would go by with small coloured lights attached to it. I found that I was singing an old song by the Kinks about Waterloo sunset somewhere inside my own head.

I stopped: the sun had already set.

I looked away from Anna Vaughan and at the other tables. To the left a couple were sitting side by side with an aura of depression around them that was strong enough to keep the other tables clear for about ten feet on either side.

Neither of them was saying anything! He was holding one of her hands in his two and. she was using the other one to dab a damp tissue at her eyes every minute or so. His blue suit with its faint stripe, the expression of glorious self-pity in his eyes and the wedding ring on his finger told it all. As usual she was around half his age and you could bet that she wasn't the one who'd been standing next to him when he'd said, 'For better, for worse.'

Not that I had anything against a little marital infidelity—how could I in my business?—as long as it brought somebody some happiness somewhere. I didn't think it did. But then, from what I'd seen neither did marriage.

When it came down to it, happiness didn't seem to be part of the natural human condition.

And if you had to choose who you were going to be unhappy with, perhaps it was more rewarding to choose with a sense of romantic self-indulgence.

At least it ended up putting more money in a struggling private investigator's pocket.

On the other side of Anna, there was another likely pair of candidates. Only this time they were at the noisy stage. I wasn't sure which I preferred.

It didn't look as though I was able to say neither. Not in this place it didn't. There must have been something about it that drew them there; the unhappy, the hopeless, those who were filled with desire for someone else who didn't want it or who wasn't in a position to receive it.

Maybe they should be like me and learn to keep it all for yourself. But there we were back on the maybes again.

I'd been so busy setting myself up as the Miss Lonelyhearts of the seventies that I hadn't noticed him come through the swing doors. I didn't react until he was almost at the table, then I didn't quite believe it until he was sitting down opposite her.

But there was no mistaking him: he wore the same suit in the same shiny brown material and the cigar in his left hand was still unlit.

-8-

He obviously hadn't seen me and I didn't think he would. He hadn't looked away from her face since he'd sat down. He had a lot to say and he was saying it fast, punctuating the speech every now and again with little jabs at the air with his right hand. The other one was in its usual position half-way down his thigh. It was a funny way to smoke cigars.

What was happening at that table wasn't funny. No one was laughing, least of all me.

I didn't like to see a man like that give a going over to a girl like that. Whatever they were really like. For all I knew, Blagden might be a doting father to his son and send off one-tenth of all he earned to help the starving millions in India. Anna might throw cats down stairs and hit passing babies on the head as they went by her in their prams.

I didn't care: I still didn't like it.

I couldn't hear what he was saying but I could see the words boring into her as she sat there. Her head was lowered and the long dark hair formed a shield around her face. I didn't need to see her face; the stoop of her shoulders, the ends of hair curling up as they met the table top—they were enough.

Either he didn't notice or he did and it was what he wanted. Whatever the case, he carried on. He talked at her straight for between ten and fifteen minutes. I was too fascinated to check my watch more accurately than that.

And then it was over. He stopped speaking, sat up straight, looked at the half-smoked cigar as though surprised to find it between his fingers, stubbed it out methodically in the ashtray, then stood up.

She didn't look at him; waited until he had turned away from the table and was standing in the gangway, gazing out over the river. Then she did look at him, quickly, with him not noticing. She pushed her chair back with her body and it was the action of a person who has suddenly realised they are very tired.

She stood up very slowly and I could see her face clearly: she had been very tired for a long time now.

He didn't look round, simply started walking towards the door as though knowing that she would follow. She did. Her step was heavy. I wondered what she was carrying with her, within her.

I followed the pair of them as they walked out into the evening on to the embankment. I hesitated in the shadows of the building as they moved across to the parapet. They stood close together and for an instant I thought he was going to take her hand, to touch her in some way. But he didn't. He talked again, more urgently than when they had been sitting inside. A boat passed by along the river. There were people shouting and laughing on board and the sound floated across the water hollowly. The speakers on the ship blared out some pop song or other.

As I stood there watching them, they could have been lovers. But they weren't.

They began to walk away, then climb the steps to the higher level. Suddenly, Blagden surprised me. He put his hand briefly underneath Anna's elbow, then turned and walked away towards the station.

Anna stood there, staring for a few moments after him. Then

she walked to the bridge that would take her across the river in the opposite direction.

I had to choose one of them and I didn't know which. It was Blagden I really wanted. After all, he was the guy who had got me into the whole mess in the first place. It was for him that I'd been hit on the head, not once but several times, and it was because of him that the cops had hauled me in, hoping to throw a nice murder charge at me. George Anthony wanted me to find Anna for him and say a few kind words in her ear on his behalf. I could tail Blagden now and pick the girl up at her office the next day.

That would be the common sense thing to do.

Common sense. That was the thing that kept the average man paying his mortgage and feeding his two point whatever it is kids and overlooking his wife's little infidelities. Common sense is what keeps a guy at his desk until he's sixty-five so that he won't lose his pension and then he drops down dead a week before he can collect. Common sense would have kept me in the police force and now I'd be running a newsagent's shop in New Cross Gate. Common sense . . .

Oh, to hell with it!

I pulled up my coat collar and hurried up the steps and along the bridge.

I had nearly caught up with her by the time she got down on to the far side of the embankment. She stopped for a moment by a waste bin that was fixed to a lamp post and fished around in her bag. Finally, she brought out the book and dropped it in. Then carried on walking.

I hung back for a while then went over to the bin. She had made me curious. I fished the book out from among a pile of empty, screwed up cigarette packs and hot dog wrappers. I held it up to the fight by two fingers. 'Playback' by Raymond Chandler. On the cover this tough looking guy was holding a girl by her arm. She was young and beautiful; her hair was long but blonde. The guy looked old enough to know better.

I wiped a splash of old tomato ketchup from the back and

shoved the book into my coat pocket, alongside Anthony's book of poems. I was getting to be a regular little library.

I quickened my pace.

At first I waited to see where she would go, but she didn't seem to be going anywhere in particular. Just wandering. Thinking. I wanted to know what she was thinking.

She crossed Ludgate Circus and turned to the left quickly. I almost thought I had lost her. But I pushed open the door of this wine bar and there she was, sitting by herself in a booth at the far end.

I went over and slid into the seat opposite her.

'Hello,' I said.

She didn't say anything.

'I think you dropped this,' I said, and pulled the paperback up into sight.

'I'd finished it,' she said.

'I know. I've been watching you read it. You're a fast reader.'

'If you've been watching me read it, then you must know that I finished it.'

'I thought you might want to keep it.'

'But I threw it away.'

'Don't you ever throw away things and then wish you hadn't. It's not often you get a chance to change your mind about things like that. This might be your lucky day.'

'That isn't funny.'

'I know.'

She looked at me then, dark eyes trying to read something without knowing what.

I said, 'Thrown away anything else lately?'

'Do you mean things . . . or people?'

'Which do you go in for most?'

'Throwing away? I throw the things. The people throw me.'

I shook my head. 'I don't think that's true.'

Her eyes questioned me again. It was too early for me to give many answers. I wanted her to give something first. I wasn't sure what. A girl in a striped dress that looked as though it was meant to be a discreet kind of uniform was hovering around the end of the table.

I looked across at Anna. Said, 'It's time you had something to eat. All that coffee on an empty stomach's bad for you.'

To my surprise she smiled. I hadn't thought I'd get a smile out of her that evening, whatever else I managed. I was glad I had. It was a pretty good smile. Not a great smile. She wasn't feeling confident enough for that. But, like I said, it was pretty good.

'What would you like?'

She turned round and looked at the menu that was chalked up high on a wall over the serving hatch. 'I'd like a ham salad.'

She smiled again. I was beginning to like that smile.

'A ham salad, a steak and kidney pie with baked potato, and a bottle of red wine. Whatever you think's best . . . as long as that doesn't mean the dearest.'

The waitress smiled as she wrote down the order.

All it needed was for me to start smiling and we'd look like an outing from the funny farm.

When the striped uniform had gone away I looked back at Anna. She was still smiling.

'What gives?' I asked.

'It's nice,' she said. 'It's a long while since anyone picked me up and then bought me dinner.' She gave a little laugh. 'It makes me feel twenty-five again.'

She reached for her bag and rummaged around for her cigarettes. I took her lighter from her and lit one. As she turned her head to one side to blow away the smoke I saw how straight the bridge of her nose was, how exact the angle as it turned under.

She drew it down into her lungs, then coughed. Once she had started she continued for some time. The food had arrived before she had stopped coughing.

I pointed at the cigarette in her hand.

'Maybe you shouldn't smoke so much,' I said.

She coughed again, just once.

'That's why I smoke so much,' she said.

Then suddenly she was smiling again and cutting into her salad as though she hadn't eaten for a week. I poured her some wine and she seemed to enjoy that too.

Between mouthfuls she said, 'You didn't just happen to follow me around a little waiting for a chance to pick me up, did you?'

'No,' I shook my head.

'What are you after then?'

'I'm not sure.'

She drank some more of the wine. 'You don't look the kind of man who's often out of his depth.'

'How far are you out of yours?'

'Don't change the subject.'

I shrugged my shoulders. She bit into a piece of tomato.

'Who are you working for? Who sent you?'

I leaned across the table and said in my best conspiratorial tone, 'George sent me.'

Instantly her face hardened, her eyes went downwards as though she had a sudden desire to study the remaining contents of her plate. She pushed it away. She had had enough. She reached over and lit-up another cigarette.

'What does he want?'

She had a way of making 'he' sound like the dirtiest word in the English language.

'Nothing,' I told her.

She didn't look as though she believed it; she said so. She said a lot of other things about George Anthony. None of them were very complimentary.

'He seemed a nice guy,' I said, 'for what that's worth.'

'Not much. George always seems a nice guy. Until you get to know him. People are always being taken in by that sincere front he carries around.' She broke off and looked at me quickly. 'But that's the way we all operate, isn't it? It's like a gigantic hall of mirrors. Only they're all distorting.' She laughed. 'Some people even think that I'm a lovely young girl when they first meet me. It doesn't usually last long.'

I couldn't think of anything to say. Not right then. I poured out some more wine.

'So what did old George want then?'

'To know how you are, where you are. He was worried about you. He thought that you were in trouble.'

She laughed again, but this time it wasn't very convincing. 'Me? What kind of trouble could I possibly be in?'

'The worst kind.'

'What's that?'

'I'm not sure yet. Not totally sure. But I do know you're in one hell of a mess and . . .'

'You'd like to help me out of it.' She finished the sentence the way she thought I was going to. Perhaps she'd been right, but I corrected her anyway.

'And George would like to help you.'

'Huh! What's he going to do? Write a sudden bestseller? The only thing George has got two of to rub together is last year's clichés!'

'He can't help it if he hasn't got money.'

'And I can't help it if I need it.'

'Can't you?'

'No!' She spat the word out and for a moment she sat there looking like a spoilt child. Then she changed her expression, almost as though she had realised what she had been doing. I wondered just how aware of herself and the games that she was playing she really was. A lot of people must have wondered that. A lot of men.

She was lighting another cigarette and the waitress was waiting to see if we wanted anything else.

'No, thanks,' I said.

'I'd like a brandy,' Anna said.

The waitress went to fetch a brandy.

'If you don't think. George can help you . . .'

'Then you can.'

'Yes.'

'You've got a lot of money.'

'No.'

'Then forget it . . . I don't know your name. You've taken me out to dinner—sort of—and I don't know your name.'

I said, 'I'm sure it isn't the first time.' I went to my wallet and gave her a card.

She looked at it and leaned right across the table so that her face was only a few inches away from mine.

'Scott,' she said softly. 'That's a good name. Strong without being brutal. I like names.' She smiled and I could feel the warmth of her breath on my face. She was seducing me there in the middle of the restaurant without even having to touch me. There were people all around us, talking, eating, drinking. Somehow that made it better still.

'You're right, of course,' she said quietly, only for me. 'I have been out to dinner with men whose names I didn't know. I've been all sorts of places with men I didn't know, done all sorts of things. There's something exciting about doing very intimate things with someone you've never seen before and you know you're never going to see again.'

For a moment I could see shadows of those things in her eyes, deep in the darkness of her eyes. I wasn't sure if I wanted to see them but I didn't have any choice. She held me, hooked.

And when she was certain, she moved her head away and lifted the glass of brandy to her mouth.

'Cheers, Scott.' She downed it in a single swallow. Her hand moved for the pack of cigarettes. My hand moved to cover it, stopping her. She pulled it clear.

'I don't need looking after like a child.'

'Don't you?'

'No. Not by you, anyway.'

'By Blagden.'

She allowed herself to show a trace of surprise. 'You know him.'

'I know him. He hired me.'

'I don't believe you. What would he hire you for? He's got men of his own to do his dirty work.'

'How do you know it was dirty?'

'It would have to be. What is he supposed to have wanted you to do?'

'Watch a flat, find out who was there. Help him get some people moved out.'

'Which flat?'

'The one you'd been living in.'

'That's ridiculous!'

'I know. Now. I didn't think so at the time.'

'What happened?'

'I got fed up with waiting around watching the same guy go in and out. I went to take a look for myself. Maybe that's what Blagden figured I'd do. I don't know.'

'What did you find?'

'A frightened guy sitting down drinking coffee. A girl who'd been beaten up and then given a lethal overdose . . . and your photograph.'

Anna didn't like what I had told her. She showed it in her face, in the way her body seemed to close in on itself.

She began to talk, abstractedly: 'Blagden let me have the flat when I was living in London, before I went down to Devon with George. I used to do . . . favours for him. He was good to me. When I went away he didn't think I'd stick it out for long. He said I could keep the flat on, use it when I came up to town. He was certain I'd be back with my tail between my legs after less than a month. Well, I wasn't. It was longer. It . . . but George must have told you all that.'

I nodded.

'While I was away I let Trevor have a key. He didn't have anywhere to stay. I'd known him for years. He was sweet, harmless . . .' Her voice trailed away.

'And the girl?'

'I don't know. Apart from the name that was in the paper; I saw that of course. It didn't say how . . . what had happened to her.'

'Does that make it different?'

She looked at me. 'It might.'

I was about to ask her another question but she stood up. She needed to go to the Ladies. She flashed me another smile from the end of the table. It really was a pretty good smile.

It kept me in my seat for a minute longer than it should have done. She had gone out through a rear exit and she must have picked up a cab straight away.

I walked back and paid the bill.

-9-

I decided to look in on my office on the way home. It was still there. Feeling pretty pleased with that I carried on to the flat. All I wanted was to put my feet up and have a drink or two and remember that smile. And forget a few other things: until the morning.

Not much to ask, you might think.

When you want very little it seems you have the least chance of getting anything. Except trouble.

They were waiting on the other side of the road, parked underneath a streetlight. This time the car was marked so the visit was official. I wondered if Hankin had come himself.

I thought back to an earlier occasion. A figure who hadn't wanted to step forwards into the light. Simply to watch. Even needed to watch. To feel the revenge for my words taken by fists and boots that he controlled as surely as his own.

The car doors opened as I walked across the patch of communal grass in front of the block. Three men: again. Hankin was definitely one of them this time. There was no disguising his size or the way he moved. On either side of him, two men in the regulation raincoats. They may have been the same two, they may not; such men are usually interchangeable. If they were the same, either their faces had healed up more quickly than mine or I was losing my touch.

Or they'd been issued with a shiny new lower-than-life mask each when they left the station.

I stood in the doorway and waited for them to arrive.

'Good evening, Chief Inspector.' I thought I would try to start things on a polite level, at least.

'Mitchell.'

'I hadn't expected to have the pleasure again so soon.'

One of the others said something under his breath that I didn't catch.

'We've questions for you, Mitchell,' said Hankin in his disinterested, blunt voice. 'For your sake I hope you've got answers.'

'Fine,' I told him. 'Where's it to be? My place or yours?'

For an answer he pushed past me and walked on into the living room. One of the other two shut the door behind us all and looked as though he was prepared to stand guard. I followed the chief inspector into the room; the second man followed me.

I thought we might all sit down and have a nice little chat and later I could serve tea. But they had other ideas.

Hankin started his first question before I was over the threshold of the room . . . and he wasn't asking for lemon and sugar.

'Yesterday, Mitchell?'

I thought about it carefully, I didn't want to make any mistakes.

'It was Wednesday,' I told him.

I must have been wrong. The guy behind me grabbed my arm and yanked it so far up behind my back that I thought it was coming off. I shouted out and lurched forwards to within under a foot of where Hankin was standing.

He looked at me with an expression of extreme distaste, like I was something the cat had left at the bottom of his bowl. I had this nagging feeling that by the end of the evening that was how I would be feeling.

'Mitchell, you're not a very bright man. When you try to be clever you only end up stumbling over your own inadequacies.'

So that's what it was! In all these years I'd never noticed. I chanced a glance downwards. If I went along to my doctor he might give me a truss.

'Are you listening, Mitchell?'

At that range it would have been hard not to, but he seemed to need convincing. I assured him that I was.

'Right. Then let's have some answers. Where were you yesterday afternoon?'

'At the movies.'

He moved away. Far enough away to give his arm a chance to get a good swing. The same old routine. Back and forth across the face, that ring catching me hard both times. And I had been at the movies, at least for part of the time. If that's what I got for telling the truth then I'd better really watch out when I started lying.

Which I was sure as hell about to do. There were several places I hadn't been that afternoon and one of them was a grotty little street in the suburbs; the other was a flat in Camden Town.

'I'll ask you again, Mitchell. This time, think. Where were you yesterday afternoon?'

I didn't want to do it but I had to. I gave him the same answer, flinching as I did so. This time I got it with the open hand first, then the knuckles. Anything for a change. The one behind me added an extra tweak for good measure.

That did it. I didn't like him getting his kicks on somebody else's time. I dug my elbow back into him hard and it must have caught him in between a couple of ribs. I felt the breath ooze out of him as he let go of my right arm. Which was just what I needed. Without that I would never have been able to get in my follow-up punch. I was aiming for the same spot I'd got a couple of seconds before and from the colour his face turned I must have come pretty close.

He staggered a few paces backwards looking like a bad heart case.

Hankin hadn't interfered, except to call the guy at the door. He came running and that was nice and handy, too. It made it easier to dodge him when he grabbed for me because he was off balance and I wasn't. It also increased the impact of the knee that I stuck up into his crutch. He went down on to his knees and didn't seem too keen on getting up.

I stood up straight and looked over at Hankin. He still hadn't moved. I wasn't too sure why.

He spoke from amongst the coughing and wheezing of his men. 'Just what do you think you're going to do now?'

'I was thinking the same thing about you.'

The guy with the bad ribs made a move towards me, but Hankin waved him back. He didn't like it, but he went.

'They're not as good as the last lot of heavies you sent after me. Recruitment must be a problem.'

He stared back at me as though he didn't know what I was talking about.

I said, 'How do you want to play it now?'

He said, 'I want to ask you some questions.'

'Okay. Only this time we'll try it my way.'

'Which means what?'

'You ask the questions and I'll answer as honestly as I can without prejudicing the interests of my clients. That's all. No comments from those ham hands of yours and no interference from the hired help. How does that sound? Apart from extraordinarily straight.'

A lesser man might have lost his temper at that; smiled even at the cheek of it all.

Not this one. Not Hankin. He said, 'You play it close to the edge, Mitchell.'

I knew he was right but in the kind of fix I was getting jammed further and further into what other way was there to play it? Like the song says, if you're skating on thin ice then you might as well dance.

He lurched over towards one of my chairs; I found another one and sat across the room from him, staring into those tired, empty eyes. The one on guard duty shambled back to the outside door. He was still wincing slightly as he walked.

We were back in business.

'Okay,' Hankin began, 'where . . . ?'

'Save your breath,' I told him, 'I know that one by heart. I was at the movies. Berwick Street.' I gave him the name of the film and the story; it wasn't difficult to let my imagination play around with the implications of the bits that I had seen.

I still didn't think he believed me, but he let it ride.

'You mentioned clients, Mitchell. Like who?'

'One's a writer. George Anthony.' From the look on Hankin's face, he'd never heard of him either. 'The other's a property man, Hugh Blagden.'

I watched him closely. There wasn't a flicker of the eye lids out of place, not a single shift of the face muscles. No sign of recognition at all.

'And what are you supposed to be working on for these two clients, mythical or not?'

I told him, without giving him any more details than I needed. I wasn't going to give him Anna Vaughan's name, but in the end there didn't seem any way round it. I wasn't even sure of a positive reason as to why I shouldn't.

'This girl,' he asked, 'you have any luck with her?'

'I found her once, then I lost her again.'

'Sounds smart, Mitchell. Did you do all that before your visit to Camden Town or after?'

I gave him one of his own blank, looks back. He didn't want it.

'We know you were there, Mitchell.'

'We?'

'You were seen. On the way there and at the flat.'

'The flat?'

'Yes, you remember the flat, Mitchell. The one where Trevor Warren was killed.'

'Trevor Warren?'

'You know Trevor Warren, Mitchell, he was the fellow you claim to have spent days watching walking into and out of that first flat. You recall that one, don't you? The one where you found the body of the dead girl.'

'I remember that,' I told him. 'I just didn't know . . . what was it, Warren? . . . was the guy's name.'

'You didn't read it in the papers?'

'Sure, but I didn't see a picture. How was I supposed to know it was the same guy?'

He got up from the chair. I hoped that it wasn't about to start all over again.

He stood in the middle of the room and looked down on me. I got the impression he felt better like that. It was more in keeping with his impression of the natural order of things.

'Sorry, Mitchell,' he finally said, 'it was a natural mistake.'

I sat there waiting for the pay-off. I didn't have to wait long.

'I suppose I naturally thought that before you shot someone you got to know their name. Obviously I was wrong.'

Now this I didn't like. Having tried to get me for one murder and not done too good a job of that so far, they were slinging a second one in my lap. That I could do without.

'Who says I shot him?'

'I do.'

'And . . . ?'

'And this.'

He made quite a business of taking it out of his pocket. Perhaps he wasn't as lacking in interest in the whole affair as I had thought. There was something of the showman about him after all.

Perhaps he'd realised that it was time to pull something a little different.

Not that what he pulled was really very different at all: just the same old gun from the pocket trick. The same old Smith and Wesson .38. The same old Smith and Wesson .38 that another guy had been holding in his hand the other night; the one I had dived at; the one that had killed a frightened youngster with curly hair and an unusual line in borrowed overcoats. The same old Smith and Wesson .38 that had been hidden away in my office until someone's prying eyes had found it and their prying fingers had taken it away.

What I didn't understand was this: if it was one and the same gun, and I couldn't see any point in Hankin waving it around if it wasn't, then what the hell was he doing with it? There wasn't time to figure that out now. Hankin was talking again.

'Do you recognise it, Mitchell?'

'I might,' I said.

He offered it to me. It wasn't loaded any longer. I looked at it more carefully than I needed.

'Sure,' I admitted. 'I recognise it.'

'You know what that little toy's been up to lately?'

'No, but I could make a pretty educated guess.'

'Go ahead.'

'Well, from what you said before, I would guess it was the gun that fired the bullet, or bullets, into the man you've said was called Trevor Warren.'

'You're being very cagey, Mitchell.'

I handed the gun back to him. 'Wouldn't you be?' I asked him.

But he wasn't about to tell me.

'I'm glad you found it,' I told him. 'Someone let themselves into my office and turned it over beautifully. It was the second time in quick succession—and much more thorough. The gun was well hidden. They found it all right.'

'They?'

'Whoever it was.'

'You can prove it, of course?'

'I can probably prove the place was broken into, I can't prove that the gun was taken. Any more than you can prove I was standing with my finger on the trigger when Warren was shot. I'm certain the gun was taken then, but it wouldn't stand up in a court of law. You may be just as certain that I fired that gun and murdered a man with it, but you haven't got the proof to take me to court on it.'

'What makes you say that?' he asked.

'You're still not going to arrest me.'

He stood there with the gun in his hand. It looked small and insignificant in those large fingers. It wasn't. He jerked his head at the man standing over by the window. The man moved. Slowly.

When he was out of the room, Hankin came up real close. 'I've told you before. Mitchell, and I'll tell you again. I've got you by the short and curlies and any time I want to I can haul you in and slap the biggest charges on you possible. But there's no hurry. If I let you bungle around for another day or so you'll stir up so much shit you'll think you've fallen head first into the sewage works.'

The face pressed itself even closer; again the faint but definite smell of brandy.

'You will have, Mitchell. You will have.'

He walked on past me and after a moment I heard the, door slam shut. I walked to the window and watched through the glass as the car pulled away from the fight.

There were only two men in it.

I let the edge of the curtain fall back into place, walked to the door and ran both bolts across from the inside. Then I went into the kitchen and pulled a bottle of Southern Comfort out of the cupboard. It was new. It was always nice, when they were new. I twisted the top against the paper seal and when it broke I peeled it off and threw it into the bin. Then I unscrewed the top the rest of the way and put the end of the bottle to my nose.

It smelt good: rich, orangey. I reached down a glass from the shelf and went back into the other room.

I put a Stan Getz record on the stereo, poured a drink and put my feet up.

A lot of thoughts ran in and out of my brain and I sat there letting them play hide and seek and wondering who would be found out. Usually it wasn't anyone.

I was worried about how he'd got hold of the gun. Assume he was telling the truth about it being the weapon that blew away Warren. Would the guy who did that walk into the nearest po-lice station after using it and hand it in to lost property? I didn't think so. Of course, there could be some very smart or lucky cops around and the gun could have been dumped and found. But why would a professional hitman do anything so silly with a murder weapon? Unless he wanted it to be found. Found and identified. As mine.

Which brought me to why it had been taken in the first place. And who had taken it. The cops hadn't been good enough the first time, so why reckon they suddenly got a lot better? Someone else could have taken it, someone who wanted to set me up in a nice frame. An even nicer frame than the one that almost dropped round me the minute I went into that first flat by the back door.

The flat that Blagden set me on to.

Then there were the two guys who had taken such an interest in where I was going the other day. Who were they working for?

And Anna. How did she fit into it all? If fit she did. Certainly she was mixed up with Blagden.

Again.

Mr Hugh Blagden and I would have to have a little talk.

I was woken in the morning by someone banging insistently on the front door. I found my way to it by instinct and tried to pull it open. Nothing doing. Then I remembered the bolts. I pulled them free and opened the door.

A youth was standing there with a telegram in one hand.

'Mr Mitchell?' he said.

I said that I was.

He handed me the dingy yellow envelope and I shut the door. This time I didn't bolt it. After all, it was now broad daylight.

I went into the living room and put the telegram down on the table. Then I left it there while I went through my morning routine of getting the fruit juice and coffee together. I thought I'd save eating until I'd seen what it said.

After I had it was possible I wouldn't have an appetite.

I pushed my finger inside the flap and tore it open, then took out the piece of white paper. I read it quickly, then slowly . . . at least half a. dozen times. I was smiling.

It read: THANKS. YOU MADE ME FEEL 25 AGAIN.

− 10 −

She was looking as tight and as brittle as she had last time, only there was something different about her. She wasn't wearing her glasses. Without them she looked strange: a tortoise without its shell.

I went in. I didn't expect her to recognise me. Somehow I thought that without those glasses she would be fallible, unable to function.

But she could. She made a cute little jumping movement in her chair and opened her mouth. Not far. Enough to let out a sound that was remarkably like, 'Ooh!'

I wondered if she had landed on a pin.

'Hi,' I said cheerily. 'It's a great morning.'

The sky was grey like it was the only colour left in the world and if the wind had stopped biting it wasn't above taking a quick snip at any carelessly exposed piece of flesh.

She fumbled for her glasses. One of the doors to the right of her desk opened a fraction, then closed abruptly. I hadn't been able to see behind it.

'I thought I told you before,' she was saying.

I turned my attention back to her. That was better. Everything was in place and she was sounding much more her old self. An attractive combination of bouncer and brick wall. On a bad day getting past her would be like going round Brands Hatch the wrong way in the thirteenth lap.

But this wasn't a bad day. Not for me it wasn't. Not the way I felt. Something had given me back some of the old bounce. If I wasn't exactly feeling twenty-five again, then I was still a whole lot less weighed down than I had been.

All I needed now was to get rid of the odd bruise and a few assorted sticking plasters and I'd be back in business with a vengeance.

Which reminded me.

'How's business?' I asked her pleasantly.

You would have thought I'd asked her to drop her pants.

She flashed me a steely look which ordinarily would have killed but she hadn't noticed my protective vest.

'You do run a business here?' I said.

'Of course we run a business.'

'An estate agent's.'

'That's what it says on the door.'

'But you don't have any flats?'

'That was what I told you last time.'

'And you don't know anything about the firm's concern with a block of expensive flats close to Earls Court where someone was found murdered. A girl, around your age. Someone had pounded one side of her face as though he was batting a slice of steak into shape ready for the grill. Then he stuck a needle in her arm. Only what was in the syringe wasn't guaranteed to cure. Quite the opposite.'

I could see that she wasn't taking it too well. One hand was holding on to the edge of the desk like there would be no tomorrow and her face was looking decidedly strained. Someone should give the girl a holiday. Before it was too late.

'That's not on your list of desirable properties? Not even at the right price?'

'It . . . no . . .' She finished by simply shaking her head. I reckoned that it was the first time in her life she'd been lost for words—ever since the nurse gave her that first sudden slap.

'Of course not. I was forgetting. And you don't know any
body called Blagden?'

Her head moved slowly from side to side and something
that might have been fear shifted along behind the frames of her
glasses.

'In fact, you've never heard the name, except from me.'

'No, I . . .'

'It isn't the name of somebody who works here for instance?'

'Uh . . .'

'Somebody who works in that office over there.'

I pointed towards the door that had opened and shut. Like the
case I'd never been given to handle. She was looking that way too.
Her bottom lip was beginning to droop. Only a little, but I liked
it. I was beginning to wish she'd take off her glasses again.

I said, 'He is there isn't he? Whatever the name on the door
reads.'

She didn't answer. Didn't look at me. Her right hand edged
along to the far end of the desk. I reached over and stopped it
before her fingers could press the button.

When I shook my head from side to side there was a smile
on it. She didn't appreciate it, though. I thought she was close to
tears. She wasn't used to losing.

I was gentle with her. Then. I said, 'You don't have to bother
announcing me. I've an idea he already knows. He's sitting in
there with a cigar in his hand waiting for you to get rid of me. But
this time it hasn't worked. Don't worry. He didn't know it was one
of my good days either. Sorry if it's left you in a mess, sweetheart,
but they don't turn up so often that I can afford to neglect them.'

She was looking at me now; looking and listening. There was
only a desk between us and the way I was leaning over that didn't
account for much.

I realised that my hand was still on top of hers. I didn't do
anything about it. I kind of liked it the way it was. I moved my
other hand slowly up to her face. Fingers lifted the glasses clear
and laid them down on the desk.

Once I got started I was a regular terror with the women.

She didn't move. I said: 'There's only one thing I can give you and that's a piece of advice. Once I've gone through that door, don't get messed up with pressing any more buttons or making any phone calls. It isn't worth putting your head on the line for. You do what I hoped you'd do last time. Walk over to the door, pull down the blind on the glass, turn the open sign round, so that it says closed, get on the other side of it and keep on going. What you do with the petty cash drawer is your business. Only don't spend too long making up your mind.'

She didn't say thanks, but then she wasn't that kind of woman. It didn't matter. I hadn't expected that. She still hadn't moved away; her hand was still under mine. I knew that if I had leaned my head forwards a little further and kissed her she wouldn't have minded.

But I didn't do it: knowing was enough.

I left her at the desk and walked over to the office door. There didn't seem to be much point in knocking, so I didn't. Just opened it and went on in.

Blagden was sitting behind his desk. But he wasn't smoking a cigar. He was too busy for that. Even for an unlit one. There was a wastepaper bin on top of the desk and he was steadily filling it with assorted papers and receipts that he was taking from a bundle of files alongside his chair.

'You might be a little late, Blagden.'

He stood up and offered me his hand. I didn't want it. I didn't want to touch that skin; I didn't think I liked whatever it was that wriggled beneath it.

He pulled back his arm and said, 'This is a surprise, Mitchell.'

'You're a liar!'

He raised one eyebrow fractionally.

'You knew damn well I was outside. You were waiting until your hyper-efficient secretary gave me the old heave-ho. But this time I didn't heave so easily.'

He sat down, again and lifted the bin off the desk. I sat down as well and watched him while he lit a new cigar.

'What do you want, Mitchell?'

'Some straight talking from somebody for a change.'

He opened his arms wide in a gesture that was probably meant to suggest that naturally he would do his best. But I didn't think he could talk straight. Not naturally.

'First, why did you get me poking around the flat in Earls Court?'

'I told you, Mitchell. There was this complicated business with the lease and . . .'

I let him carry on for a while and concentrated on the smooth urbanity of the accent, the tone of genteel persuasion that got up my nose even more than the other kind of persuasion he got others to apply on his behalf.

When I had listened to it for long enough I stood up. I don't think he was certain what I was about to do. I'm not too sure that I did either. But he was puffing at his cigar enough to actually keep it going.

I walked round and sat on the corner of his desk with my foot resting on the edge of the wastepaper bin.

'I'll tell you, Blagden. You stop me if I get it wrong. This business doesn't deal exclusively within this country. You've got offices abroad. You buy up properties in other parts of the world and sell or rent them over here to people who've got more money than they know what to do with. Or who want to get out with what they've got before the taxman gets more than they want to give. It's a big operation. Not just the Continent. The West Indies. The Middle East . . .

I stopped and leaned down far enough to lift a torn piece of paper out of the bin. It was a receipted hotel bill. I scanned it quickly, then opened my fingers. We both watched as it floated down and perched on the corner of the steel bin, wobbling precariously like some drunk and almost opaque butterfly.

Then it toppled inside.

'. . . and India. As I say, big, impressive. Enough bread to be made to satisfy anyone.'

He was staring down at the blotter on his desk now. He was trying to give the impression that he wasn't listening to what I was saying but I knew that he was.

'Except that it gets to the stage when there isn't an enough. Money's like syphilis: you don't know you're riddled with it until it's too late. When it gets too deep a hold it's almost impossible to find a cure. So when the chance came along of making some more bread on the side, you couldn't resist it.

'Because we're not talking about peanuts. What I'm guessing you're into is big, big money. The other week the cops in Sweden or some place like that found a haul of thirty pounds of heroin. That, was reckoned as being worth around thirteen million pounds.'

He stopped taking an interest in the blotter; shifted his chair harshly and stared over at the wall. I reached out for his arm and pulled him back towards me. The material of his suit slid under my grip like a loose second skin. But I didn't let go. My fingers increased their pressure.

'Do you realise what that means? It means that every junkie you supply has enough of that shit running round his blood stream to keep me in food and booze for the rest of my life.'

He tried to loosen my grip but I wasn't having any. He couldn't even get his cigar to his mouth.

He started to say, 'You can't say that I have anything to do with supplying . . .'

That was as far as I let him get. My foot kicked the bin across the room and before it had clattered against the far wall I was standing up and the pressure on his arm was increasing second by second.

He was a big enough man, strong enough—but he wasn't used to having to show it.

'Of course you don't do the supplying. Not you. Not while there are lesser mortals to do that for you. All you're concerned about is getting the stuff in and selling it in bulk. What happens after that isn't your concern, isn't that right? I bet you've even got a nice handy line in rationalisation all worked out in case you should ever need it. Something to do with the laws of supply and demand and how if you didn't provide what was wanted then somebody else would. Does that ring any bells inside that thing you carry around on your shoulders under the pretence that it's a real human head with a real human brain inside; a human brain with human concerns, human cares and human weaknesses.'

I could sense my voice getting louder and I knew the pressure I was applying to his arm was increasing with it. He tried to prise my fingers away again but they weren't shifting. Beads of sweat started to roll down his face and his eyes started to bulge in their sockets.

Then there was a strange sound in the room and I realised that it was him, shouting.

'What's the matter, Blagden? Don't like it, huh? You're lucky it's me and all I'm using is my own hand. If it were somebody else then it could be a nasty looking needle. You know about needles, don't you, Blagden. Even if it isn't you who pricks the skin and slots them into the vein.'

He was getting paler every minute. I thought he might be going to pass out, so I released the pressure. He had a funny way of saying thank you. He tried to ram his knee up between my legs.

Now I didn't think that was very nice.

I told him so. Then I thanked him . . . for giving me the opportunity I had been looking for. I looped a long left into his face and enjoyed watching his chair keel over in what was a passable imitation of slow motion. He didn't go with it, not exactly. More slumped down to the floor where the chair had been.

There was a dark line of blood issuing from his nose. He lifted an arm and wiped it away with the sleeve of his jacket. A few seconds later he was having to do the same again.

I pulled him to his feet and told him to get his chair. Then I sat him down in it and watched the drips of blood falling on to the desk blotter where they spread in darkening circles.

It was still one of my good days.

'Right, Blagden. Two things. First, I want the Earls Court thing off my back. So you take a clean sheet of paper and make a statement to the effect that you hired me to watch the flat and find out who was in there, to the extent of making entry into a building over which you hold a controlling interest. State the retainer you paid me and then sign it. When you've done that you can dig into your wallet and give me the rest of my fee.'

He wasn't about to argue. He sat there like a real good boy and did as he was told. I got an envelope from the desk drawer and addressed it to Tom Gilmour at West End Central. Then I found a stamp and stuck it in the corner.

'Okay,' I told him, 'that brings us to the second matter. Anna Vaughan.'

He almost jumped. He didn't quite but it was a matter of touch and go. The right hand side of his face twitched a little by way of compensation.

'You've got your hooks into her. Again, I'm not absolutely sure how but if my guesses are as good as the earlier ones they won't be far wrong. You've got her worried and frightened and I don't like it. So lay off. Keep right away from her. If I see you messing her about again I'll finish what I just now began. And if you send one of your bully boys round to find her, I'll take him to pieces and send them back to you through the post. One at a time.'

I thought that was about all for now. There were a few more things I could have asked but I didn't figure it would do any good. Like, I could have asked where Anna was, but I figured that if she gave him an address it either wasn't the right one or she would have split by now anyway. And to ask him meant letting him know that I didn't have an idea where to pick her up—presuming she would be too worried by now to go back to work.

I could have squeezed a lot of other things out of him, but they weren't any of my business. Two things were: saving my own neck and trying to save the girl's at the same time. Anything else could wait until those were settled. One way or another.

While I'd been thinking, Blagden hadn't exactly been over-active. He'd got as far as finding the cigar he'd started and had jammed it between the fingers of his left hand. He hadn't bothered to light it.

I had a sudden memory of a silent movie with a guy who's got a face full of cigar and some other character comes along and slams his fist into the end of it. The cigar splits open and rams up against the first guy's face.

I had enjoyed it at the time. And sure as damn it seemed a good idea now.

But then. . . . why be vindictive?

Blagden wasn't looking too good anyway: at least the way he was I couldn't see anyone buying a used car from him.

I stuck the stamped envelope in my pocket and moved over to the door. When I went out into the reception room it was empty of one receptionist.

I was glad she had taken my advice—for her sake. I wondered what she had decided about the petty cash. If I bumped into her one day I thought I might ask her.

Hell! The way I was feeling I believed she'd tell me.

-11-

I spent a lot of the remainder of the day trying to track Anna down. It wasn't easy. The telegram gave no real clue and there wasn't very much else to go on.

I tried the air line office but I'd been right; she hadn't showed up. I finally got an address out of the woman in charge, after using a mixture of bribery, threats and my own simple, good-natured charm. I needn't have bothered.

Ten minutes in the reference library close by Leicester Square showed me that the house didn't even exist. Neither, the exchange, operator informed me, did the telephone number.

When my feet were aching enough I got a cab to the office. I picked up the usual selection of circulars advertising three pence off everything and tore them in half without looking at them. There was a conveniently large bin close to the door in the outer office and I dropped the pieces into it and walked on through.

Somewhere I thought I could recall reading that we were in the middle of a serious paper shortage. I'd even known a girl once called Lynette who used to get abusive when assistants in shops tried to stick what she bought into paper bags. The last I saw of her she was heading for this commune in the middle of East Anglia surrounded by massive tanks in which they were going to recycle their own waste and turn it into power for fuel and light.

Knowing her, she probably had a scheme for recycling the toilet tissue too.

I sat behind my desk and waited for inspiration to strike. Or luck. Coincidence. Something. I'd been out doing all the routine leg work I knew how and it had brought me the usual rewards. I guessed it was okay if you had a hell of a lot of men and you saturated somewhere with them, asked a few thousand questions, then asked them again; checked and rechecked every bit of information you'd received. That way, sure, you could get results.

But that way wasn't my way. Partly because I didn't have a lot of other guys to walk their feet off for me. Mainly because I didn't like to work that way. I didn't see things that way. I didn't believe life was like that. Life was luck, a little of it good, most bad. It was coincidence. It was . . . something.

I sat there for another ten minutes. Through the window the sky still looked grey. So did the inside of my head. It had to be time to get up, stretch my legs, get down to the coffee shop and see what was brewing.

I was half-way down the stairs when I heard the phone ringing.

I ran back as fast as I could. I knew what would happen. It did. As soon as my hand lifted the receiver I heard it go dead. Great! Still, I reassured myself, if it was important they'll ring again. I told my stomach to hang on and sat down.

This time it was five minutes. Precisely. The phone was in my hand half-way through the first ring. At first I thought it was a wrong number, then that someone was kidding around and doing the handkerchief over the mouthpiece bit for a laugh. It wasn't either of those things. It was Gerry Locke. What was left of him. He sounded as if someone had done their best to take his mouth off. He wasn't making a lot of sense but I got something about Anna and an address.

I checked where he was and said I'd be round. There was a first aid box in one of the drawers of the desk. I grabbed it and left the office fast.

*   *   *

Gerry Locke had tried to get back up the tall flight of stairs to his room. He hadn't made it. He was stranded half-way up, his right leg pulled in underneath his body, both arms stretched high, reaching for something they hadn't been able to grasp.

I leaned down next to him and checked that he still had a pulse. I couldn't find it straight away. Then, as I moved the tips of my fingers over the side of his head, something fluttered against them like a frightened bird.

It wasn't easy, but I managed to get him up the rest of the stairs and on to his bed. I went over to the window and opened it; you could almost see the foul air slink out through the gap. Then I went back to the bed.

I wished I hadn't had that thought about his mouth: it was too close to being the truth. What had been his lips certainly couldn't be called that any more. Instead there were traces of purplish pulp which fell back shapelessly against his face. His mouth was open. I watched fascinated as a bubble formed from nowhere; swelled; burst, scattering tiny specks of pink in its wake.

Where the bubble had been an instant before I could see his gums. The last time I had visited Gerry Locke there had been teeth there as well. Not now. Not at the front, at the top. Someone, something had wrenched them out. They hadn't been very careful about how they had gone about it. One tooth had obviously snapped across the root, leaving a single fragment behind. The rest was raw and bloody: blisters of red had formed over the empty sockets.

He wouldn't be able to bite down on a reed for a long time.

Not that it mattered. He wasn't going to be playing for a long time anyway.

They hadn't only worked on his face: there'd been his hands as well.

The little finger on his right hand stuck out obscenely at right angles to the palm. The others were not quite so obviously broken.

Until you looked at the knuckles more closely. They hadn't just been pulled out of joint, bent and twisted by other hands. Someone had used something heavier, nastier; it could have been the edge of the heel of a hard boot which had been raised a long way into the air; it could have been a length of piping; simply a hammer. Whatever it was had been systematically smashed down on finger after finger until the fourth one on the right hand. The thumb remained intact.

It must have been at that point that he had told them what they wanted to know.

I looked at the mouth, then back at the hands. No: Gerry Locke wouldn't be blowing sax for a long time to come.

I hunted around for something clean enough to wipe his face without smothering him with germs. Finally I came across a half-way decent shirt that he must have used when he was depping in the pit at the Palladium.

I ripped this into strips and fetched some water in a pan from the kitchen. I wasn't a trained nurse and I'd never got my badge for first aid from the boy scouts, but I did as good a job on him as I was able.

Then I tried to get him to talk. There was some whisky left in the bottom of a half bottle that had got shoved under the bed. I lifted his head a little and tried to pour some down his throat without touching what used to be his lips.

He started and gagged, and when the Scotch ran back down on to the blanket it was stained red. But there had been a reaction. I poured him some more. This time he made an attempt at a swallow and promptly choked on it.

It was doing him good, though. His eyes opened. I gave him a dribble more. This time he spoke. He didn't say much, just, 'Mitchell' and I don't think I would have recognised that if it hadn't been my own name.

I got my face right down close to his and started to ask some questions. I wanted to know why he'd phoned. I wanted to know what had happened before he'd done that. Most of all I wanted to know about Anna's address.

It came slowly and painfully: but it came.

Two guys had come to see him. They'd come early when he was still asleep. They'd let themselves in just the way I had done. He couldn't tell me much about them, except that one had been big and the other hadn't. They'd both been strong. They'd woken him up and pulled him out of bed and told him that they wanted to know where Anna Vaughan might be. He'd told them what he told me: he didn't know. It could even have been the truth. But what they did sent things back to the surface of his mind that had lain forgotten for a long time.

Anna had talked to him once about a cottage in Hampshire. Some artist she knew owned it, but he was usually wandering about all over the place catching butterflies and things like that, sticking a pin through them, then painting them. It was a living, much like any other.

Locke had been down there with her once. A village outside Andover. He couldn't dredge up the name. You drove out of the town through these new council estates and kept on going. The road seemed to be disappearing into nowhere until suddenly you were in a village. The cottage was on the right of a crossroads, behind a high hedge.

I didn't like it. He'd remembered too well. Though I could understand why. After they'd gone he'd lain there and thought about them doing the same to Anna as they had done to him. That was when he'd crawled downstairs to phone me. He hadn't fancied the police. They would have come round and probably turned the place over and found some things he didn't want them to find.

So it was down to good old reliable Mitchell! Once a knight errant, always a knight errant.

I phoned a man I knew who really was in the used car business: I needed to borrow a charger: mine had laid down and died a long time ago. Not only that, but my lance had been impounded.

A fine knight I made! The nearest I would have got to the Round Table would have been a stool in the corner.

Barrie agreed to lend me a car for a couple of days. He also promised that the wheels wouldn't fall off . . . at least, not all at once.

After that I phoned for the ambulance.

                    *   *   *

All the way down I was trying to work out what was likely to
have happened. If Gerry Locke's guess about the cottage had been
right—and it seemed reasonable to think that she would have
wanted to get out of London, then certainly the other two would
have got to her first. Presuming they went straight there without
reporting back for instructions.

Then, supposing it was Blagden they were working for, would
he have done as I'd told him and warned them off? I tried to console myself with the thought that he might, but there was no way
I could make it come out convincing.

His kind didn't allow themselves to get warned off. Not with
the amount of cash at stake that I reckoned there to be.

I increased the pressure on the accelerator and did whatever my
personal equivalent of praying might be called. Hoping against hope?

Andover had been a sleepy country town for as long as it could
remember, until some planners from London decided it would be
a good idea to move out a few thousand people, build a lot of
instant homes and make it into a larger sleepy country town, only
now it was overflowing with disorientated people from the city.

No, I haven't been doing a quick course in social history. I
knew somebody from Andover once: a few hundred years ago.

I turned away from the town centre and found the road Locke
had spoken of. Found the crossroads. Parked the car along a lane
and walked back. Found the cottage.

Habit forced my hand into my pocket, feeling for my Smith
and Wesson. Of course, it wasn't there. I pushed open the lopsided gate and stood at the end of the path.

There wasn't a sound. There should at least have been a bird
singing, somewhere, but there wasn't. The door was back a foot or
so under a porch that someone had tried to coax a couple of rose
bushes to twine themselves around. I listened again for any sound
from inside the cottage.

Dead.

The evening seemed to darken perceptibly as I stood there. Then . . . the faintest of noises. From inside. A loop of light curled out from under the door.

I moved away from the porch and round the solid wall of the cottage which faced the hedge. At the back there was a window. There was just enough space to squeeze myself up to it. I bent down and peered through years of cobwebs and dust that had been allowed to accumulate on the outside.

I could see a tiny kitchen with a stone floor; a deep sink into which a tap dripped noiselessly. I looked beyond and into the next room.

The door was half open and I could see a wooden table by the far wall. A couple of chairs, one of them in the centre of the room, the other pulled up to the table itself. Someone was sitting at the table, arms resting on it, head resting on hands that I guessed were cupped round it. Her hair looked duller, but that was probably the light. A part of it had got caught up in the high neck of the jumper she was wearing, breaking the otherwise even line of its fall. I don't know why, but I liked that.

I stayed there a while longer, watching her, telling myself that I was waiting to make sure there was no one else in the room. When I could fool myself no longer I moved back to the door and knocked twice with my knuckles.

A voice said, 'Go away!'

The response was instant, as though she had been waiting for my knock—somebody's knock.

I tried again.

This time she said, 'Who is it?'

The voice sounded edgy, tired.

'It's me,' I told her. 'The guy who goes round picking up books after you.'

She opened the door. She stood in the dim light of the room looking at me. She said, 'Hello.'

I didn't know what to say. I stepped into the room and closed the door. She walked round me quickly and slid the bolt back across. She was on the way back when I caught hold of her. She stiffened for a second, tensing herself against me, but then she let herself fall forwards and I was holding her and she was crying. I held her for a long time.

Eventually, she pushed herself away and sniffed a few times, then went wandering off to find a tissue. She couldn't wander far. I looked around the room; there wasn't much more than I had seen already. A small armchair. A low table with a candle on it that was providing all of the light. In the fireplace a fire was laid but not lit. I lit it.

Anna came back down from upstairs and she was obviously making an effort.

'Would you like some tea?' she asked.

'Sure,' I said.

'It's herb tea.'

'What?'

'Herb tea. It's what I always have.'

'Isn't there anything else?'

She shook her head and her eyes gleamed in the candlelight. 'There's only herbs because I brought them with me.' She smiled. 'I take them everywhere I go. Those and my nightie and my toothbrush.'

I said I'd try anything once and she went into the kitchen.

I nearly told her what it looked like, but I thought I'd better not. But it didn't taste like that . . . not that I'd ever tasted that either.

'See!' she said triumphantly. 'You like it!'

I wouldn't have gone that far but at least I was drinking it.

'How did you find out I was here?'

'Would you believe me if . . . ?'

'No,' she interrupted.

'Okay, then. It was Gerry Locke. He told them as well.'

'Them?'

'Don't bother lying. They've been here haven't they? They've been and they're coming back. You can't afford to buy them off and you can't afford to run.'

She stared at me, then sipped at her tea. There was no need for her to answer.

'I think you'd better tell me about it.'

She drank some more of her tea. In front of us the fire was catching and starting to throw its first shadows around the room. Anna got up and put out the candle with her fingertips. Then she came back and sat down and started to talk.

'I was in India. I'd started out the usual way, on a transit van overloaded with passengers and baggage, and the usual thing happened. We broke down. I got there by hitching and making the occasional bargain. It was incredible. I felt so . . . it's difficult to explain . . . calm and peaceful and yet at the same time I was alive to everything that was going on around me. I really have an affinity with India.'

If anybody else had said that it would have sounded empty, pretentious, but from her it didn't. She believed it: for her it was true.

'One day I met this American. The place is full of them. Young hippies who've finally made the biggest trip of all. He fascinated me because he was so typical, so full of things that I resented, hated almost. Yet there was something about him I liked, I don't think I'll ever forget him. That David. That summer.

'We came back to England together on the plane. David had been doing a little dealing out there and when he'd scored enough he bought two tickets. Said he wanted to see the Changing of the Guard. Anyway, he had this sitar thing that he'd bought and he asked me to take it through customs for him. He had a lot of other stuff anyway and they'd reckon he was overweight for the flight and . . . well, it doesn't matter now, does it? I took the thing on the plane and then hauled it through customs. They searched David, but not me. I thought it was just the long hair thing, you know.

'When we got to London and found this room for him in Bayswater, he opened up the case. The instrument had been specially made in lightweight wood so that no one would notice a difference in how it felt when they picked it up. He prised off the back: it was full: clear bags the size of a man's wallet: inside each bag it was packed tight; pure, white.

'I just thought it was clever. I didn't even mind that he'd taken me for a ride. Especially when he paid me. About a month later this man came round to see me. He wanted to know if I'd like to go on another holiday—all expenses paid.'

She stopped abruptly and stood up.

I said, 'Why?'

'Why not? I liked the money, the freedom it got me. The excitement. I met people I would never have met otherwise. Saw places I would never have visited. People would phone me up from the South of France and say we're having a party, hop on a plane and join us. I stayed on yachts with millionaires and in chateaux with pop groups.'

Her voice was defiant, daring me to contradict the rightness of what she had done. She had had her young life to the full, and now . . .

'And now?' I asked her.

'Well?'

'Now you're hiding away in a tiny cottage scared half out of your mind that someone's going to walk through that door and force you to get back on the treadmill again or do some very nasty things to you if you refuse. And they won't want you to refuse because in their eyes that's turning your back on them which is the next best thing to betrayal. Close enough to it for you to become a risk.'

I stood up and put my left hand on her arm, just above the elbow. She wouldn't look at me.

'You know what they do with people they consider risks, Blagden and his friends, don't you?'

Still she wouldn't look up, wouldn't answer.

'They send a couple of guys after them, one short and the other tall.' I felt a twitch underneath my fingers as something inside her responded. It still wasn't enough.

'They might be kind and kill you. They might be nasty and leave you to face the rest of your life with a very ugly face indeed.'

She turned away. I let her get a couple of paces. I gripped her by the shoulders, hard. Then I moved myself up against her. My hands moved down her jumper and found her breasts. After a few minutes she turned back into me. She lifted her face and I thought it looked great and then I couldn't see it at all because my eyes were closed and I was kissing her and it was as good as I had thought it would be.

After a lot more of that, she pulled herself away and tried to make it to the stairs. I didn't know if she was making a getaway or leading me on, but either way I didn't want to know. I grabbed her wrist and held on tight.

She grinned and made as if I was hurting her something terrible.

'You're a brute!' she laughed. 'You're nothing but a brute and you're only taking advantage of me because underneath this old pair of jeans I haven't got any knickers on.'

And she wasn't lying: she hadn't.

It had been a long time since I had lain with a woman and known that the only thing between us was the firelight.

We were still like that when I heard the car draw up on the road outside.

I wanted Anna to go upstairs but she'd only sit on the chair across from the door. I slid back the bolt and let them in. Locke had been right. One of them was pretty big and the other was a lot smaller . . . that hadn't stopped him holding the gun that had poked round that other door and sent Trevor Warren off on the big sleep.

They didn't like me being there. I could tell that from the way they scowled and pushed past me on their way into the room.

The big guy stood over Anna and jerked his thumb in my direction. 'Who's this monkey?'

His accent was Anglo Italian with a strong overtone of New York nasal. He'd seen *The Godfather* at least twice. The second time to try and understand the plot.

His buddy had his hair slicked back from his forehead by half a hundredweight of grease. His skin and the set of his face suggested that he was Maltese. Not that it mattered.

'I said, who is he?' The thumb jerked again. I thought of the sax player's broken hands.

'The name's Mitchell,' I told him. 'What's yours?'

If he meant me to take what he said seriously, his father had a very strange sense of humour. The priest would have gone the colour of his robes and dropped the baby head first into the font. That could account for a lot.

'Get lost!' he said next.

I noticed that the little one wasn't saying much, but with a partner who's got that kind of touch with dialogue who needs to go shooting off at the mouth every minute?

I looked at him and wondered where he kept his gun. I presumed that he'd replaced my Smith and Wesson with a little something of his own.

I finally figured it was clipped to his belt in front of his left hip. I hoped so. It was a hell of a place to have a hernia.

'You heard me. I said to beat it!' He came over the room to where I was standing. In that room it didn't take him long. From close up he really was fascinating. I could see his muscles rippling under his suit.

Somehow I wasn't worried about him; my eyes kept shifting to the other guy's right hand. Whenever it hovered close to the front of his jacket my stomach began to tighten.

I kept watching his hand and talked to the big fellow. 'Don't start pushing me around, pal. I'm here and I'm going to stay where I am. Anything else you've got to say to the lady you can say in front of me. Only say it fast and then be on your way.'

I thought if I put it like that there was a good chance he'd pick up most of what I was meaning. I think he did.

'Look, scum! I'd like nothing better than to pull you to pieces with these.' He lifted up his hands for me to inspect: sausages with bone. 'And if you don't shift your arse through that door I'll do it right here. In front of the lady.'

He was a simple-minded soul. He needed to look at Anna when he mentioned her. His head didn't turn far, but it was enough.

I slammed my head straight into his and hit him in the side of the temple. He was still falling while I was diving to the side. I did my best to grab the gun hand but somehow I didn't make it. I landed my shoulder into his body okay, though, and he dropped like a body through a trap door. Only this time the floor met him half-way and hammered the rest of the wind out of him.

But still he didn't let go of the gun. I was reaching for it when something lifted me into the air and slung me in the general direction of the kitchen. At that angle there was no way I was going to make it through the gap.

My head chipped some plaster down to the edge of the carpet. I used my hands and feet to lever myself backwards off the wall as though I was starting back stroke in the pool.

He tripped over my back as he rushed in and somersaulted into the kitchen. There was an odd slapping sound as his face made contact with the stone floor.

When I got focused on the Maltese guy he was sitting in a strange cross-legged pose near to the fire. His eyes looked very small; tiny black points. They weren't looking at me. They were fixed on the gun.

The gun was in Anna's hand. She was holding it very steady. She was standing in the middle of the room. A sudden flare of flame lit her face. It was very pale and very, very calm.

I didn't move. The big guy behind me wasn't moving either; not for some time to come.

I watched the little man as he sat on the floor, gazing up the barrel of his own gun, trying desperately to figure the odds.

Desperation never helps judgement.

I thought I saw his mind click into place a split second before it happened. His hands pushed downwards and he hurled himself at the gun. He was quick. Agile.

In the middle of his leap the gun went off.

The room was filled with the sound and when the echoes finally died away he died with them.

-12-

He lay back against the edge of the fireplace and there was a hole at the front of his chest that went through his clothes and looked as though it kept on going.

There was a lot of blood. Some of it was coming from his mouth but mostly it came from that hole in his chest.

There was a smell of scorching in the room and it wasn't from the firing of the gun. His arm had fallen close to the fire and the sleeve of his jacket was beginning to smoulder. I got up and went across and moved it over in front of him.

Anna was still holding the gun. Her arm had dropped to her side. When I moved towards her, she lifted it again. The gun was still at the end of it. The arm, the gun: both were pointing at my stomach.

I looked into her face. It should have been looking back, seeing me. She wasn't seeing anything. Not anything that was there, in that room.

I took another step towards her and took the gun from her hand. Her fingers were cold.

There was a movement in the kitchen. I went over and hit him on the back of the head a couple of times with the butt of the gun. Then I found a towel and wiped away any prints that might have been on the gun and slipped it into my pocket.

When I got back to Anna she was sitting in one of the chairs, staring at the body by the fireplace. I stood her up and swung my arms under the backs of her legs and carried her up the narrow stairs. I laid her on the bed.

There was a candle beside it in a chipped white enamel holder with a blue ring running around its edge. I went back downstairs and got a box of matches.

I lit the candle and she closed her eyes. Something fluttered against one of the squares of window pane. It was dark outside now: totally dark.

'Listen,' I said. 'Anna. There are things that have got to be done and done fast. Do you understand?'

She opened her eyes and looked at me.

Her mouth formed the word, yes.

'We've got two problems downstairs. One of them isn't going to move out of there without a couple of other guys carrying him. That's the first problem. The other one is going to be coming round and moving out of his own free will before very long. That's our second problem.'

Anna pushed herself up on the bed until she was sitting up. I was sitting facing her. I didn't need the spread of wax around the top of the candle to tell me that time was running out.

'I've got to let the cops have those two. Unless I do that there's no way I'm going to get off the hook. If I can let them have a couple of names to throw a few murders at, then they just might agree to forget about the corners I've been cutting. Not that I've stopped yet.'

I could see what she was thinking.

I carried on: 'Nobody needs to know what happened downstairs. Not exactly. But you never went near that gun. D'you understand that?'

I reached out for her hand: it was still cold.

'You never touched the gun!'

I stopped. I realised that I'd been shouting.

'Get your things. We're driving to London. I'll stop on the way and phone the police. I still want to keep a jump ahead of them. For now.'

I helped her off the bed and down the stairs. I gave the guy in the kitchen another little pat on the head and before we drove off I let his tyres down and pulled a few bits and pieces out of his engine and threw them in the bushes . . . just in case.

I drove the car to my flat. Anna needed to sleep and I wanted to know where she was. I showed her the bedroom and the bed and left her to it.

Then I got hold of the telephone directory and looked up Blagden under Hugh Barnard, which had been the name on his office door. The address was in Highgate and it sounded pretty impressive when I tried it over once or twice inside my head.

By the time I got back into the bedroom Anna was sitting on the side of the bed. Her face was still white and, although I didn't touch them I knew that her hands were still cold. She was wearing a pink nightdress that looked as though it didn't belong to her.

It might have belonged to somebody she once had been—but that was a long time ago.

She looked like a child.

I told her that I was going out. That I'd be back before morning. That I would phone before I did so and wake her up so that she could let me in. That she should bolt the door as soon as I had gone. That if anyone knocked without ringing first, on no account was she to unlock the door. That she should trust me and not worry.

Then I went quickly. I heard the bolts slide home behind me.

The house was along what was little more than a lane that led off a steep hill. I parked the car and walked. The houses were large and set well back behind high brick walls and wrought iron gates. There were lights still on in some of them, mostly in the upstairs rooms.

In one of them a telephone rang. When I had passed almost out of earshot it was still ringing.

Suddenly there were no more houses on the left. Behind a white railing, grass sloped down to a thicket of trees. Further over, to the right of those trees something shone in what little moon-light had escaped through the cover of clouds.

It was a pond. I was walking on the edge of Parliament Hill Fields. On a different night I thought it could have been pleasant. Now it didn't matter.

There were things which did.

I recrossed the narrow strip of road and began to look more closely at the names at the entrances to the houses. It was the fourth one along. The brick had been covered with a kind of pebble dash effect and painted white so that it showed up clearly even in that light. I lifted the latch on the double gate and stepped on to the gravel path.

There was a light on in one of the downstairs windows at the side. I made for it carefully, not wanting to make too much noise with the tiny stones under my feet.

I must have been successful. No dogs started barking, no raised voices of enquiry were heard. I suppose I could have triggered off some anti-intruder device simply by being there, how-ever silent, but Blagden obviously didn't feel the need for that style of protection,

No, I thought, as I looked around the edge of the window frame. He's sitting much too comfortably for that.

He was at the far end of a long room, leaning back against the arm of a leather settee. He was reading. On the table in front of him there was a half-filled glass and a decanter of what might have been port. A large glass ashtray held the inevitable cigar. It seemed to be out again.

It was time I went in.

I wondered if he'd put out the cat yet and locked the back door. I went round to see. The door was locked, but the kitchen window wasn't. Living in an area like that he should have known better. It took me a couple of minutes to get inside. I looked quickly around the kitchen.

There was a pin board over one of the work tops. I went over and looked at it. There was a shopping pad with detachable sheets of paper, each of which had a cute little picture of a vegetable along the top. Written on the uppermost sheet, neatly in red ink, were: aubergines, fennel, garlic, sweet potatoes. To the right of that hung a diary with a page for every week. There was only one entry for this week: Mark, dentist, 10 a.m.

Arranged in precise random order around these two central items were an assortment of postcards from friends who'd been to Spain for Christmas or skiing in the Swiss Alps, the stubs of a couple of theatre tickets and a leaflet advertising a school jumble sale.

It was nice to see that Blagden enjoyed a full and normal family life. I walked across the tiles to the kitchen door, wondering how much longer he would be able to enjoy it.

I stepped inside the long room. Blagden looked up from the settee and as he did so he let go of his book. It slid down his lap, then tumbled to the floor. A leather marker flew out before the book finally fell shut. I didn't think he'd worry overmuch about losing his place.

He started to get up but I told him to sit down. Partly to my surprise he did. I pulled a chair from against the wall and stuck it on the carpet about six feet in front of him.

If it had been a movie I would have set the chair down backwards and straddled it, but I preferred to be comfortable. I sat down and crossed one leg over the other. So far so good. I even found myself smiling. Only a little smile . . . and it was for me, not for him. Not at all for him.

'You didn't, did you?'

'What?' His voice was pitched higher than it should have been, as though he was remembering what had happened in his office.

Which was good . . . only I wanted him to remember what had been said as well.

'You didn't take any notice of what I said.'

'What are you getting at?'

'Those men. You went ahead and sent them after her anyway.'

He sat forwards and moved his arm away from where it had been resting. A vein had started to throb immediately over the edge of his left eyebrow. When he spoke it was with the desperation of a man who knows his back is up against a very shaky wall and that the bricks are starting to crumble away even as he speaks.

'Look, Mitchell. I don't know how you got into my house, but I imagine it was by some illegal means or other. You have no right to be here and absolutely no right to cross-question me. As for what passed between us this morning, of course I forgot it. That was the best thing to do with the totally unsubstantiated allegations you were making. Luckily for you, they were made without witnesses being present, otherwise my lawyers . . .'

I could take so much and then no more. Right at that moment I was stuffed up to the top of my gullet with Hugh Blagden and the diseased crap that he'd been sending in my direction ever since our first meeting. I didn't want another lie, another posture, another minute of deceit.

I reached down and pushed the table out of the way as hard as I could. The cut glass decanter bounced twice on the rim and then landed on its side, the rich looking liquid lapping out into the carpet.

Blagden had flinched as though I had hit him. I was standing in front of him, my hands back by my sides. When he thought I'd calmed down I sensed him relax. Then I did hit him. Only once and I didn't give it any backswing. But I wanted it to hurt.

From the way he slapped against the back of the settee and the sound that came out of his suddenly opened mouth, I thought I'd succeeded.

In the silence that followed I heard a quiet tapping at the door to the room. I pointed to Blagden and he said, 'Come in.'

We both watched as the door opened and the little boy came in. His hair was tousled from sleep and he was wearing striped pyjamas and blue slippers with pictures of Mickey Mouse on them. He stood there, looking from one to the other of us.

Then Blagden said, 'What is it, Mark?'

The boy said, 'I had a dream.'

His bottom lip started to quiver and tears formed in the corners of his eyes. His father put out his arms and the boy ran past me and into them.

'What sort of a dream, Mark?'

'A nasty dream. There was a monster thing and it was eating us up.'

Blagden hugged him tight and then released him a little.

'But you know there aren't really monsters, don't you? Only in stories . . .'

'And films, Daddy,' the boy interrupted, suddenly sounding very serious.

'Yes, Mark, and in films.'

He bent down and lightly kissed his son on top of his head. The child looked at his father's face, at the trickle of blood that was running still down from the split in his lip.

'What's that, Daddy?' he asked, pointing.

Blagden touched his face and seemed surprised to feel, then to see the blood. 'Oh, nothing. There was an accident. Look, see what happened to the table.'

The boy looked. 'You fell over it, Daddy,' he said.

'That's right.' He reached for him and kissed him again, this time on the cheek. 'Do you think you can get back to sleep now? It's school in the morning, remember.'

'Yes, daddy, all right.' He walked backwards out of the room, watching his father all the while he did so. He hadn't given me more than a couple of hasty glances all the time he had been there.

'He's six . . .' Blagden began.

'Shut it!' I shouted. 'I don't want to know. I don't care. It doesn't matter. He doesn't matter. Not to me. Not to what I'm doing here.'

'What . . . what are you doing here?'

'I'm here because I need to let you know you were wrong. You were wrong about a lot of things, Blagden, but most of all you were wrong about me. You thought I was nothing. A shifty private eye, with one foot already in the grave and one in the cess pit of other people's lives. Well, you were right about the second part but you were way out on the first. I'm a long way off from being finished. I may not look much and I may not be very bright, but there's one thing I don't do; I don't give up. I'm not prepared to lie down and let you or any of your strongarm boys walk all over me. What you thought you were buying with those few notes you passed me across the table in that pub was a dupe, a nobody you could use as you liked and that wouldn't kick back.

'You were wrong, Blagden. All the way down the line. You were wrong today when you didn't believe me when I said what I'd do to you if you went after Anna again.

'You were so wrong.'

The pulse against his forehead was racing enough to break through the skin. He huddled back into the settee, trying to get away from my hands as they reached down for him. But there wasn't any way out.

I lifted him up on to his feet and he just stood there, arms down by his sides, looking at me.

At the last moment, he started to say something but it never got out . . . I'd already started hitting him, I hit him a lot. At first it was random, a mixture of temper and frustration finding an outlet in my fists. After that I became more methodical.

If he fell down, I picked him up and started over again. If he cried out too loudly, I struck his mouth with my open hand.

I thought about the dead girl with a flayed face.

I thought about the young man with a bullet between the eyes.

I thought about the musician with smashed fingers and torn mouth.

I thought about Anna; the thing she saw in her eyes: the coldness of her hands.

And I hit him again and again and again.

I was still hitting him when they came into the room and pulled me away.

I was sitting on the same settee that Blagden had been on earlier. But now it was later. Blagden was on his way to hospital and I was staring at a pair of hands that were wrapped up in two towels. They were my hands.

Hankin was sitting on the smaller chair now, but he wasn't straddling it either. Occasionally one or other plain clothes officer would come into the room. Sometimes they spoke to Hankin in quiet, guarded tones. Sometimes they busied themselves with other things.

I was trying hard to think. Right from the first I had nursed the idea that Hankin had been involved; that he had been on the take from Blagden or someone else with a connection, an interest. Now he was here and he had been through my story three times already. Hadn't said anything, I shown any emotion save the usual one of tiredness. At least, he hadn't slapped me this time. Though now he had reason enough.

Even if he had been involved, I guessed that things had got to the stage where he couldn't avoid moving in. If Blagden laid a complaint against him and tried to take Hankin down with him, then he would have to prove it to A.10's satisfaction.

I was still worried about the gun.

Finally I thought the only thing to do was ask him about it.

'A grass came in with it. A put-up job, of course. Whoever stole it from your office and later used it to kill Warren wanted to set you up for it. From what you've said, Blagden or whoever pulled his strings, must have started getting panicky about the way you'd begun poking your nose where they didn't appreciate it.

'They tried warning you off but that didn't work. So they thought up the business with the gun. They realised they would almost certainly have to get rid of Warren, who knew too much for his own good. It was a way of killing the proverbial two birds . . .'

He lit a cigarette and blew the smoke in a lazy curve across the space between us.

'You said, Blagden or whoever pulled his strings . . . ?'

'Right. Blagden's big but he's not the one at the top. We wanted to wait a little longer, find out more. Pull in the really juicy one. But after your caper down in the country we couldn't very well wait around any longer, could we?'

'You got the big guy all right?' I asked.

He nodded. 'We had to chase him over a couple of fields, but in the end he came quietly.'

There should have been the glimmer of a smile as he said that last phrase, a wrinkle at the edges of the mouth even. But there was nothing.

He held the cigarette between the middle two fingers of his hand, so that when he stuck it in his mouth the whole of the lower half of his face was covered.

I found myself thinking idly what big hands a lot of people had. Hands and rings.

Hankin stood up.

'Your friend, Tom Gilmour, seems to think you're worth bothering about, Mitchell. I think he's wrong. You're just a nothing running round in circles sending yourself dizzy. You didn't have a bloody clue what was going on in this case, did you? Not a clue. I told you that if I let you run about for long enough you'd stir up a lot of shit.'

'But not enough to suffocate in,' I told him.

'Not yet, Mitchell. Not yet.'

I could have said a few more things. I could have said what about the couple of murders I'd sorted out for him, what about the drug smuggler I'd brought out from under cover. But I thought he'd only say that they could have done those things themselves any time they'd wanted to.

So I said nothing.

Hankin turned on his way to the door. 'Get home and get some sleep, Mitchell. Come in first thing in the morning and make a full statement.'

He hesitated a moment or two. Perhaps he was waiting for me to say thanks. I didn't. He stopped waiting and left. I arched back my head and closed my eyes: I was feeling tired, tired, tired.

I drove back to the flat very carefully. I was in a hurry right enough but I didn't trust my reactions and this night—this morning—was the last one on which I wanted to wrap myself round a convenient lamp post.

I even waited a couple of minutes at a red light that seemed to have jammed, although there was no other traffic and no one walking the streets.

I slid the car into the kerb at minus miles an hour. My hands were aching from holding the wheel. I looked at my watch. It was too early to be late and too late to be early.

I pushed my body out of the car and locked it. As I was walking across the grass I started to sense the tiredness falling away from me with every step.

It was going to be all right. It might even, with luck, be more than that. I remembered the glow that the flames from the fire shot across her body and how her skin tensed when I touched it.

I was almost knocking on the door when I realised that I said I'd phone first. If I didn't do that, she'd wake up and start to get scared all over again.

I found a coin in my pocket and walked the fifty yards to the nearest phone box. I dialled the number and waited. No answer. She must be asleep. I put down the receiver and tried again. She'd been pretty whacked too; it would take a lot to wake her.

But the phone was by the bed.

I was half-way through dialling a third time when my finger froze in the middle of a curve. I could see her right inside my head. Only she wasn't warm in front of the fire. She was cold. Cold.

I jumped out of the box and started running. I pounded my legs down on to the pavement but it was like racing through water. I could see her eyes now, staring the way they had when I took the gun away from her. Staring at nothing I had been able to see.

I thought that now maybe I knew what it was.

Hammering on the door wasn't any use. I pulled off my shoe and smashed its heel against the frosted glass of the high window alongside. In my haste I must have cut myself as I reached through but I didn't notice at the time. I just wanted to get into that room.

The bed was empty, the covers thrown back.

I checked the living room, the kitchen.

Nothing.

The bathroom door was locked from the inside. I kicked it down. My eyes jammed shut and I could feel something climbing up my throat and at the last moment I realised I was going to throw up. I leant my hands on the edge of the bath and watched the vomit hit the white porcelain and splash back up the sides. When I was sure I'd finished I wiped my mouth and my eyes and then, only then, did I look at Anna.

She was sitting on the toilet. Her nightdress was hoisted up almost to her waist and you could see the long fall of dark hair down between her thighs. Her legs were spread quite wide; wide enough for her arms to be pushed down between them. Her fingers were curled into the water at the bottom of the toilet bowl. Only the water was red because she had cut her wrists. The razor blade floated on the top, where she had dropped it.

Her head had fallen sideways, against the wall and the way her hair hung across it I couldn't see her face. I was glad. I didn't want to see her face.

I thought I might throw up again, but I didn't.

When I got out into the living room I found the note. It was written on the back of a plain post card. It said: 'I didn't think I'd ever feel 25 again.'

That was all.

I went and sat on the bed and looked at the telephone. I knew I should pick it up but I didn't. Not for a long time. I sat there and thought about Anna. I thought about George Anthony waiting down in Devon for me to find her, waiting and worrying.

I thought it was all right for George Anthony: at least he'd be able to write a fucking poem about it!

After a while I did pick up the phone.

NEON MADMAN

This is for Libby Houston: poet.

-1-

It was hot. The circles of darkening sweat that spread from my armpits reached almost to my waist; my new navy blue cotton briefs were welded to my body. Inside my shoes, my feet were carrying on an argument with pain that had started several hours earlier and never had they felt less like winning. When I shifted my position in the chair and lowered one foot to the floor, it sang back at me with a flat note of suffering.

I reached up my right hand and wiped away the moisture that dripped from my scalp. Before I had finished more had appeared. Like most things, it was a losing struggle. I gave up and allowed the lines of sweat to run into and through my eyebrows, from there to drip down on to my cheek, the side of my nose. When I couldn't take the gradually increasing irritation any longer I shook my head and watched the drops fall on the blotter on my desk. This time they had met more than their match. I thought I knew how they felt.

It was something after four in the afternoon and I'd been on the go since that morning. Seven hours and much of it on my feet. Walking around, pretending to be looking casually in shop windows or at the dying fragments of roses in other people's gardens; walking around or standing still; standing and watching; watching and waiting.

I don't know what I was complaining about. That was how I earned my living. If living wasn't too strong a word for what I did. I was a private detective.

All day I'd been out on a case. Following this guy's wife as she went through her daily routine. A routine which he suspected to include more than a soupçon of infidelity. Though where she was going to get the desire from in that heat I couldn't understand.

Her old man drove the Rover out of the garage at around eight thirty and she leaned her head through the window and gave him a good long kiss on the mouth. He headed off towards the city and she went back into the house. Half an hour later she opened the door to a smart young man in an off-the-peg suit and a ready-made smile. It was a little early for the man from the Pru, I thought, and it wasn't the kind of area where the tally boys had to get up with the dawn in order to scrape in a few overdue payments.

She was still wearing her housecoat and there was a welcoming burst of cleavage to accompany her good morning smile. Okay, I thought, so my better days begin with scrambled eggs and orange juice, but out here in the land of plenty, who knows?

I got out of my car which was parked fifty yards down the road on the other side and walked up to the house. A neat gravel path led alongside the garage and into a hundred feet plus of garden. I have a way of walking on gravel that's as soundless as treading on silk. It comes with years of practice.

They hadn't gone upstairs, nor had they bothered to draw the curtains. You could have ridden a bike through the gap between them, never mind aimed the telephoto lens of a Pentax SP 1000. Oh yes, we professionals only use the best. Scott Mitchell's Pentax, it will say when you open your colour supplement one of these fine Sundays and flip through the ads gazing at all those things you should have. That's before you read in the news pages how you can't afford them.

This lady could afford more than most and from the earnest look on the guy's face he was explaining to her how she might make even more. There were some brochures open on his lap and some forms lying on top of one of those smart black brief cases that are too thin to take a decent-size sandwich. I snapped away for a few minutes, but without any enthusiasm. If this was voyeurism, it had all the eroticism of yesterday's cold potatoes.

I went back to the car and waited for him to come out so that I could get a few shots of his face. It had all the smugness you'd expect from someone who'd made his first commission before his first cup of coffee.

I waited around some time while she took a quick bath or a shower or something. She was looking very new and shiny when she reappeared with a shopping bag and made for Kingston High Street. She was wearing a halter top over a loose skirt that finished somewhere around her knees. Her skin was a beautiful, even brown and she was showing a lot of it. Her hair was cut short and shone with a dull coppery colour. She had too much money in her purse and too much time on her hands. She went from shop to shop parading her sensuality as though it was next year's original model.

The only thing was, nobody appeared to be buying. The hottest thing on view apart from the weather was a little double-entendre with the butcher's assistant about how big a piece of steak she wanted that morning.

She broke off her exhausting routine to drink some vile and overpriced coffee in a mock Tudor place called somebody or other's pantry. Then it was back on the shopping trail. I nearly offered to push her trolley in Sainsbury's, but thought better of it. I wasn't into gestures of devotion.

So it went until lunchtime, when she was whisked away by a guy driving a plum-coloured Datsun with the certainty of someone who knew nobody else had a right to be on the same road. They drove down to the river and parked outside a discreet looking hotel with so much ivy on the walls that if it was cut down the brickwork would disintegrate with it.

I parked my own car and made for the dining room. A hasty glance around told me that they hadn't come for lunch. Their hunger was of a different kind.

It wasn't easy getting past the sweet grey-haired old lady who sat behind the reception desk with all the benevolence of a cobra. I finally managed to twist her arm with a five-pound note and got myself and my camera up in to the first floor. The keyhole didn't yield much, so I tried the balcony which ran along the back.

It was turning into the sort of job I would have used a double for if I was making a movie. But this was real life. Or so I kept telling myself as I considered the possibilities of falling from the narrow ledge which led from one section of balcony to another.

I made it all right and thanked her for being so untroubled about the curtain again. Whatever she was suffering from it sure wasn't a guilty conscience.

I stood there for a while taking all the usual pictures while they did most of the usual things. I will say this, though, what they lost in originality they more than made up for in enthusiasm.

Most of the time I could only get shots of his back—you see what I mean about originality—with the occasional glimpse of her face from underneath his arms. I didn't think it would matter much. As long as she was clearly there and doing what she was clearly doing, I didn't think my client was going to be too bothered about her companion's identity.

I was about to make my way back when they stopped and he rolled over on to his side. She lit him a cigarette and put it lovingly between his lips. I caught him three times. He was an impressive looking man. The sort of face which inspired confidence.

Well, I'd buy a used car from him any day. Even a Datsun.

I slipped back downstairs. Now that I'd got what I'd come for the ledge didn't seem to be any kind of problem at all.

I waited in the bar for them to come back down. A little more arm twisting told me that they came every Tuesday and Thursday, always at the same time. I wondered if his secretary wrote it in his diary for him and then reminded him of his engagement if he seemed in danger of forgetting.

There's a meeting of directors at eleven, an appointment with a merchant banker at twelve and your twice-weekly screw at one.

Nice work if you can get it.

Unlike mine. Mine was a reel of film, a few neat pages giving names of places, descriptions and times. Those were my business. Those and nothing else. As long as I stuck with them I guessed I would be all right. There had been occasions in the past when I had stepped too far outside my league and got myself mixed up in nasty things like murder. It hadn't been nice; it hadn't been easy; I'd been warned by my friendly neighbourhood policemen that my nose was getting in where it wasn't wanted. And I nearly got myself killed.

I hadn't liked that. I had no intention of getting beyond myself again. I was going to stick with nice easy divorce cases and large brown manilla envelopes filled cram full of photographs and notes. I pass the envelope across the desk; the client passes me back a cheque in exchange.

What could be simpler?

I looked up and saw the silhouette against the glass of the office door. For a big man he walked softly. He paused then opened the door and stepped through. He was big. He shut the door with the same decisiveness and leaned back against it. I guess he wanted me to take a good look at him and I could see why.

He was four or five inches over six foot and broad enough for his height not to be the only thing you noticed about him. Some of his muscles were housed in a short-sleeved satiny white shirt, but mostly they bulged outside it. There was a rich scrub of dark curly hair on his chest that made my office doormat look positively threadbare. Above this he wore a plain silver chain necklace.

His legs were threatening the seams of a pair of yellow slacks above a pair of light tan casuals. Both hands were open and spread with their knuckles towards me so that I wouldn't miss any of the rings that adorned his fingers. They weren't just pretty—I bet they hurt some, too.

His hair was curled on to his scalp as tightly as that on his chest. The nose that spread across his face was broad enough to have been broken at least twice.

He was both the most handsome and the most dangerous looking West Indian I had seen for a long time.

I opened my mouth to say something, but there didn't seem much point.

As soon as he had finished making an impression I was sure he would tell me the score. I just hoped the way he read the game I wasn't going to lose by too many.

He moved away from the door and came over towards the desk. I tried to stop them, but my eyes flicked down to the barely open desk drawer anyway. This boy didn't miss a trick.

He gave a funny sort of grin and pointed. 'Don't do that, man. It would be a mistake, like I'm telling it to you.'

From where I was sitting he looked awfully big. I knew that if I stood up he would still be a few inches taller and a hell of a lot heavier. I thought that he was right about the drawer. There was no way I could get the gun out in time. I grinned back at him and tried anyway.

His right leg kicked up under the far side of the desk and the next thing I knew I was trying to chew wood. By the time I had given it up and was spitting out the odd splinter, a few changes had taken place.

Like I was on my back and the chair I had been sitting on had spun away across the room. The desk had rebounded off my mouth on to my legs and tried to knock a tune out of my shin bone with all the delicacy of Lionel Hampton in his third successive chorus of 'Flying Home.' Except the only sound was me—yelling.

The desk drawer had banged itself shut. My visitor had come round between me and it, though he couldn't have thought I was going to be so stupid as to try that trick twice. In case I was he gave me a short, sharp kick into the top of my shoulder. I grunted and pulled my head to one side till it was staring at his shoes. The one he had kicked at me with hadn't got scuffed in the process and I was glad, I felt that if it had he would have blamed me and taken a second shot.

I moved my head and looked up at him. For the second time, I grinned. He pulled his lips back to reveal the usual set of fine, white teeth—then he spat right in my face.

I reached up with my left hand and wiped the thick mixture of spittle and phlegm from my eyes, my cheeks and mouth. I scraped it off on me carpet and did my best to look as though nothing had happened. But I knew that I would remember what had.

So did he.

He took a couple of paces back and told me to get up off my fat white arse.

I did exactly as I was told: I got up off my fat white arse.

'You're Scott Mitchell, right?'

'Right. How did you guess?'

He looked at me with scorn. 'For one thing your name's all over the outside door. For another, from what I've heard about you, that's the kind of dumb trick you would try.'

'Too bad,' I said. 'I'll have to stop them sending copies of my references to every cheap hood and heavy in town.'

This time he laughed out loud. I went over and got the chair and sat down.

'So what is it?' I asked. 'Or did you just come over to grab a few laughs and have a little work out on the side?'

He had something against me sitting down. This time he kicked the chair from under me and grabbed me before I bit the floor. He yanked me into the air and jolted me down on to my feet.

As if I wasn't having enough trouble with them already.

'Look, man, you don't try games with me. You listen. See?'

I did my best to show him that I was going to do exactly that and without any trouble. Apart from anything else, I was anxious to know what he wanted.

'You were down south of the river today. You were at a place called the Three Swans. Asking questions. That right, man?'

I could have denied it but I was feeling tender and tired—and hotter than ever. I didn't want a going-over. Not right then and there. Later maybe.

'Sure,' I said, 'I was there.'

The large head nodded. 'What you doing there?'

'I was following somebody for a client.'

'Who?'

It was my turn to shake my head. Only I did it in the opposite direction.

He took a step towards me and I saw his fists begin to bunch up. They looked like over-ripe bananas.

'You've got to know I can't tell you that. Once I start giving away clients' names as soon as I'm asked, there goes my hope of getting any more work.'

I knew that if he really went to town on me, the question of work would be purely academic. I had to say something, and fast.

'Look, I'll give you this much. I was following a woman. Divorce business. She was supposed to have showed up at the hotel. Nothing happened. I asked a few questions and got nowhere. Her old man's obviously some kind of nut. It was all a big waste of time. Now there's nothing in that to interest you—or whoever you're working for.'

There was a long pause. I was conscious of the streams of sweat that were pouring down my face more strongly than ever. Across the room a dumb fly had managed to get itself trapped between the two panes of the open window and was buzzing and banging in an effort to get out.

Somehow I didn't think he was going to make it.

Somehow I thought I knew how he must be feeling.

The West Indian didn't have a crease in his shiny shirt and there wasn't a bead of perspiration on him. Perhaps he wasn't human. Perhaps he wasn't really there at all. I could simply walk around him and let myself out of the office and nothing would happen.

And maybe some magic or mysterious hand would move the window and the fly would slip out into the early evening air.

I stood there and looked up into the man's face, watching his expression change to a nasty sneer. Behind us, the fly buzzed on with increasing desperation.

I had to have one more go. 'If we got our paths crossed, that was nothing but coincidence. There wasn't anything going on for you to get disturbed about. Not on my account. I'm sure not going back there. No reason to.'

He flexed his muscles in the right arm and I held myself tense in readiness, but all he did was say, 'You being square about that divorce thing?'

'Sure.'

'You better be. 'Cos if I ever have to come back to you, man . . .'

He didn't need to finish his sentence. My imagination was working well enough to fill in the details.

He came right up to me and lifted one fist level with my face. He allowed the edges of the rings to graze my skin, finally pushing one hard into the flesh underneath my right cheekbone.

'You got me, Mitchell?'

It was difficult answering with a faceful of fist, but I did the best I could. Finally he lowered his hand and stepped away. Which was when he saw the camera in its case on the floor. He stooped down and picked it up.

'You have this with you today?'

'Yes.'

'You got the film still in it?'

'Sure. There's a film there.'

He began to walk towards the door, camera in hand.

'Only it's not the one you're looking for.'

He swung round and glared at me.

'How come?'

'I took that out—the film I used today—took it out and mailed it off to be developed. It should be back in four days.'

'If you're lying . . .'

'I'm not lying. My client wants those pictures of his wife walking around shopping all day. The film that's in there's brand new. Take a look for yourself.'

He hesitated, looked down at the camera, then swung back his arm and threw the Pentax at me as hard as he could. I held it on the third attempt. It had cost me a lot of money and I wasn't about to be able to afford another. Certainly not the way this case was going—whichever way that was.

He stood in the doorway and pointed a finger at me.

'Pray you been telling me the truth, Whitey, or I might have to come back and get myself a little righteous with you.'

It didn't call for an answer.

He glared at me over the outstretched arm for a few moments longer, then turned and slammed the door so hard I thought the glass would break. It didn't.

The outer door was shut with the same force. I walked over to the window and watched him as he emerged from the front of the building and walked off in the direction of Leicester Square.

He didn't waste his energy looking back up at me. Why should he?

I eased down one half of the window and released the frustrated fly into the air. I felt pretty good about that. Kind-hearted Mitchell, they call me.

Amongst other things.

I went back over to the desk and set it to rights. I fetched the chair and sat on it with my arms resting on either side of the blotter. It was still hotter than hell and I still had that report to type out.

That and a few dozen questions to which I didn't have any answers.

−2−

＊

I finally got the thing finished and decided there was nothing I could do to stop it looking like a script for a bad film. Like a friend of mine said to me once, most people write their own script then spend the rest of their lives playing the part.

The husband had come to me a few days before. He sat there in the client's chair and fidgeted around under the discomfort of the heat and what he had come to say.

But hot as it was, there was no way in which he was going to either loosen his tie or remove his jacket. That was the kind of script he was into. He shuffled his feet a lot and stalled for time while he told me about how something important had come up at the bank and he'd nearly phoned and cancelled the appointment. Unfortunately for him he hadn't and sooner or later he was going to have to come out with it.

And when he did it was the oldest story in the world: he thought his wife was playing around with other men behind his back.

I'd looked at him as evenly as I could and asked him if he was sure he wanted me to follow her around and check her out. Perhaps things were better left as they were. Or maybe he should confront her with it himself.

But no, his mind was made up. He took out his wallet and passed the inevitable photograph across the desk. You know, the one that was taken a few years back when they had that wonderful holiday together. It had been just like when they'd first met, both of them so happy. And then . . . and then what?

He was sitting here in the office of a private detective asking for his wife to be treated like a suspected criminal. I took the photo from him and passed him a card with my charges on it in exchange. I always felt a certain embarrassment talking about money. In those situations, anyway.

It wasn't only the coppery hair that made Marcia Pollard a good-looking woman. She had a figure that wasn't about to allow anyone not to notice it and a way of standing and holding herself that suggested a good deal of pride, even arrogance. When she wanted a thing, she looked as though she'd do her damndest to get it.

I looked quickly at the man with thinning fair hair and the definite beginnings of a paunch. I guessed he wasn't getting in quite as many games of squash as he used to. Marcia had wanted him once and she had got him. It looked as if she didn't want him any longer: not just him.

My eyes went back to the photograph. She was in her early to middle thirties—the classic age for infidelity. The time when you needed reassurance so badly you would make all kinds of fool of yourself to get it. And never count the cost until it was too late.

'Your fees are not cheap, Mr Mitchell,' Pollard had observed.

'If you want to shop around, go ahead. You could get some-one to do it for less. Only don't come squawking to me if they hold out on you or try to put the squeeze in for themselves.'

I knew that I wasn't sounding very sympathetic but I didn't care. Pollard wasn't the kind of man I found it easy to be nice to. He rubbed me up the wrong way without even trying.

'No, no. Don't misunderstand me. I have no intention of going elsewhere. I am sure that your charges are—er—commen-surate with your expertise.'

I wasn't impressed by the words or the vestiges of a public school accent that spoke them, but the sight of the man's cheque book coming out of his pocket did a lot to reassure me.

I handed him back the photograph of his wife.

'Don't you want to keep it?' he asked, surprised.

I shook my head. 'I don't think so. I'm not likely to forget her now that I've seen her.'

I was on the point of adding, maybe that's the trouble, but I decided against it. There didn't seem to be any fun in hitting anyone as down as he was.

And that had been four days ago. Bowed down by his job and the heat and the nagging weight of suspicion. Tomorrow I was going to deliver a little package of reports and photographs which were going to drive him right under. Possibly for good.

For an instant I wished he had taken my advice and left things as they were. With the kiss at morning and evening and a lot of doubts. That would have been better than . . .

But then I realised I would only have been talking myself out of a job. And I had already banked the first cheque.

To hell with it!

I got up and went out of the office, locking both doors as I did so. It wouldn't stop anybody who was half-way serious, but it might discourage ten-year-old kids and little old ladies but to supplement their pension.

Once on the street, I turned left and headed for some coffee. I went down the stairs and smiled over the top of the coffee machine. The girl smiled back. We exchanged a few pleasantries and I bought an open ham and tomato sandwich and a piece of cheesecake to keep my stomach in check.

I gave her the money and she smiled again as she handed me the change. Her name was Tricia and she was nineteen or twenty and outside that coffee shop she didn't exist. Not for me anyway. For someone else I guessed that she did, but not for me.

Which was why we were still able to smile at each other after a couple of years.

I sat down in the corner and stirred the coffee for several minutes although I hadn't been taking sugar for around six months. I was thinking and it wasn't about what I was doing.

I was thinking about a big Spade heavy who had shown how easily he could take me apart. Trying to figure out how our lines had become crossed. It didn't sound as though he'd been at the hotel himself, so that meant someone else had seen me and either recognised me or followed me back to my office. Someone who was there for a little more than pleasure.

They could have been using the hotel as a meeting place or a pick-up point and got spooked at seeing a private investigator suddenly snooping about the place. Or they could have been watching it themselves . . . it or him. The guy who had taken Marcia Pollard there for a little after-lunch romp. Just to make sure that the avocado didn't go to waste. The guy who went there every Tuesday and Thursday. As regular as a work out in the gym—and probably a hell of a lot more enjoyable.

There hadn't been a name in the register, of course, and Pollard had told me he didn't want to know who was involved with his wife, just if anyone was. But I had a natural curiosity.

Murdoch, the grey-haired woman had told me. James P. Murdoch.

'He's a very important man,' she had added in an awed whisper.

At the time I hadn't thought twice about it, but now it seemed as though she might have been telling the truth.

I realised that I had eaten all of the roll and half of the cheesecake without noticing what I was chewing. I got up and ordered another roll. I didn't want to get involved in a long argument with my stomach later about whether I'd fed it or not.

'What's the matter, Mr Mitchell? You look worried.'

She stood there smiling, a flap of dark hair, falling down over her forehead and the light over the counter making the slight down of her arms shine whitely. She was a very pretty girl. I wondered what she'd be like when she was ten or twelve years older and starting to get the itch once her old man was off to work and the kids were in school I didn't want to know the answer.

'It's nothing,' I said, 'Only the heat.'

She smiled sympathetically and agreed. I took my bread roll back to the table and thought about eating it. It tasted good. Only by that time the coffee had started to get cold.

James P. Murdoch. I tried the name out inside my head a few times. It sounded convincing enough. The sort of name I felt I should have been able to place but couldn't.

I drained my coffee cup, ate the last mouthful of cheesecake, said goodbye to Tricia and went back to my office to play with the London telephone directory.

It was a game I was used to. I must have been one of the few people who could recite whole sections of it from a relatively early age. While other kids my age were marvelling at Roy of the Rovers or Jack Slade, I was sitting there with a volume of E–K open on my knees.

The plot was lousy but the list of characters was fascinating!

Later, when I was working as a young CID copper attached to Holmes Road police station, it was to come in more than useful. And since I had left the force and taken to working for myself, I used it even more.

Only this time the name wasn't there.

There were quite a few J. Murdochs, but I figured that if he was as definite about using the full Christian name and initial as he seemed to be, then he would have filled in the entry that way. Which meant he was either out of London or ex-directory. It never occurred to me that he wouldn't have a phone at all.

I pushed the book down on to the floor and called a girl called Pat whom I knew and who worked on the local exchange. If my memory was right she would be working late and she was. A very regular girl, Pat, which was just as well in itself.

We worked our way through the I haven't seen you for a long time, I've been busy I'll give you a call as soon as I'm free stuff and then she asked me what I wanted.

I told her.

I heard her swear at me half under her breath and thought for a moment she wasn't going to play. But a couple of minutes later she read the number out to me.

'Where's that?' I asked.

'Richmond somewhere.'

'Okay, thanks a lot, Pat. I'll . . .'

'You listen to me, Scott,' she interrupted. 'I'm fed up with conducting our relationship strictly in terms of what information I can feed you with over the telephone. I'm beginning to feel like the speaking clock. I think it's your turn to feed me.'

There was a slight pause during which I could hear her breathing. 'What with?' I asked.

'To start off with a nice juicy steak and a bottle of wine. And then you can take me dancing. It's a long time since I went dancing.'

'All right, Pat,' I promised. 'The next time I call it will be to fix a date.'

'It had better be,' she said and broke the connection.

I dialled the number she had given me and it rang a lot of times before anyone came to answer it. It was a woman's voice: smooth, assured, cultured. The sort who always gets to stand in the royal enclosure at Ascot and picks the winner as well.

'Mrs Murdoch? Mrs James P. Murdoch?'

A few seconds of hesitation, then the answer came with thoroughbred assurance. 'This is Mrs Murdoch. Who is that calling?'

'My name's Mitchell. Scott Mitchell.'

'The name means nothing to me Mr Mitchell. With whom did you wish to speak?'

I liked the with whom. I said, 'Is Mr Murdoch there?'

'Does that mean you want to speak with him?'

'Could be,' I said. 'Or it could be I want to make sure he's out of the way before I start chatting you up over the phone.'

'I presume you're joking.'

'Why presume? With a voice like yours it must happen all the time.'

I waited for the line to go dead, but it didn't. After a while she said, 'How did you get this number, Mr Mitchell? It is ex-directory, you know.'

'Yes, I know.'

'Well, are you going to tell me how you came by it?'

'Perhaps I saw it written on a wall somewhere. Who knows? Are you going to tell me whether your husband is in or not?'

'My husband is out.'

'When will he be back?'

'I have no idea.'

'Well, is he anywhere I can get in touch with him?'

'I have no idea of his precise whereabouts either.'

'He is your husband?'

'Mr Mitchell, I don't know why I persist in talking to you in this inane and undignified manner instead of putting down the receiver.'

'That's right,' I agreed. 'Nor do I. It's interesting; isn't it? Maybe you get fed up with talking broken English to the au-pair and reading last month's "Homes and Gardens".'

She might have laughed. Then again, it could have been in-terference on the line. She said, 'Actually, it was "Harper's and Queen".'

'Would it be worth my trying again later? To talk to your husband, I mean?'

'It might and it might not.'

'You mean sometimes he doesn't come home nights?'

'He's a grown man, Mr Mitchell, and he does as he pleases.'

'If I were him I reckon it would please me to get home to you pretty quick.'

'I'll give you the benefit of the doubt, Mr Mitchell, and take that remark as being gallant.'

'As opposed to what?'

'Merely suggestive.'

I waited a little, then asked where I could get in touch with her husband the next day.

'He should be at his office by ten o'clock.'

'Which is?'

'The Everyman Insurance Group. My husband happens to be the chairman, you know.'

I didn't but I thanked her anyway.

'That's quite all right, Mr Mitchell. I hope I don't have occasion to speak to you again.'

And she hung up with a shade more speed than natural elegance required. Just when I had been thinking we had been getting on so well.

I checked my watch again and dialled another number. Patrick was at home and he'd be pleased to see me in an hour. I got up and walked over to the filing cabinet. It was time for a whisky.

Frances let me in, giving me one of those half-smiles that were a mixture of shy beauty and distrust. She showed me into the study where her husband was waiting. He got up quickly and shook my hand. Behind me I heard the door close. We were going to be left alone.

I looked at Patrick as he poured me a strong shot of one of his precious malt whiskies. Heavy spectacles, unfashionably short hair that was dark and thick. He was a couple of years younger than myself but he didn't look much older than he had when I'd first met him, which was over fifteen years ago.

I had been learning the ropes in my job and he had been doing the same in his. When you're learning, you make mistakes. Patrick's had been more serious than most. I had been able to help him cover it up. It was never mentioned between us again but always after that I knew that I could turn to him for help if I needed it.

And always after that Frances had regarded me with suspicion, as if she were afraid I might be tempted to use the hold I had over her husband.

I hoped she was wrong, that she needn't have worried. Though I could understand why she did. Most human relationships work in the same way: we all have strangleholds on those we hate as well as those we love. It's why those we hate return that hatred and probably why those we love return that.

Power—that's what relationships are about. Unless you can keep them to the occasional smile over the coffee machine.

'It's been a long time, Scott.'

I agreed. It had. I knew that, as with Pat at the telephone exchange, I was guilty of getting in touch with him only when I wanted to use him. Perhaps that was something else relationships were about. My relationships.

'Yes, I know, Patrick. I'm sorry. It's just that . . .'

'You've been busy,' he finished for me, taking his pipe from his mouth and grinning a boyish grin.

I nodded and looked down at the chess board that was set out on the table between us, the pieces in mid-move.

'Have I interrupted you and Frances?'

'No. I was working through a set piece. Frances was seeing to the children.'

I nodded again.

'What did you want, Scott? I'd like to think this was a random social call, but I'm sure it isn't.'

He sensed my unease and waved his pipe at me. 'No. That wasn't mean for censure. I know the rules of the game as well as you do.'

'You're still writing your city column?'

'Until tomorrow,' he smiled. 'The way things are going, there could be no city column within any twenty-four hours.'

'It's as bad as that?'

Patrick sucked at the stem of his pipe and his eyes flickered over the top of it. 'Not really. I don't suppose it's ever that bad. We just like to think it is.'

Frances came into the room with a pot of coffee and some cups on a tray. Patrick moved the chess board carefully down to the floor and the coffee things were set on the low table.

Frances paused behind her husband's chair a moment. She let her fingers bend against the back of his neck and he arched his head backwards. She looked at me quickly, then walked out of the room, shutting the door behind her.

'She still doesn't like me, Patrick, does she?'

He handed me a cup of coffee. 'What was it you wanted from me, Scott?'

'You know a man called Murdoch? James P. Murdoch.'

'Naturally. He's Chairman of the Everyman Insurance Group.'

'Know much about him?'

Patrick sipped at his coffee. 'Usual kind of background. Public school, Oxford, a spell in the Civil Service, merchant banking— he was abroad for a while, Africa, Central America—then the Everyman. He's been Chairman there for nearly four years.'

'Successfully?'

'They're still paying quite a good dividend.'

'Has he got any other interests—business ones, I mean?'

Patrick thought for a moment. 'He did have a couple of directorships, though I'm not sure how active a part he played in those. His name might have looked good on the letter heads.'

'Can you find out for me?'

'Certainly. Tomorrow morning?'

'Fine. And Patrick?'

'Yes?'

I balanced my cup against the rim of the earthenware saucer. 'You don't know any reason why he might be mixed up with a bunch of hoods? Or why they might be interested in him?'

Patrick chewed his pipe a little more, but finally shook his head. 'I write a financial column, not a gossip column, though there are times when you could be excused for thinking that the two are one and the same. But sorry, there's nothing I can think of.'

'Can you ask around?'

'Yes. But I shall have to be discreet.'

I smiled. 'Of course. That's one of the reasons I came to you in the first place.'

He sat back in his chair, and I sat back in mine. When the pot of coffee was empty, we went back to the malt whisky. We talked about people we'd known in the past and about movies we'd seen; about who would be the best to open the batting for England in the third test against the West Indies and whether Spurs were going to have a really good season again at last. He got up and put on a record of the late Sandy Brown playing some of the best clarinet in the world and we finished the whisky.

By the time I stepped out into the night I had almost managed to forget that I was a private investigator at the beginning of a case that had started out simple and got progressively complicated ever since.

I put my arm round Patrick's shoulders and gave him a hug, waved to Frances, standing in the doorway behind him, and made my way down the steps. I suspect that my walk was slightly unsteady. That malt whisky was smooth as silk, but the power that lay beneath the smoothness was all the stronger.

For an instant I remembered Murdoch's wife, her voice on the phone. It seemed to have much the same qualities. If he was playing around behind her back, then I couldn't imagine her not knowing. And if she allowed it to continue, I couldn't see her caring.

I shook my head and looked up at the sky. There were a few stars and a wedge of cloud had pushed across in front of an almost full moon so that I couldn't see that clearly either.

Hell! I couldn't see a lot of things.

But I could see the dark saloon that was parked across the road; the darker shapes of two men sitting in the front seat. I could have turned around and made it back to Patrick's, but I didn't want to get him involved any more than I already had.

I shook my head again and pushed my hands down into my jacket pockets. I kept on walking. The cloud shifted away from the moon and if there'd been any doubt as to the identity of the lonely guy walking down that silent street that vanished with it.

-3-

It was something over half an hour's walk from my flat to where Patrick McGavan lived. For that reason I'd not bothered to use the car. Right now I was beginning to think I had made a mistake. That kind of walk seemed all the longer when you were being followed. It made you feel all the more vulnerable.

It was one thing for a couple of guys to pick you up and try to shake some answers out of you, but when you didn't even understand the questions it was more difficult. What usually happened was that they thought you were being clever. They didn't like that. That was when they started to get nasty.

I could still feel a dullish pain high in my shoulder where my West Indian friend had been taking a little kicking practice. There were a lot of things I wasn't feeling like and top of the list was getting beaten up by two anonymous hoods in some anonymous street at well past midnight.

I knew what would happen: the car would increase its speed until it had drawn up alongside me; the door on the passenger side would open and a pair of hands that looked as if they belonged to King Kong would reach out. There'd be a few shouts and bangs and up and down the street a number of bedroom lights would go on behind curtains, anxious faces would peer out;

then the lights would go out again. Nobody would come out, nobody would phone the police; if anyone asked them the next day, nothing would have been heard at all.

Who was I to blame them?

I had known what I was doing when I chose my job. I hadn't been forced into it. There hadn't been any false sense of civic duty behind what I opted into. Those people in the street—they didn't owe me a thing and I didn't owe them a damn thing either. Not until one of them came into my office and hired me.

As it was, there was just me walking along with my hands still in my pockets and the saloon still edging along the kerb fifty yards behind me. Two guys biding their time, toying with me, enjoying the knowledge that all I could do was wait for them to make their move.

Well, fuck them!

I pulled both hands from my pockets and turned round. I started to walk back towards the car and I walked fast. The side lights flicked off and then the engine cut out. They waited. Fine! I'd see they got something to wait for.

Who the hell did they think they were anyway?

By the time I drew level with the saloon they were doing their best to sit there as innocently as a couple of sightseers outside Buckingham Palace.

I bent down and stared in at them. Thick set, dark coats, trilby hats, a day's growth of stubble on their chins and less than half an ounce of sense inside their heads.

I reached down to the car door and they hadn't even had the sense to lock it. I yanked it open and pulled at the first guy's arm. He was pretty heavy but he wasn't that heavy. I got him half out of his seat and stranded over the gutter.

It suited him that way. He looked up at me with piggy little eyes and what was probably meant to be an angry scowl. To me he just looked like any other cheap hood.

I let go of his arm and grabbed for his lapels. At the same time I chopped down on him with my right fist. There was a very sat-isfying feeling of hitting something hard and then he came all of the way out of the car and sprawled on to the pavement. Half of him was still in the gutter but now it was the other half.

His friend had got out of the car and was moving round towards me. He had a length of piping in his right hand and was in the process of raising it high over his head. Which was fine by me. I threw up my left arm to break the blow and punched him in the gut twice. He folded forwards like yesterday's dirty washing and I stepped sideways fast, pulling the arm that held the piping round behind his back. I slammed him down over the bonnet of the car and lifted the arm as high as it would go.

There was a scream and then a clatter as the weapon fell from his opened hand and bounced off the metal on to the roadway. I played with his arm a little more and enjoyed the sounds that came from his mouth. Then I stepped back and kicked at the base of his spine with the underside of my shoe. His groin went into the front edge of the bonnet as though it was trying to make close friends with the engine.

I stooped down and picked up the length of pipe. As I did so, something drove into my side and sent me staggering backwards. It was the first guy and he was moving in for a second go, but there was no way he was going to make it. Not the way I was feeling.

I let him come for me, blocked his lunge with an open palm and suckered him one across the temple with his buddy's piece of pipe. He closed his eyes and took a nose dive into the tarmac. There was a queasy sort of squelching sound as his face bounced back a couple of times before settling down for a nice long sleep.

The driver was now standing with his weight leant back against the car and his hands massaging his balls. He winced as he saw me coming towards him so I pretended to be going to kick him down there for luck. He shut his eyes tight and lowered his head forwards and I hit that instead.

He sat down!

I pulled him back up again. I had a message to give him while he could still listen.

'Okay, you stupid shit! Get back to whoever sent you and take this message from me. If anyone wants to see me, then I've got office hours and a telephone number that's in the book. I don't like being followed and I don't like being threatened—especially by cheap trash like you. There might be people around who can take me, but you're so far away from them you're not playing the same game, never mind in the same league.'

I stopped talking to get my breath back. One of his eyes had started to close and there was a thin line of blood snaking out of the corner of his mouth. He looked dumber than ever.

'You got that?' I gave him a shake and he grunted.

I slapped his face a couple of times for good luck and let him sink back down to the ground. The other one was still stretched out and didn't show signs of moving for a long time.

I left them to it and walked the rest of the way home. I was feeling kind of tired. But good inside.

I woke next morning to a thickish head, a bruised right hand and a vague feeling that I had done something pretty damned stupid. By the time I had made the coffee and was two mouthfuls into the first cup the vagueness had gone. I had been stupid all right.

Whoever had sent those heavies cruising after me wasn't likely to be thrown off by what happened last night. All it meant was that next time the men would be more carefully chosen and instead of lead pipe it would be a gun.

I seemed to spend half of my life making sure that the other half was as close to impossible as made no difference. And I would have to remember to go easy on Patrick's whisky in future.

I thought about phoning him but it would have been too early for him to have got the information I wanted. I thought about making myself some scrambled egg on brown toast but it was too much effort. I thought about a lot of things I should have known better than to have given head room to.

Only some mornings waking up alone brought memories of her crowding back into my mind with an insistence that wouldn't be denied: When you've spent a year sharing your toothpaste and your breakfast with someone who manages to be beautiful even at seven thirty then it isn't easy to forget. Like stretching across the table and kissing the smear of butter from the corner of her mouth. Like the look in her eyes when she told you to take care. Like staring out of the window at her as she walked away, knowing that all she had on under the long flowered skirt was the tiniest pair of pants and that underneath those she was still damp because you'd made love before getting up.

Watching her walk away . . .

I got up and poured myself another cup of coffee.

Half an hour later I called Patrick. His secretary told me he'd ring me back in ten minutes. He did. Exactly. He was always an efficient man.

He also sounded a little confused. That was surprising. He was not a confused man.

'What gives, Patrick?'

'Not very much.'

'How do you mean?'

'I made the usual kind of enquiries, phoned the usual people. Up to a point it was all right, but there was one place I kept getting stuck at.'

'Which was?'

He paused, then said, 'Mancor Holdings.'

I sensed that it was meant to bring some kind of reaction or recognition from me, but it didn't. When that became obvious, Patrick went on.

'The name doesn't mean anything to you?'

'No. Should it?'

'Not necessarily. It came up in connection with Murdoch's other interests. He was one of the directors until six months ago, then he resigned. I got on to the number given as their head office and suddenly everyone started being so cagey it just wasn't true. First of all they said they'd never heard of a James P. Murdoch, then, when I told him he was clearly listed as being on their board until recently, they agreed they knew him but all links had been severed. I tried to ask a few more questions, but they stone-walled then hung up. Since then I've been asking around but it's like trying to find out about Watergate.'

'Any ideas what they're covering up for?'

'None.'

'And did you get anything?'

'Not much, but here it is. You've got something to write with?'

I said that I had.

'Right. Mancor Holdings appears to be a parent company for a host of other businesses that drift in and out of existence with some regularity. But it includes Mancor Amusements, Mancor Pleasurama, Mancor Marinas, Corman Films . . .'

'You don't mean . . . ?' I started to interrupt him.

'No. Not those Cormans. This is some kind of distribution set-up for super-8 stuff.'

'Blue movies?'

'Could be. Anyway, there's also Mancor Security and some-thing called Corman Enterprises. But, as I said, trying to get information about any of these operations or Murdoch's involve-ment with them was hard work. The more I wanted to know the more jumpy they became.'

'Did you try any of the other companies?'

'I rang a couple of numbers but no one was answering. I can let you have the numbers I've got.'

He did so and I wrote them down.

'What do you feel about it all, Patrick?' I asked.

'Well, it could be one of two things—or both. Whatever Mancor is they don't want people poking their noses in too far. And that means past the front door. And however much they might have wanted Murdoch on their board at one time, they don't want him now.'

A pause, then, 'I'm sorry I couldn't be more use, Scott.'

I assured him he'd done fine, promised I'd drop round for a meal with Frances and himself as soon as I could, then put the receiver back on the rest.

I seemed to be getting somewhere only I didn't know where the hell it was. I rang the numbers Patrick had given me. Two were engaged and three weren't answering.

I needed to talk to someone and fast. Before somebody else came to talk to me.

I ran a hand through my hair and brushed it down at the sides. I didn't want to talk to Murdoch's wife looking a mess. My hand was a couple of inches above the telephone when it rang. I picked it up immediately. It was her.

'Mr Mitchell?'

'Good morning, Mrs Murdoch.'

'It was almost as if you were waiting for me to call.'

'Perhaps I was. What can I do for you?'

'You could talk to me.'

'What about?'

'A number of things.'

'Like your husband?'

'He's one of them.'

'And Mancor Holdings? Is that another?'

She drew in her breath and I could almost hear her thinking.

'What did you say?' she asked after a few moments.

'You heard what I said.'

'Mr Mitchell. You aren't about to try and . . . lean on me, are you?'

It made a pretty picture. I told her so. She warned me not to get saucy down the phone.

'You mean I have to wait until I'm there in the flesh?'

'Don't be obscene, Mr Mitchell.'

'Listen,' I told her, 'there's nothing obscene about my flesh. Why only last night I had a work out with two real tough guys and left them looking like something that had been in a car wreck.'

'Mr Mitchell, are you being altogether serious?'

'Sure I am. Altogether. You want me to flex my muscles down the line or can you hang on until I get there in person?'

'I'm beginning to wonder if I should see you at all.'

'Suit yourself. But I've got to talk about Mancor to someone and if your old man's still not around it had better be you. He hasn't showed up, has he?'

'How do you know that?'

'Just a hunch.'

'Do you know where he is?'

'How should I know where he is? What do you think I am? His old lady?'

Mrs Murdoch hung up with all the precision of a wounded aristocrat.

A minute later she rang back and made sure that I had the address. I told her I'd be over in an hour and to get the coffee brewing. When I put the phone down again I was feeling pretty good. Maybe it wasn't such a bad day after all. Maybe I wasn't as stupid as I'd started off thinking.

I went over to the window and looked out across what was left of the grass. If I could afford to get it baled up there was a good chance I could sell it as straw. I didn't need to check the barometer to tell that it was going to be another hot day.

I stepped into the bathroom and gave myself a few quick squirts with a deodorant. I wasn't too sure what my chances of getting in a little close-up work might be, but it didn't hurt any to be prepared.

I was half-way to the car when I heard the phone ring. It could have been important or it could have been the local dancing school offering me a course of free lessons. Either way I wasn't interested. By the time I reached the car the phone had stopped ringing.

The handle of the door was almost too hot to touch and I wafted air through the open windows for a few minutes before I climbed inside and set off to drive across London.

It was going to be one hell of a journey and I just hoped that it was worth it.

Apart from an argument with a taxi driver going round Hyde Park Corner and a near collision with an ice cream van at the entry to Putney Bridge, it was a pretty uneventful trip. I only lost around five pounds in weight and it didn't take more than two minutes for me to scrape myself off the driving seat and pour what was left out into the scent of red roses that hung over the front of the Murdoch house.

I left the car in the drive and went up to the front door. The bell push was one of those discreet affairs that resembled the Kalahari diamond on a bright day. I wiped my fingers on my handkerchief and pressed it. I could hear bells echoing from the other side of the panelled wood door and then foot steps.

It was a little oriental guy wearing a short white jacket and a slant-eyed smile that he pasted on each morning right after cleaning his teeth. I told him who I was and offered him my card, but he just kept on smiling and opened the door wide enough for me to get in. It was real nice inside and cool enough for there to have been some kind of air conditioning at work.

The Chinaman disappeared and I was left in the hallway with nothing to do but admire the quality of the rug and count the Hockney prints on the walls.

He came back and opened another door and gestured for me to go through. There wasn't anyone else in that room either and it didn't look the kind of room that took too kindly to people.

When I looked round for laughing boy he'd gone again, but not for long. He came back with a silver tray and a couple of bone china cups and saucers. He set this down on a table and walked back out again. There were two cups, so I guessed that someone might be joining me. I looked at the tea and wondered if I should wait.

Hell! I was thirsty enough to let my usual good manners slide a little.

The saucer was lime green with gold leaf edging and a yellow daffodil painted on a black background at its centre. The outside of the cup was white, except for the obligatory gold leaf. The entire inside of the cup was another hand-painted daffodil, along with green leaves and blotches of white and black. The china tea was translucent and there was a jasmine petal floating on the top. I looked at the second cup; there was a petal there as well.

I was tasting the tea and wondering if you got a petal every time when the door opened and she came in.

'Don't get up, Mr Mitchell,' she said coolly as I sat transfixed.

She reached down and took her tea and walked away so that I could get a better look at her. Either that or my deodorant hadn't worked at all.

Whatever her reason she was worth looking at and it didn't matter a damn that she knew it.

There's a late forties movie called 'Out of the Past' that's supposed to star Mitchum and Douglas. It doesn't. There's this smooth, beautiful woman in it played by Jane Greer and every time she's on the screen there's no looking at anyone else.

Maybe she doesn't have Lauren Bacall's wit and she misses the ice coolness of Veronica Lake, but there's something that's all her own. The waved hair that clung to one side of the face; the face made up to look like satin sheets; eyes that were brown pools you wanted to dive right into. That was what she had.

It was what Murdoch's wife had, too. It was to her advantage that forties dresses were back in style for they suited her figure as well as the rest of her. I looked her up and down and then down and up but each time I came back to those eyes.

I didn't understand a whole lot of things but right now most of all I didn't understand what her old man was doing hitting the sack with other women when she was around. But perhaps that was the trouble. Perhaps she wasn't around as far as he was concerned.

In which case . . .

I tried a wry smile and turned my head to one side as though asking her a question. I didn't think I needed to spell it out and I was right.

'I thought you came to talk business,' she said without so much as a flutter of her eyelashes.

'That depends what you mean by business.'

'I mean my husband's business.'

I gave her a long look. 'That might be exactly the kind that I'm interested in.'

'Do you think you can handle it?' The right eyebrow rose a questioning quarter inch.

'I'm not sure, but I'd like to give it a try.'

'We'll have to see what we can do later.'

'Why leave it tighter?'

'Because right now your tea's getting cold, your mouth's hanging open like a dog on heat and there are things that are more important.'

There was nothing I could say. Jane Greer had someone else write her words for her, but this one, she just took them off the top as she went along. I kept my mouth open and tried pouring some tea down it. She was right. It had started to get cold.

Mrs Murdoch came over and put down her cup and saucer; she was close enough for me to reach up and touch her through the silky material of her dress; close enough for me to know that her perfume was as expensive as I had thought it would be; close enough for me to forget what I had gone there for.

What had I gone there for?

'You phoned me yesterday and asked some questions about my husband. You wanted to see him. Why?'

I looked back at her and then moved my gaze away. With eyes like that I was going to tell her too much too soon.

'Don't get coy, Mr Mitchell. It doesn't suit you.'

'All right,' I said, 'maybe we should level with each other. You let me in on what you know and I'll do the same.' I wasn't looking directly at her when I made the promise. 'Only call me Scott, all this formality is making me feel important.'

She made a few gestures in the direction of a smile. 'My name is Caroline.' She turned her back and walked towards a shelf where she started toying with a small black statuette.

I wondered why she was suddenly so jumpy. I didn't figure it was just because we were getting down to first name terms at last. It had to be what she was going to say next. It was.

She said: 'I think my husband may have been murdered.' The words came out very quickly. Quickly for her anyway. All the time she never stopped running her fingers over the smooth surface of the statuette.

'You've got to have a reason for that.'

She faced me and fixed me with those brown eyes. 'Why? I'm a woman. I have feelings about these things. When some thing dreadful happens to someone you're close, to, well . . . you know. Somewhere inside you.'

Suddenly she wasn't saying her own lines any more and the eyes ceased to matter. I stood up and went towards her.

'Don't give me that crap! Last night you didn't know or care what your husband was up to. You gave me the impression that you lived separate lives and I believed you. Now you're making like some kind of romantic mystic who can tell if he farts fifty miles away. There might be a few things about you that are soft but your heart isn't one of them. If you really think he's dead then it's because you've got good solid reasons for suspecting it and not because of some story book intuition. If you want me to stay and listen to what's on your mind you'd better start levelling with me and do it fast or I'll be out of the door before your Chinese house boy can start quoting the thoughts of Chairman Mao.'

I thought I'd said enough. She seemed to have wilted a good few inches and she was clinging to that damned statuette as though it was saving her life.

'Come on,' I said, 'let's sit down and talk.'

I went over and took hold of her arm. The dress felt the way I had known it would and underneath it her flesh was both firm and yielding against my fingers. We made it to the settee without too much difficulty—considering.

She began talking straight away. 'You're right, of course, there is something definite, though not in the way that perhaps you mean. What you implied about James and I leading separate lives is also true. But we did hold on to at least the vestiges of a normal relationship.'

'You mean in front of mutual friends?' I interrupted.

'Yes, but to ourselves as well. I'm not sure why. Possibly it made us feel more civilised. One thing was that if James was not coming home he would phone and let me know. He wouldn't tell me where he was really going to be, but he would make some kind of excuse. Then, in the morning, he would telephone again, usually when he got into work.'

'Sounds cosy,' I said, 'did you work the same thing?'

She froze more than a few degrees even in all that heat. If she'd been any closer the beads of sweat along my hair line would have turned to tiny balls of ice.

'Don't get too presumptuous! I assure you I am not in the habit of behaving like an alley cat!'

'But your old man was—or whatever the male equivalent is?'

'Does that matter?'

'It might, but for now we'll let it pass. I guess you were going to tell me that you didn't get your phone calls.'

'Exactly. Neither of them.'

'Maybe he's out on a blitz. Perhaps he got drunk, fell asleep, was having so much fun getting laid that he forgot all about it. I guess he's only human like the rest of us.'

She was shaking her head and I wasn't too clear what to.

'He'd always phoned you before?'

'Yes, always.'

'So you figured something had happened to him and you called me. Why me and not the police?'

'That's obvious. The police would say that twenty-four hours wasn't long enough to start worrying without any more facts and . . .'

'And you thought that a few shots of those brown eyes of yours would divert me from asking the same question?'

'I didn't say that.'

'You didn't have to. You also didn't have to say that if the cops did get involved then they might start probing around in the wrong places. And you wouldn't like that, would you, Mrs Murdoch?' I paused and looked at her. 'Caroline.'

Her hand reached out for mine and hovered over it like a butterfly about to land; then it thought better of it and returned to rest on the white silk of her thigh.

'What do you want me to do?' I asked.

'Find James.' She blinked her eyes shut. 'Or find out what has happened to him.'

'Is that all?'

She looked at me uncomprehendingly. Or she did her best to. She wasn't the kind of woman to whom looking dumb came easily.

'You left out the bit about saving the family's good name and fortune.'

I thought she was going to go into her ice maiden routine again, but she decided against it. She said, 'I'll be honest with you, Scott, I'm not awfully worried about the former, but the money is important to me. Perhaps I shouldn't say that . . .'

She let the sentence trail off into visions of hard-earned luxury that made my heart break into a hundred pieces, each of them gilt-edged.

'You're hiring me?' I wanted to be sure she didn't think I was going to find her old man for a favour.

'Of course.'

'All right. I shall want a nice cheque for a retainer and something to cover expenses. Then you'd better give me a list of places your husband might be, as far as you know them. I can't promise to turn up too much, but I'll try. And one other thing . . .'

'Yes?' She hadn't really believed I was going to let her off that easily.

'I had a friend asking questions about your husband's business interests. For reasons of my own. When he came across the Mancor connection he also came across a line in brick walls that makes the Great Wall of China look like something you might have at the bottom of your garden. Come to think of it, you probably have. Then when I mentioned the name to you on the phone this morning it was as though I'd suddenly said a very dirty word in the nursery.'

'So?' The ice was back with a vengeance. It hadn't done anything about the line of sweat that was chasing down my back and threatening to stick me to the settee. It hadn't done anything about that but it was wreaking havoc with what little composure I might have had left.

'So,' I managed, 'before I'll agree to act for you I want you to know something about what Mancor is and how your old man came to be mixed up in it. Remember, you didn't say disappeared, you said murdered.'

She closed her eyes and allowed me to stare at the perfection of her face. For a sickening instant I was gazing at a mask, a death mask. Whoever she had been, whatever living, breathing woman had once existed beneath that exterior didn't seem to exist any more.

Then she sighed and stood up; walked over towards the door and pressed a discreet bell alongside the frame. Almost immediately the little Chinaman appeared like a character out of pantomime.

'I want a drink. What would you like?'

I realised she was talking to me and said a Scotch and ice would be fine. She relayed the order and asked for a Campari soda for herself. We both filled in the time before the drinks appeared by pretending we were characters in a play who had suddenly found ourselves between acts and with the curtain down. Only it was between us.

When she'd finally downed half of the contents of the glass, she went back to her black statuette. It seemed to be some kind of a familiar and I didn't like what that suggested about her.

I took a swig at the Scotch. It was good. I said, 'You were going to tell me about Mancor.'

She gave that beautiful sigh again and began. 'Before he took over his present position, James worked abroad. He got involved in the wrong company—he loves gambling you know, with cards as well as women. Somehow, some rather unscrupulous characters got their hooks into him. At first they were content to bleed him for money. But when he returned to this country and became a comparatively big name in the city, they realised that there was something more they could take from him. His name. They were anxious to set themselves up a legitimate business front and James' name on their board of directors would give them a respectability they could not hope to achieve otherwise.'

'And he agreed to compromise himself like that?' It didn't sound too likely.

'Scott, he was already compromised in ways it is best not to consider. My husband's sexual appetites are not always what might be considered normal.' She gave a look that was a mixture of distaste and pain.

I nodded. 'But what happened six months ago?'

She stared back at me blankly.

'Your husband's name was taken off the Mancor letter heads. Apparently he resigned all connections with them.'

Again the hand made as if to move towards my own, then thought better of it. I wished she would stop practising her self control. I had the feeling that if she ever let go the results would be spectacular.

'There was a scare at Mancor. Someone tipped the police off about some irregularities in their finance. James resigned before the Fraud Squad moved in.'

'They allowed him to? The Mancor people, I mean.'

'Apparently.'

'And what happened?'

'Nothing. Either it was a false alarm or someone managed to effect a cover up in time. Certainly there was no talk of any prosecution.'

'Possibly someone was reached.'

She gave me a look which was meant to suggest that she didn't understand. Maybe she really didn't.

'A little cash in the right hands can work miracles.'

'I'm afraid I wouldn't know about that.'

'Is he still paying them money?'

'I don't know. I don't think so. We have quite separate accounts now and James no longer discusses such things with me.'

'And you don't go through his cheque stubs like a good wife?'

She put down her empty glass and stood up. 'I believe you wanted a cheque from me, Mr Mitchell. And a list of names and places. If you will excuse me for a few moments.'

She turned and walked out of the room. It was some sight. While I waited for her to return I tried to think but it wasn't easy. I'd made some progress with Caroline Murdoch even if we were finishing the interview back on last name terms. I could always work on that one another time.

Ten minutes later the Chinese servant was smiling and holding open the front door. I had a substantial cheque in my pocket and I reckoned I was lucky to be leaving having lost nothing more than a few pounds of weight. I said goodbye and stepped out into the sunlight. It was approaching its strongest and I reached for a pair of sunglasses and slipped them on.

In a way they helped, but overall they only added to the darkness I was wandering around in. Every time a few more facts got added the number of possibilities grew so large that there didn't seem to be any direction to take.

I looked at my watch and wondered what sort of plans Marcia Pollard had for lunch—like who was she eating today?

Hell! It was too damned hot and after sitting that close to Caroline Murdoch I couldn't rouse more than a nicker of interest. I got into the car and headed for Covent Garden and my office.

-4-

The garden was one of those places that had been declared dead but refused to lie down. The authorities had moved the fruit and vegetable market out to a new and more hygienic home and set out to organise the demolition of what was left behind. They wanted to knock all the old buildings down and erect a lot of new blocks of offices and flats in their place. They smashed down a whole street and the next time they looked a landscaped garden had appeared amongst the rubble. They put up ugly bare fencing and overnight it was covered with multi-coloured murals. They ordered tradesmen and shopkeepers to quit and when they came back to check found that they were still there.

I held fast along with them. Partly it was because I didn't take any too kindly to being pushed around; partly I was lazy. I liked it where I was and I didn't fancy setting up office somewhere else.

It was a good office. When you didn't look too closely at the cracks in the plaster or the dust between the floorboards; when you didn't notice that it was too cold in the winter and that at times like this the only way you could stop yourself withering up was to leave all the windows open and take off most of your clothes.

Whoever had got there before me must have found that out pretty quickly. I'd left the windows shut last night but now, looking up to the first floor, I could see that they were open wide. I wondered idly if whoever it was had taken their clothes off. I parked the car across the street and decided that I might as well find out.

It might be good news. It might be another client. It might be a couple of sixteen-year-old girls who wanted nothing less than to have their wicked way with me and to hell with the heat.

Only half a dozen steps up from the entrance I knew that it wouldn't be any of those things. The kind of fantasies that came true in my life were usually other people's and seldom my own.

The outer office was wide open and through it I could see the other door had been left ajar. A curl of bluish smoke moved lazily through the air in the inner room. I could see the edge of my desk and I wasted a few thoughts about the Smith and Wesson .38 that was nestling down in the drawer along with a handful of old letters and a few packets of photographs.

I shut the first door behind me and held my breath. Nothing happened. They weren't going to come to me. I shrugged my shoulders and flicked some of the sweat away from my eyebrows. Wiped my finger along my trousers and went on in.

The West Indian was making an attempt to sit on one of the office chairs and looking decidedly uncomfortable about it. He might as well have tried to get his feet into a pair of size fives. He looked up at me and opened his mouth as if to say something. I caught a quick flash of gold-filled teeth before he changed his mind and remained silent.

By then I was looking elsewhere. And with good reason.

The second man was standing in front of the window, both hands behind his back. He took a little looking at; he wasn't the kind of guy you saw every day. Every other day perhaps.

He was the same height as me. Around an inch over six feet. That was where the similarities ended. He was thin and wiry; his patterned mauve and yellow shirt was open to the waist and it was possible to count the ribs from across the room. He had on a pair of light blue jeans that he could only have got into by using a shoe horn. A pair of open buffalo sandals showed bony and dirty feet. None of that mattered.

What did were his hair and face. The hair was dark brown except for a broad streak of white which began behind his head on the right and swept across it diagonally until it fell across his left temple. The face was as thin and gaunt as the rest of him, with two high cheekbones threatening to break through the stretched skin. His right eyebrow didn't exist and the dull roundness of the eye beneath it looked out oddly on the world. On my office. On me standing in the middle of it.

Or did it?

He reached upwards with the middle finger of his right hand and slowly, slowly, so that I could not miss what was happening, he pushed the edge of the finger hard into the socket. The eye plopped out and down, to nestle in the open palm of his other hand. The space that remained was deep pink.

As I watched the other eye winked.

''Ello, Mr Mitchell. I can see we'll 'ave to keep an eye on you.'

The laugh that followed his own joke was strange and high-pitched; it didn't seem to come from inside his body at all, rather from some hideous mechanism hidden inside that weird head. It was mechanical, jarring—yet as hollow as the empty eye socket I was trying unsuccessfully not to stare into.

'You've met my friend, Big G, before. My name's Charlie. You won't go and forget that, Mr Mitchell, will you? You wouldn't forget a nice lookin' feller like Charlie?'

I didn't answer. The trouble with characters like Charlie is that you never knew the best way to talk to them; whatever you said was almost bound to be wrong. If there was one thing I couldn't cope with it was a nutter. And take it from me that's what Charlie was: a nutter. A down-and-out head case. Only his best friends wouldn't commit him.

In that heat his fake eye had to be getting pretty hot inside his hand. It was probably sticking to it right now. I don't know why, but the thought bothered me. I think I just wanted him to cover up the obscene pink space on the right side of his face.

'You see, Mr Mitchell, I thought Big G and I ought to come over and see you, like, and make a few things clear. After all, that was what you said, wasn't it? If we wanted to say anything to you, come over to your office. So that's what we've done. I 'ope it proves to you 'ow we're reasonable men. Reasonable men, Mr Mitchell.'

He lobbed the glass eye up into the air a few inches and caught it without looking what he was doing.

'Though I do think as 'ow you might 'ave treated our two friends with a little more consideration last night. Real bad, they looked. Real bad, Mr Mitchell. They was only put on you to let you know we was watchin' what you was up to. They wasn't told to fix you nor nothin'.' He grinned a lopsided grin. 'If we'd wanted to do that, we'd 'ave got Big G to settle you earlier. I mean, that stands to reason, don't it?'

He smiled and I sensed the big West Indian get off the chair and move close up behind me. I thought I knew what was going to happen and I wasn't sure if I could prevent it.

'Maybe,' I tried, 'we could do a deal.'

Charlie liked that. You could tell by that high laugh that cut through the heat of the room. I could smell the perspiration of the West Indian's body and the stink of the cigar he had been smoking.

'Sure,' Charlie sniggered, 'we'll do a deal with you, Mitchell. Only it'll 'ave to be afterwards.'

He threw the eyeball upwards from his left hand, caught it with his right and jammed it back into place. I hoped that the one behind me was watching it too. That would give me a split second's start. Even then it probably wouldn't be enough; but at least I would know I'd tried.

I feinted to my left and rammed my elbow back into what I hoped was his gut. It was like hitting an orthopaedic mattress. The looping left I threw next was a little more successful. But success hitting a guy like that could only be relative. At least it turned his head to one side long enough for me to be encouraged to take a sock at his unguarded chin. My right fist got as far as an open palm that caught it as easy as Pat Jennings making a one-handed save. Then throwing it back out.

I went back against the side wall and fell heavily on one knee. With a shout and a scramble I headed towards the desk. He came after me. He wasn't trying awful hard and that should have worried me a whole lot more than it did.

Behind him I could see the freak show standing patiently watching what was going on. Perhaps it was nice to be the audience for once. I hurled a few things off the top of the desk in Big G's face and followed that up by trying to ram the desk itself into the top of his legs.

The impact jarred my wrists. But so what: I had the right hand drawer open fast and my hand went in for the gun.

'Jesus fucking Christ!' No wonder the big black bastard wasn't in a hurry. And no wonder one-eyed Charlie thought he could stand back and let it all happen. Nothing much was going to happen. Not from me, it wasn't. They'd taken the fucking gun!

Charlie's high-pitched laugh cut through the atmosphere and I was reminded of a film I'd seen about hyenas in the African bush. His friend pushed the desk out of the way without the least effort and came for me. There didn't seem to be much future in trading punches with him, but then again I couldn't figure out an alternative. As it was he swopped one combination shot of his own for a flurry of mine and it was all over. As far as I was concerned.

If there'd been a towel around I might have tried throwing it in, though there might not have been time even for that. The last thing I saw was Big G turning his back on me and walking away towards Charlie, who was scratching at his cheek with the barrel of a Smith and Wesson. My Smith and Wesson.

But I wasn't about to complain. I was about to take a little sleep.

Something was pushing itself between my teeth. Op at the top on the left hand side, forcing itself between a gap that I couldn't remember having been there before. I sat there and tried very hard to concentrate on it. I wasn't certain why, but it seemed important. What right had it to be messing around with my mouth? The gap didn't feel even; there were jagged little edges and a crevice that seemed much deeper than I hoped it could possibly be.

I started to hear voices in the background and somehow they seemed to bring my mouth into perspective. The hole in my teeth got smaller and I realised that the probing thing was my tongue. I told it to stay still and then listened to the voices.

It should have been the two guys who had waylaid me in the office, but it wasn't. One deepish voice, talking fairly constantly with another, colder and more authoritative cutting across at intervals. I kept picking up the word snow and wondered if there'd been a sudden change in the weather. Then I tuned in on the fact that it was a commentary on the Test Match.

My mind clicked slowly into gear. Second day from Lords. It sounded as though the West Indies were batting and not doing all that well. I opened an eye and risked a quick look out. I was still in my office and it appeared to be empty of anyone else but me. Perhaps they'd nipped out for something to eat.

I tried the other eye and made to move my arms. I couldn't. They were tied to the chair with red flex. I tested the strength of the knots. They were tied tight. But no one had bothered about my feet.

The window across the room was still half open.

Without being too sure what I was going to do when I got there, I began to rock and hop over the room. It wasn't easy progress and half-way there I almost toppled right over backwards. I had another delve between my newly broken teeth just as a means of reassuring myself of what was going on, then headed for the window once more.

I was five feet away when I heard them coming through the outer office.

There wasn't anything else for it: I looked round my shoulder and prepared to give them my best smile.

The huge shape of Big G filled the doorway and from the expression on his face smiling wasn't going to do me any good.

The West Indians must have been more wickets down than I had thought. Maybe they were playing the wrong men. If they had this fellow out there in front of the stumps the ball wouldn't get past him all day. And if he hit it, it would lift right out of the ground.

He grunted and moved aside to let Charlie into the room, looking just as cute as ever.

'Hello, Charlie,' I said, still doing my best to be pleasant.

After all, when two guys break into your office, knock a couple of teeth out of your head, bruise your jaw and send you unconscious for an hour or so, steal your gun, tie you so tight to the office chair that your circulation is seriously threatened, and thoughtfully leave the cricket commentary on when they step out for lunch, the very least you can do is be nice to them.

Well, isn't it?

There just isn't any pleasing some people. The thin one came over to where I was sitting and held out his right hand towards me. I would have shaken it, but on account of all that red flex it was more than I could manage. Then the hand moved up towards his face and I thought we were going to get the eye-popping routine again. In a way I was right, only it was my eyes he was going to try it with, not his own.

The thin hand lashed around the upper part of my face like a whip and by the fourth stroke I was stinging like all hell and I opened my mouth and called him a nasty name. A very nasty name.

It wasn't a very politic thing to do in the circumstances, but at times like that your instincts take over. And my instinct had been to make one or two slightly outrageous suggestions about the possible causes of his rather strange appearance.

I should have known better.

The bony back of his hand struck me once more, at the side of the mouth this time. I hardly had the opportunity to lick at the trail of blood before he stepped away—far enough so that he could take a kick in my direction. I gasped as the toecap dug in underneath my ribs and the chair shifted backwards a couple of feet. He wasn't about to finish there. The same leg sprang back at me, the toe going into the centre of my stomach this time and the heel missing my balls by a miracle and less than an inch. This time the chair overbalanced and I went with it.

I shouted out as my wrists clashed with the floor awkwardly and rolled over sideways.

'Stand the pig up!' Charlie ordered.

Big G reached down and lifted the chair with me in it off the floor as though it was empty. He held us aloft in the humid silence of the office. I hadn't noticed earlier that the radio had been switched off. Not that I thought it mattered. The West Indian brought the chair back down to the floor with a force that broke two of its legs and almost did the same for mine.

I wondered if they were intending to play with me for the rest of the afternoon, or whether they had anything more serious in mind. Big G must have been thinking the same thing. He said something I couldn't catch to Charlie and as a result of that the two of them came and stood in front of me, blocking out the window and increasing the almost claustrophobic feeling of heat.

But at least they might be going to talk to me for a while instead of making as though I was some kind of oversize rag doll.

They stood there like that for several minutes and all I could do was wait and see what would come next. There didn't even seem to be any point in smiling. By now they'd made it clear it wasn't a friendly visit

Eventually they got fed up with the silent intimidation bit and Charlie went and fetched another chair. The other chair. He placed it down a few feet away from me with its back towards me. Then he sat astride it and glared with his one good eye. I tried to remember which movie I'd seen that in first. It was probably some hard-boiled New York cop movie, something like 'Detective Story.' Only they wouldn't have cast Charlie in a movie: no one would have believed him.

As if to prove me right, he did the popping thing with his glass eye again, only this time he rested it on the top of one of the legs of the chair.

I hoped it would pick up enough dirt and dust either to infect his goddamned socket or else to mage him itch to death. He didn't seem any too worried. His attention was on other things. Like the knife that had appeared in his right hand.

It was a cute little thing with a black shiny hilt and a curved blade that was about four inches long. Little but very, very sharp.

He proved this by making a few simple cuts into the top of the chair. It was like carving butter someone had forgotten to put back in the fridge. I thought that if he started on me the result might be the same.

Maybe he didn't have anything like that in mind. Maybe all that he wanted was a chance to put the frighteners on. If that was so, he was doing a pretty good job.

'Mitchell, I don't know 'ow to say this, but you're a fool. You're so fuckin' stupid that if someone showed you a fieldful of shit you'd dive into it headfirst. An' if that didn't bleedin' suffocate you the first time, you'd get up and try again.'

He started to make patterns on the back of the chair with the edge of the knife. I was conscious of the way the line of sweat down the centre of my back was running twice as fast; the palms of my hands were dry and starting to itch; at the side of my temple a pulse was flickering crazily. I looked from the empty pink socket to his one good eye. It leered back at me in a way that I couldn't at first understand.

Then I did. I'd seen that expression before. In a kid of seventeen I'd come face to face with on the landing of a block of flats in south London. He'd had a knife, too; only his had been taken from the butcher's shop where he worked. It was nine inches in length and was used for carving joints of raw meat away from the bone. Usually. Nine inches long and the blood close to the hilt still hadn't dried. That kid hadn't been carving dead meat.

I knew. I'd just come out of the ninth floor flat where he lived. There was blood there, too, but that was splashed up on to the walls and clogging the pile of the carpet. Some was still left in the bodies of his parents and his twelve-year-old sister, but it couldn't have been much. Nobody has that much blood in them.

The kid was wearing plimsols and they'd left a ribbed pattern of dark red on the stone stairs. He stood there with the knife in his right hand, the left one open, extended, waving me forwards, wanting to feel the juddering impact of the blade entering flesh and forcing against bone. He looked at me and the look had been the same as that which now came from Charlie. Except that Charlie only had one eye.

I knew what had happened with the kid because it was over—except on long hot nights when it was impossible to sleep and he stepped carefully down the steps from my dreams. What happened was that there'd been a shout from below and I'd looked round to see Tom Gilmour standing four steps down. There were two uniformed men behind him, but it was Tom who held the gun.

After three weeks on remand awaiting trial the kid had got hold of a razor. Nobody had ever worked out how. It wasn't a new blade and it hadn't been easy to slash his wrists and his neck the way he had. It had been too blunt and rusty to make a clean job of it. He'd had to make a lot of strokes before it had been enough.

Charlie's one eye was still staring at me hard and he still looked as crazy as anyone I'd ever seen: as crazy as a seventeen-year-old with a butcher's knife.

He moved the short blade away from the chair and passed it across in front of my face. I didn't want to blink but I couldn't help myself. And then the point pressed against the bone at the centre of my forehead. Pressed in until it had pierced the skin. Charlie drew a line across the front of my head and pulled the knife away.

Back in focus, I could see a single bubble of blood at the knife's point. It was surprisingly scarlet, bright. I watched as he lifted the blade to his lips and licked the blood away.

Then he opened his mouth and gave out with another of his high-pitched hyena laughs.

The big West Indian moved closer to him and put a hand down on his shoulder.

'Charlie,' he said. 'Charlie.' The voice was low and deep and there was a lot more feeling in it than there might have been.

The knife rested against the back of the chair; the eye blinked. Along my forehead blood mingled with sweat and ran round the ridge of my eyebrow and down the side of my cheek.

Charlie said, 'See, Mitchell, you just don't want to learn.' He carried on as though the last few silent minutes had never happened. Perhaps they hadn't. 'Big G 'ere came round to see you and listened to the little story you told 'im. Almost believed you, 'e did. We sent a couple of the boys out to let you know we was watching and what do you do? Attack 'em for no reason at all. It wasn't a clever move, Mitchell. Especially since you'd been seeing that little Irishman who writes about all them money things. Now, I don't see as 'ow that could be to do with divorce. That was what you said you were workin' on, wasn't it, sweetheart, divorce?'

My tongue against the roof of my mouth was sand against sand.

'He's just a friend, it had nothing to . . .'

A hand flashed at my head but fortunately it was the other hand. It slapped my face hard.

Charlie's voice was getting higher, closer to losing control. 'You stupid, fuckin' liar! Who d'you think we are? Mugs? Fools you can unload your crap on? You were asking questions about Murdoch, weren't you? Same as you were creeping about down the river after Murdoch. We know, Mitchell, we know!'

He stood up and a hand came for me and it was the one with the knife and my eyes closed themselves and I waited. Nothing happened. I opened my eyes again. The knife was inches away from my throat. The veins bulged from the wrist beyond it. Behind that a huge brown hand was clamped across the wiry arm, holding it fast

'No, Charlie. No. Not now.'

I watched as the veins relaxed, the fingers around the handle became less white; the intervening hand opened and loosed its hold. I breathed for the first time in a lot of uncountable seconds.

Charlie reached out his left hand and retrieved the glass eye. The knife disappeared from sight. Big G moved the now empty chair away from in front of me.

'That's telling it to you, man. There won't be no more warnings. You got yourself mixed up in things that don't concern you. Stay clear. Whatever it is you think you got hold of, let go. If you don't, it's going to turn right around and bite your head off. If you don't, then Charlie's going to come and see you again. And next time, he'll come alone.'

I think I nodded my head. I can't be sure. I watched as the two of them walked out of the inner office; listened as the footsteps moved out of earshot.

Now it was just me in a hot sweaty room with red flex round my arms and a line of steadily congealing blood across my face. For a long time I sat there, thinking; then for an even longer time I tried to get myself untied.

By the time I managed that the first West Indian innings, against all possible expectations, had almost totally collapsed.

–5–

There was usually a bottle of Southern Comfort in the office to console me during those hours when I thought I was the only human being left on earth. Some weeks it got emptied pretty fast. The week before this had been one of those. And I'd only been able to replace it with a bottle of Scotch. It was good Scotch, but to a Southern Comfort man that isn't any excuse.

Right then, though, it didn't seem to matter. I could have lit up at the thought of a bottle of Vimto and a straw.

Whatever happened to Vimto?

After the second shot, I had sufficient circulation back in my arms to be able to hold the bottle aloft for long periods at a time. Which was fine. It meant I could dispense with the glass and to hell with good manners.

I didn't see anyone around who was about to object.

I didn't want to see anyone around.

Most especially I didn't want to see a tall skinny one-eyed cockney freak with a penchant for knives and a big West Indian who could have doubled for any three good heavyweights you could care to mention—or any five British ones. I didn't want to see any worried, suspicious little husbands or randy, bored housewives from the upper mortgage belt. I didn't want to see any master financiers with murky pasts who might or might not be inhabiting a murky present. Nor did I want to see any elegant doe-eyed brunettes who could have me eating out of their hand just as easily as they could get me mixed up in murder.

To hell with all of them!

Why should I care?

I hit the bottle to my lips one more time and with a perfect sense of occasion the phone rang. I carried on drinking and listened to it. It may have only been Scotch but it sure tasted good. It had blood and sweat beat by a long, long margin.

I lowered the bottle just as the phone stopped. We should go into partnership.

It could ring again for all I cared. I was strictly out. Why should I get any further involved in the whole business? All I was supposed to do was to find out if one guy's wife had been doing a little cheating on him and find this woman's husband after he'd been missing for all of one night. That was all. Only it had been pointed out to me no less than twice that there was more to it than that and that if I persisted in making my enquiries I would end up in a rather nasty predicament, or, to put it another way, dead.

All right. So I'd do the sensible thing and opt out right now. Wouldn't I? I mean, the fact that I'd taken a couple of retainers didn't count for much. Whoever heard of an honest private eye outside of a book or a movie?

Like, who the fuck do you think I am? Philip Marlowe?

I was just drinking to that when the phone did it again. I picked it up and got half-way through telling the party at the other end that I was the answering service and that Scott Mitchell had been called away from town for an indefinite period when I recognised her voice.

'What is it, Mrs Murdoch?' I asked.

I didn't remember that I was supposed to be calling her Caroline and she didn't remind me. She must have been thinking of other things. I also managed to forget that she was one of the last people on the world I wanted anything to do with.

It's amazing how forgetful you can be when you're listening to a voice as smooth as that and you're a quarter of a bottle into some Scotch.

Besides, underneath that smoothness, she sounded frightened. And I didn't think she was acting.

'I . . . I've had a telephone call. A short while ago. I tried phoning you but there wasn't any reply.'

'Sorry,' I said, 'I've been sort of tied up all afternoon.'

'Can you come to the house?'

'Can't you tell me about it now?'

'I'd rather not, if that's possible.'

'Was it from your husband?'

'Yes.'

I hesitated and she tried saying please. She said it very nicely. It took me a while to make up my mind. All of five seconds.

'I've got one or two things to do first, but I'll get over there as soon as I can.'

I thought about telling her not to answer the door to anyone except me, but I thought that might get her more worried than ever. So I contented myself with saying, take care. It was only after I'd put the phone down that I realised it was a long time since I'd said that to anyone. And meant it.

I checked my watch and dialled Robert Pollard's office number. All I raised was the cleaning lady. I thought about ringing him at home but decided against it. He'd either have to catch me himself or endure the wait until the weekend was over.

Next I called the guy who did my photo work for me. He was still hard at it—probably yet another set of blue prints for the tired-eyed raincoat trade. Prints to be held in the left hand only.

He wasn't too pleased that I hadn't collected them sooner. After all a rush job was a rush job. I told him I'd been busy and apologised. I didn't waste my tied up line on him. There wasn't much point in sharing a joke with someone who wasn't going to be able to see the point.

I told him I'd be round inside half an hour and made the third call.

Frances McGaven answered the phone and when she heard who it was she became as distant as the farthest star. She went and fetched Patrick anyway but God knows she didn't like doing it.

Patrick had rather an abstracted air, as though I'd dragged him away from the middle of yet another chess problem. I asked him if he knew who at the Fraud Squad had investigated the Mancor group and produced the whitewash.

He thought a little, as though contemplating shifting one of his pawns into a position of some danger. It gave me time to think about chess: the most powerful figure was the queen.

'Is that what it was? A whitewash?'

'Could be.'

'But you obviously think so.'

'Well, Murdoch got his name out of the limelight as soon as they started sniffing round which suggests that he, at least, thought there would be some dirt flying about and didn't want too much of it to get stuck to him. Then nothing happened.'

'He could have been wrong.'

It didn't sound probable and it didn't really need me to say so. It wasn't likely that Murdoch would be involved in a company without knowing something about the way they were operating. And with the information I'd had from his wife about the sort of people they were, it seemed pretty conclusive. I said as much to Patrick. It brought on another spell of thinking. He did a lot of that, Patrick, thinking. I'd never gone in for it much myself. Not unless you include self-pity.

'You think someone was bribed, then?'

'It's possible. A nice little bundle of unsequenced fivers wrapped in newspaper and left on the table in the quiet corner of the pub before the evening trade picks up.'

'You sound as though you were there.'

'I was,' I told him. 'I've been there dozens of times. Policemen are as honest as the next man and he's probably fancying your wife, envying your car, and he's got his left hand in your wallet pocket while he shakes hands with you with his right.'

'You're a cynical bastard, aren't you?'

'Only since I woke up.'

'When was that?'

'The day I realised that the world didn't stop at the end of my pram.'

Patrick didn't say anything to that. I didn't blame him. He was a married man with kids and a good job, a retirement pension, and a savings account in the building society.

To agree with me would be to make a lie of his own life.

'Okay, Patrick, you're right. I'm a bitter, cynical sod and I exaggerate and our British policemen are still wonderful. Or most of them are. But not all. Just possibly not the men who looked at the Mancor books.'

'What do you want from me?'

'Is there any way of finding out who did the inspection?'

Another pause.

'I know an inspector in the Fraud Squad. He comes to me for a snippet of information sometimes. He might know; or find out. If I wanted to know badly enough.'

'Could you put me on to him?'

'Sorry, Scott. I couldn't do that. Besides, he wouldn't talk to you. And after that he wouldn't talk to me either.'

'Well, can you . . . ?'

'How important is it?'

'It could be very.'

Silence. Possible moves ran through Patrick's mind. Sometimes there were reasons for running risks, for offering an opponent the opportunity of check. As long as it wasn't checkmate.

'I'll try to see him, Scott. Will Monday do?'

'You can't manage it this weekend?'

'All right, if it's that urgent.'

'Thanks a lot, Patrick, only . . .'

'Only what, Scott?'

'Take care.'

I'd said it again; meant it again. Perhaps I was softening up. In the head, perhaps, not the heart.

'I mean it, Patrick, there are some very nasty people involved. I don't want you to get hurt.'

'Don't worry, Scott. I won't get hurt talking to a friend of mine who happens to be a policeman.'

I didn't answer. I was too busy hoping that he was right. Probably he was. After all, I had a friend who was a policeman, too. One.

We said our goodbyes and hung up. I wondered how he would explain it to Frances and didn't envy him the expression on her face when he did so. Not that I blamed her at all. She had every reason to feel about me the way she did. I hoped that she wouldn't have any more before this thing was over.

I collected the two sets of prints and the negatives. He said that if the chick in them ever wanted to earn some good money he could fix her up with some sessions. The kind of sessions he had in mind, I reckoned that she'd probably jump at the chance.

I went in for a coffee and gave the prints the once over. They were hot stuff all right. Perhaps I was missing my vocation. The girlie mags would welcome me with open legs.

Tricia had gone home and her replacement was a coffee-skinned youth with oddly purplish lips and a small silver ring in his left ear. The coffee didn't taste the same.

I left without having my usual second cup and started the drive across London. I guessed that somebody might be trying to follow me, so I made a few sharp changes of direction and followed some pretty odd routes with the hope of throwing them off. Once I'd crossed the river, I slowed down and found myself some clear, straight roads. I couldn't pick out anybody behind me so maybe they weren't bothering. Maybe they were just very good.

Either way, there was nothing to do but get to Richmond and see what was up with Caroline Murdoch.

She opened the door herself. The miniature Chinese didn't seem to be anywhere around. It must have been his night off. I followed her into the same room where we'd had our first little chat. It didn't look any more cosy, but perhaps that suited what she didn't have in mind.

I let her pour me a drink and sat toying with it, watching her doing her best to appear settled and unconcerned. She wasn't very good at it.

She was wearing a black dress that seemed to have padded shoulders and a healthy opening at the front. The material clung closely to her chest and she wasn't wearing a bra. A fold-over belt in the same material pulled the thing in at her waist, allowing it to fall away loosely towards where her feet would have been if she'd been standing up. As it was, it had got carelessly arranged so that there was a nice amount of leg showing. She had small feet inside funny little shoes, with straps that wrapped themselves quite high up her calves.

One hand rested along her thigh. It seemed long and white and still. Very still. As though she was willing it not to move. The nails were painted dark red and were curved into elongated points. Perhaps they were false.

I didn't think it mattered.

The waves in her hair seemed less pronounced than they had before; some of the bounce had gone out of them. She lifted up her other hand and ran it through one side of her hair. She did it slowly, time after time after time. Nothing else about her moved. Not even her eyes: deep and brown, as could be: staring unblinkingly into the pinkish liquid at the bottom of her glass.

She stayed like that for more than five minutes; the fingers combing through the hair.

I wondered if she had forgotten that I was there.

I set my glass down on the carpet and walked carefully across the room. It was the sort of room that encouraged you to go across it that way.

I went round behind her and put both my hands down on to her shoulders. I'd done that before; I used it sometimes when I wanted to reassure people. There were times when it was the right thing to do. This wasn't one of them. Or perhaps it wasn't the right person—I wasn't, she wasn't.

I felt her body stiffen under my touch; she held herself in tight. Her shoulders pushed backwards and her spine moved forwards into a slight arch. I didn't have to look to know that her eyes were clenched shut.

I moved my hands away and walked round where she could see me. It hadn't been the reaction I had expected. She didn't look the kind of woman who freezes when she's touched. Perhaps she was more particular than most who did the touching. Perhaps she was more afraid than I had thought.

I stood there for a little with my hands in view and what was meant to be a neutral expression on my face. I didn't want her to think I was about to make any more dumb moves.

I wanted to say something to get the conversation going, only I wasn't sure what to say. It didn't matter. Suddenly she was talking as if nothing out of the ordinary had happened.

I stood there and listened.

'There was a phone call in the very early evening. It was James. I didn't know who it was at first; I didn't recognise the voice. The line wasn't very good, but it wasn't only that. He sounded worried, frightened. I was surprised. I'd never heard him like that before, not even once or twice when he's been in a state in the past. It was as if he was physically frightened. As . . . as though he genuinely believed his life was in danger.'

'So did you.'

She looked at me sharply.

'The first thing you said when you phoned me before was that you thought your husband had been murdered.'

She nodded. 'Yes, but although I said the words I don't think I really knew what they meant. Not physically meant. I don't even know if I believed them. I just thought something wrong had happened to him. But hearing his voice like that was different. It was as though he was trembling on the brink of some horrible, hurtful thing and desperately wanted to escape.'

'Could someone have been there with him while he was making the call? Someone who was forcing him to talk to you?'

'No. I don't think so. But I do think he believed that they might arrive at any moment.'

'They?'

'I don't know and he didn't say, but it must be something to do with those people who had a hold on him before.'

'Mancor?'

'I suppose so.'

'Anyway, what did he say you were to do?'

'He told me to get some money from the bank. Quite a lot of money. Several thousand pounds. And his passport.'

'Clothes?'

'No.'

'Did he say what for?'

'Yes. He's going to leave the country. He didn't say where to. I don't think he wanted to implicate me more than necessary. At least, that was what he said. The less I knew about where he was and what he was doing the less I could be forced to tell anyone else.'

Great! I thought. That means they could play pretty little games with you for hours on the assumption that you did know and were holding out on them.

I didn't say so. I didn't say anything.

She was talking again. 'I can't do anything until Monday, of course. Then I have to deliver the passport and money to him.'

'Where at?'

She shook her head. He really was being cagey. 'He wouldn't say where he was staying. He said he would phone on Monday morning and tell me where to meet him.'

'Did he say anything about you going with him?'

The hand on the leg made its first move. It twitched. Just once, but I saw it.

'No,' she said.

I didn't understand it. It sounded as though that mattered. The last time we had talked about her husband I had got the impression that she wouldn't have cared much if he had disappeared from her life forever. Now . . . I didn't know why exactly, but she was reacting differently. It could be that his fear had communicated itself strongly to her and was getting at her in the same way. Or maybe she saw herself losing a grip on all of his money.

I went back to my drink and rescued it from the carpet. It was nearly empty and I drained what was left in half a swallow. She got up and took the glass from me without asking; she walked out of the room and came back with it refilled. I noticed she had got herself another too and that the level was twice as high as before.

I sat down and looked at her. She was beautiful.

'What are you going to do?'

'Just as James says. Go to the bank and draw out the cash, then take it to him with his passport.'

'Very dutiful.'

'I couldn't refuse him.' She ignored my sarcasm.

'What do you want me to do?'

'I'm not sure. He said I wasn't to talk to anyone about it . . .'

'But you did,' I interrupted.

'Now you sound as though you're reproaching me. I needed to tell someone and, besides, you are supposed to be finding him for me.'

'And now you've found him yourself. More or less. I'll let you have your money back.'

'No. No.' There was a quickness, a firmness that I neither understood nor trusted. 'I want you to come with me. To the bank and then to wherever James wants me to meet him. You don't have to come as far as where he actually is.'

'You're worried about carrying all that money round?'

She nodded her head. I still didn't like it. She shouldn't have been worried by toting round a cool million. The Caroline Murdoch I had talked to before wouldn't have been.

I took my cheque book from one pocket and my pen from another. I opened the book and started writing. I wondered how far she would let me get.

Caroline Murdoch got up and came over to where I was sitting.

'What do you think you're doing?' she asked, when she could see perfectly well what I was doing.

'I'm making you out a cheque for the retainer you paid me.'

'But I've told you . . .'

I let the pen drop between the folds of the book and stood up. There wasn't much space between us. Across it I said, 'I'm sorry, but there's no way I can carry on working for you if you're not going to level with me. You've paid me too much to do a simple bodyguard job and if you want more than that you're going to have to spell it out good and clear. And you're going to have to tell me a whole lot more about Mancor.'

She took it well. The expression on her face didn't falter. The eyes didn't leave mine. They were her trump card and she was playing them for all she was worth. I only had to lift my arms away from my sides by less than nine inches and I could hold her. She would let me hold her. Now. She wanted something and she knew what she might have to pay to get it. It wasn't something you could let her have back by making out a cheque.

Her eyes still didn't leave me. I knew that I could have her right there in that room if I wanted her. I wanted her all right.

I turned away and made space between us.

'What's it to be?' I said. 'Do I carry on writing that cheque and drop it in your lap as I walk out of the room or do you do a little more talking?'

The eyes tried again but for now they'd lost me. She knew and she didn't like it; she didn't like it one little bit. But she sat down anyway and started to tell me some more. She didn't tell me everything still, I was certain of that, but she said enough to stop me feeling a total dupe and enough for me to back down without making it too obvious.

There was no way I could afford to turn down that money. I thought she probably knew that as well.

'When James wanted to get off the Mancor board he persuaded them that he had valid reasons—as far as they were concerned as well as for himself. If he became involved in any kind of serious financial scandal then he wouldn't be any use to them in the future. As it was, if he could step down out of the limelight then after a while he would be able to go back on the board and things could go on as before.'

I put the glass to my lips but didn't drink a drop. I was listening.

She was talking. 'Once he was out of it, James wanted to stay out. His career in the city was becoming increasingly successful. There were all kinds of possibilities in the offing. The first trace of scandal would lose every one of them.'

'So he tried to resist the pressure—that and a little more,' I suggested.

'What do you mean?'

'I'm not sure. But if there was a cover up of irregularities in the Mancor group's finances and if those irregularities were as serious as I'm beginning to be certain they were, then he could have tried to turn their blackmailing back on them. It would be a hell of a bluff to make and hope to get away with, but if they as much as half-way believed him, they'd be rattled. To put it mildly.'

I stopped and looked across at her. She was interested in what I was saying, right enough. The left hand was back in her hair and her mouth was turned up a fraction at one corner. In most women you'd never notice that, but on her any deviation from perfection stood out like a fat blue fly on top of a wedding cake.

'Do I seem to be making sense?'

'Yes. I think so. James was certainly up to something and there were often phone calls at all hours. Arguments that ended up with James slamming down the phone as often as not.'

'Do you know who was phoning him? Was it the same person all of the time?'

The waves rippled slightly as the head moved from side to side.

'I'm not sure. Sometimes he would use a name. Two I remember: Don and Franco. Franco would be Franco Tabor. He was the man at the top. The one who made all of the decisions. He came, to the house once with James. I didn't like him. He had an awful way of leering at you through half-closed eyes. I didn't trust him. He's a dangerous man, I'm certain of that.'

I remembered his name from somewhere and I wasn't able to put my finger on it. Not then, maybe later when I had more time to think.

'And Don?' I asked, while she was still feeling helpful.

'Don Allen. He was the chief accountant.'

'What do you know about him?'

'Nothing much. I met him once at a party. He was not the sort of man you noticed at all. Fiftyish. Rather fat with dark horn rimmed glasses and wine stains on his tie. I think he drinks quite a bit. On that occasion he did. He even . . .' She paused and looked at me for all the world like a young girl about to confess to something dreadfully naughty that had happened in the dorm. 'He even put his hand up my skirt. Well, not that far, actually, but he tried. I couldn't believe it. Suddenly there were these fingers rubbing against my tights and when I looked behind me it was him. Don Allen. He didn't even apologise. Just pulled his arm away and moved on.'

'Did you say anything to your husband?'

'Of course not. What would have been the point?'

I didn't know. None, probably. I got the impression that he wouldn't be very bothered. But then I could have been wrong. I'm often wrong about a lot of things.

My glass was empty again and I thought it was time to go before she refilled it. I stood in the middle of the room and she came and stood in front of me. Even closer than before. This time she had her eyes begging me to touch her and I knew she wouldn't be frigid or stiff. Not now. She wasn't frightened any longer. I didn't understand that either.

I looked downwards slightly and I could see that her nipples were erect and were pressing through the black material of her dress. She would let me have her because she thought it might be necessary. If I were fat, grubby Don Allen with groping hands she would still let me have her.

I moved around her and went towards the door. She let me get as far as the hallway before she came after me.

'What should I do?' she asked.

I felt like telling her. I didn't. Instead I told her to ring me if anything else came up, especially if her old man got in touch with her again. I wrote my home number on the back of a business card and passed it across to her. Her fingers rested on mine a fraction longer than was necessary.

'Scott.' The red lips opened just enough to say the word.

'Great,' I said with my more sardonic tone. 'You did it.'

'What?'

'You remembered my name.'

I turned around and walked out of the house. I thought as I made for my car that it was getting cooler, but I couldn't be certain.

– 6 –

It was still warm enough for me to drive with the car windows wound down. I drove slowly, partly since I was still expecting a tail and partly because I figured I had a lot to think about. For a time I reckoned it was a dark green Viva, but when that left my route at Victoria nothing else seemed to pick me up. Which meant I could devote all of my energies to thinking.

By the time I was passing through Trafalgar Square I hadn't managed one relevant thought. I gave up and pushed the button of the car radio.

It was some character who thought he was a close relation of Wolfman Jack only he wouldn't have made fifth cousin twice removed. He shouted and screamed about a lot of stuff in the charts but apart from Gladys Knight and yet another reissue of 'Leader of the Pack' not much of it was worth the fuss. Then he got into his oldies bit and let us have Lou Christie's 'She Sold Me Magic'.

I lasted the first sixteen bars then pushed the button hard. The trouble was that she had. Only it didn't have a maker's label that warned you about the fact that a certain time everything changed back to normal.

The horses were white mice; the coach was a pumpkin; the beautiful young girl not only didn't fit the slipper any more she wasn't interested in wearing it. As for me I suppose it was the same old story, only worth half a column on page four: Frog Made Prince For A Day.

All right, it was longer than a day, but maybe that just made the business of finding out it was all over that much harder.

Jesus Christ! How did I get into this?

I swerved across all four lanes of traffic in the Tottenham Court Road and cut up a taxi, four yelling Italians in a Mercedes they'd probably bought from peddling ice cream, and a Morris Minor. I felt a little better.

I managed to stay that way until I got back to my flat. I parked the car and got myself inside. Put some water on to boil and ground some coffee. Then, while the coffee was brewing, I ran myself a bath. I grabbed a pile of newspapers that I'd never had time to read and chucked them on to the bathroom floor where they'd be within reach.

By now the coffee was ready, so I poured myself out a large mug of the stuff and took that into the bathroom as well. A few minutes later I was sitting with warm water up to my armpits, a folded paper in one hand and the coffee in the other.

Every man should afford himself a little luxury and this was mine. It was all the luxury I could afford but I'd made sure it wasn't going to be wasted. I'd taken the phone off the hook.

Half an hour later I knew all about the effects of the hot early summer. In Leeds and a handful of other cities they were about to ration the use of water; racial outbursts in the streets of South-all and other parts of London had resulted in five stabbings so far, with two dead; the prophets of doom were claiming that we would reap the worst harvest for several generations. It had been hot, all right. Oh yes, and England had got the West Indies out for less than two hundred in their first innings and were all set to knock them for a high score tomorrow.

I could hardly wait.

I dropped the papers back and pushed the pile out of the way so that I could get out and get dried. I was feeling much better. Ready for the rest of the coffee, something light to eat like an omelette with a tomato salad, a book to read that wouldn't keep sending me back to the dictionary every other page and some good music on the stereo.

I put on a robe and went into the kitchen. Not until the omelette was cooked did I put the phone back in action. He was very considerate; he didn't ring through until I was on my third mouthful.

It was Robert Pollard and he was still in central London. He'd gone for a meal with a couple of friends after work and wanted to know if I had anything for him. I thought about stalling him until Monday but reckoned I'd have my hands full with the Murdoch thing. I told him that I had something for him and he said would it be all right if he came over and collected it.

I said it would be fine and gave him the directions. The omelette was getting cold and slightly solid by the time I got back to it. I finished it and stuck a Stan Getz record on.

I put my feet up and waited.

He was quicker than I'd anticipated and he looked as if he'd run all the way instead of driving. Which only showed how out of condition he was. All sorts of condition. I poured him some coffee from a newly brewed pot and sat him down.

On the table between us there was a large brown envelope. It had his name on it. Inside it were the typed notes of what I'd seen, along with one set of photographs. I wasn't sure why I was hanging on to the other set, but I was. And I wasn't about to tell him of their existence.

He sipped at the coffee as though he didn't like it but wasn't impolite enough to say so. Maybe he did like it but had other things on his mind. Like what was waiting for him inside that envelope.

'Is that . . .'

'Yes.'

His left hand moved out and touched the brown manilla. Picked it a couple of inches off the surface of the table, then dropped it back down again.

'I . . . I want to . . . I mean before I look . . . was she? . . . did she?'

I nodded. 'Yes, Mr Pollard. She was and she did.'

The hand leapt away from the envelope as though it had suddenly given him an electric shock. He tried to put the coffee down before spilling it and didn't succeed. Brown liquid ran down his fingers and the back of his hand. He looked down at it as though not knowing where it had come from. He wiped at the spilt coffee with a white handkerchief, which he pushed back into his suit pocket.

Both hands went to his head, pushed up through his thinning hair and then came back down and fidgeted with his tie.

'I don't . . . I don't want . . .'

He swivelled round in the chair so that he was hunched forwards with his back to me—and to the envelope. He began to rock backwards and forwards and a faint mewing sound came from his mouth.

I watched him for a while, then got up and fetched him a glass of brandy. I put it down on the table beside the envelope and then got hold of his shoulders with both hands. This time it worked.

Gradually he stopped moving, then the little mewing sound stopped too. He sat up and turned his head so that he could look at me. I gave him one of my ready-to-wear line of reassuring smiles.

Have confidence in Mitchell. Bring him your problems. Is your wife getting it on the side? Call in Mitchell and soon you can have close-up photographs of her on the job. Then you can enjoy the fun yourself.

Yes, sir, Mitchell is the man for the cuckolded husband to turn to in his hour of need. He'll dispel your doubts and turn them into sickening reality.

Pollard's expression shifted as if he had realised for the first time that I was holding him. I moved my hands away, but without rushing it. I didn't want to set him off again, but neither did I want him to think that I was making a pass at him.

We could safely leave the sexual inconsistencies to his wife.

I got him to drink the brandy, then to pick up the envelope. I thought he was going to take it away without opening it, but no, I wasn't about to be spared that one.

I sat tight as he ran his finger under the flap and anticipated getting him some more brandy, at least. He took out the notes first and read them through carefully, slowly, as though reading a dense company report. When he'd got to the end, he turned back to the top sheet and read them all through again. Only then did he take out the photographs. I watched his face over the top of them, waiting for it to crumble, crease.

It did neither. Nothing happened save that the blood drained out of it and by the time he was on the last print I was looking at the face of someone who might have been dead. In a way I think he was.

He put them back into the envelope and stood up. It took him a long while and I almost thought he wasn't going to make it. When he had he put the envelope in his left hand and held out his right.

It took me a second or two to realise what he was doing. He was going to thank me.

I stood up and shook his hand and listened while he said the words. Then I showed him out of the front door. I could have watched him walk to his car but somehow I didn't want to.

I didn't want to do anything: I went to bed.

Several hours later I realised that I was awake. I levered myself up with one elbow on the pillow and listened. Something wasn't right. It bothered me and it took me a long time to realise what it was. Then I did. It was raining.

The rain was hissing off the concrete path that ran by the flat and singing against the windows. I pushed back the covers and slid myself off the bed. I pulled back the curtains far enough to see through. The rain was heavy and from the look of the ground it had been falling for some time. The air that came through the opening at the top of the window was cooler, fresher than any I had felt or smelt for days.

Yes, it was good.

I moved away and let the curtains fall back into place. I thought I'd better take a leak before I went back to bed. But I never made it.

Something stopped me, turned me round and had me opening

the curtains again. I opened the main window and felt the rain on my arms and on my face as I peered out. I didn't mind and anyway I wanted to be sure.

I was sure. I shut the window again but it didn't go away. Parked behind my own car was the Rover that I had seen Robert Pollard in before. From the shape that sat slumped forwards over the wheel, he was still there.

I got dressed quickly, got hold of a torch and let myself out. The rain still felt good and I knew a lot of people would be glad of it; it was going to make a lot of dying things grow but it wasn't about to do anything for Robert Pollard. Not anything at all.

The car door was unlocked and I reached across behind the body and flicked the passenger door open then went round and climbed in. Very carefully, I eased the body backwards on to the leather upholstery. The eyes were still open as though they were looking for something they knew they were never going to find. I couldn't easily see how he'd done it, so I assumed he'd taken some kind of overdose. I looked for the bottle on the floor but it wasn't there. I'd forgotten that he was a methodical man; it was back in his jacket pocket.

Whatever had been in it was all gone. He'd chosen it well. There didn't appear to have been any other reaction. He hadn't thrown up or convulsed sufficiently to make a mess of his clothes. To anyone passing he just looked like a drunk who'd taken a nap at the wheel. Which was why nobody had done anything about him. And that's being charitable.

On the back seat lay the brown envelope. I picked it up with my handkerchief and let the contents slip out on to my lap. Carefully, I extracted the pictures which showed Murdoch's face. These I put into my own pocket. The rest I returned to the envelope and it all went back on to the rear seat.

I looked for a note and couldn't believe it when I couldn't find one. A man like Pollard would surely have left everything nice and tidy at the end. But no. There wasn't any note.

Maybe he wanted to leave something unpredictable at the end

of his predictable life. Maybe writing anything would have meant he would have to blame his wife and he couldn't face doing that.

Although he'd done it: and far more powerfully than with words on paper. He left her his own body as a rebuke; the body she had already turned her back on; probably did so night after night after night. Now she could live with it—or try to.

Notes you can burn or tear up and they're easy to forget. Bodies you can burn as well, or bury them down underneath the dark earth but it isn't so easy to forget them. Especially if you were the main cause of their being there.

I left my prints on the car door but made sure they were off everything else. Then I walked back through the rain and let myself into the flat. I poured myself a drink and then poured a glass of brandy for Pollard. I sat down in the half light of the room and drank them both.

After that I phoned the police.

When they came it was in some numbers and quickly. They could have been waiting all night for something like this to happen. The blue lights revolved and revealed the slanting lines of rain and the tyres swished on the roadway.

I picked out the one in charge as soon as he got out of the back of the leading car. I don't know if it was the world-weary yet nevertheless brisk manner of his movement or the appearance of his lightish grey raincoat. Whatever it was, he was walking through my door soon enough. The methodical stuff with the body and the car could be left to those who were best suited to it.

Inspector Jones looked as though he deserved a more interesting name but that wasn't his fault He gave the immediate impression as he looked around the room that he was a policeman who liked as much personal contact with people as he could get. He would be good at talking, good at finding out what he wanted to know; I didn't think that there would be many men better at conducting an interrogation. His concern was with the living rather than the dead: so he had left Pollard's body downstairs in the car and come looking for me.

Well, he'd found me. I filled him in on who I was and showed him the necessary proof. Then I offered him some coffee and was surprised when he said yes. I offered to lace it with something stronger and he didn't say anything. I took it that he wasn't refusing, so I let it have a quick taste of the brandy but I was careful to make sure he could see what I was doing.

He said thanks and sipped it hastily. He put the cup down at a tilt in the saucer and sat back with his legs crossed and his raincoat draped over the back of the chair. He asked me what I knew about the man in the car and I told him. I told him almost everything: I only omitted Murdoch's name.

I wasn't certain why I was doing that, any more than I had been certain why I'd removed some of the photographs from the envelope. But it seemed the right thing to do. I hoped that I wouldn't be proved too painfully wrong.

Jones nodded and listened, saying exactly enough to keep me talking but no more. He wasn't bothering to take notes. A uniformed constable behind him was doing that. Which meant the inspector could drink his coffee while I was talking.

When I'd finished he sat forwards and uncrossed his legs. He looked as if he was rather glad something like this had broken. It was a lot more interesting than muggings or break-ins or whatever other minor matters might have come up. It was certainly better than sitting in his office going through the latest crime statistics or pretending to read Home Office reports.

He was between forty and fifty. He had a head that was rather too small for the shoulders on which it was perched. His hair was cut short and parted on the left with a lot of precision. He hadn't shaved in more than twenty-four hours.

I thought that if I had to, I could probably get along with him. I didn't think I'd ever like him and I guessed that was the way he would prefer it.

'There's one thing that doesn't fit,' he said.

'Yes. I know.'

'You wouldn't have had any reason for taking it?'

'No.'

We both knew we were talking about the non-existent suicide note though neither of us said so.

'And you didn't see that he was out there until immediately before you phoned?'

'That's what I said, inspector.'

He sat back again and crossed his legs. Behind him the constable looked studiously down at his notebook, as though he'd just noticed a full stop out of place.

'People have been known to say things that aren't exactly true.'

'Sure,' I agreed, 'but usually when they're confused or they've got something to cover up. I'm feeling pretty good for this time of the morning and I'm clean all the way through.'

He gave me a look which suggested he was a long way from agreeing.

'You don't accept any blame for what happened out there, then?'

I didn't say anything. He flexed the fingers of his right hand in a gesture that I might have been meant to notice, cracked his knuckles and clenched the fist again.

'Let's get this straight. The man out there comes to you and you give him a packet of juicy pictures of his wife having it off along with a set of notes that read like a mucky book. He immediately—if you are to be believed—goes out to his car and kills himself. And you say that none of that lies on your doorstep. Well, Mitchell, if you think that then you stink even more than I thought you did!'

The young copper was writing away furiously. I knew Jones was only trying to rattle me and that I shouldn't rise to the bait. I knew all right. It didn't stop me standing up and letting him have a few moments of my mind.

'Look! That guy out there knew what he was doing when he hired me. A man knows when his wife's been playing around. He simply wanted confirmation. He paid me to get it and that was his choice. I warned him that he might be better off not knowing and he wouldn't listen. Okay, that was his privilege. When he came round here this evening he knew what he was going to find.

He knew what was going to be in that envelope. Not exactly, but he knew the kind of thing he'd find. That was why he got half drunk before he got here and why he had his little bottle of pills with him in his pocket. He knew what he was going to find and he wanted it proved and he must have known what he was going to do about it.'

Jones jabbed a finger in my direction. It was the most violent thing I had seen him do. So far.

'And you, knowing he'd been drinking and wasn't feeling exactly great about his wife let him go wandering off into the night without caring twopence about where he was going. That's fine. What's known as being compassionate, I think.'

I didn't like it. I didn't like the way that finger was pointing accusingly at me and I didn't like what the man had said. I didn't like the way the copper with the notebook was looking at me as if I was something that had just crawled out from under a stone. I didn't like the fact that a client had killed himself outside my flat. I didn't like anything. Much.

'Look, inspector, I did my job. Nothing more and nothing less. And nobody can expect me to do any more. If someone asked you or your men to dole out a little compassion in the line of duty you'd probably tell them to go fuck themselves because you were busy. Well, fuck you, inspector! The fact that I'm working by myself doesn't make me the child-minder of the world!'

There was a silence that took all three of us firmly by the hands and held us close. In the midst of it I didn't notice anything and only after a while did I realise that the rain had stopped. There were no longer noises coming from the road. I touched one shoe against the other and it sounded like an explosion.

Behind us the young copper was having difficulty keeping his eyes in his head. And he had stopped taking notes. I wondered at what point.

'Sit down, Mitchell.'

I sat down.

'You've got a very hasty temper.' It was a casual observation. The tension was evaporating fast.

I agreed. There didn't seem to be much point in doing otherwise.

'What else are you working on at the moment? Or was the Pollard thing your only case?'

He'd lobbed me the ball and I hadn't expected it, though I should have done, I wanted to say it was the only one, but I hesitated and the hesitation was so long that it made it impossible to make the lie.

'There's one other thing. Some anxious wife who thinks her old man's disappeared.'

Jones crossed his legs, then recrossed them the other way. He lifted an eyebrow and waited for me to continue.

'It won't amount to anything.'

'How can you be so certain?'

'She called me after he'd been away one whole night. By the time tomorrow comes properly around he'll be back home. She's just another over-worried wife.'

'I didn't think they made those any more. I thought it was husbands who did all the worrying nowadays. Like Pollard.'

I didn't answer. I thought maybe I'd try crossing my legs but I didn't manage it with his degree of style.

'Is that what most of your business is? Husbands chasing wives and wives chasing husbands?'

I shrugged my shoulders. It was a gesture I felt more at home with. 'Mostly, I guess. Though there is the occasional high flier like an old lady losing her bingo money down a drain.'

'Don't underestimate yourself too much. Weren't you the fellow who was involved in the Cathy Skelton kidnapping thing?'

'Sure.'

'Tom Gilmour from West End Central, he's a friend of yours, isn't he?'

'He was the last time I saw him.'

'I know Tom. He's a good bloke. A good copper—even if he is a bit flash.'

I grinned. Tom would like that.

Inspector Jones stood up and signalled for the uniformed man to leave the room. 'It all seems pretty straightforward then. Providing everything you say is on the level. And I've no reason to believe that it isn't. Not yet anyway. Come in to the station in the morning and go over it all again and we'll get you to sign it in duplicate. With luck you won't have anything more to do except say a few words at the inquest.'

I thanked him and he went over to the door. Once there, he turned. 'This Mrs Pollard, nice looker is she?'

'If you like everything well displayed and readily available.'

'A lot of people do.'

I nodded. 'So she found out.'

'You've nothing going there yourself, have you, Mitchell? No relationship of any kind?'

'No, inspector. Not of any kind.'

He thought about it for a few seconds then walked out. I watched him go over to his car and then went to the kitchen. There was some coffee left in the pot. I poured it out and took the cup back to bed with me.

It had started to get light and the rain had begun once more. Only drizzle but it looked set in for a long time. It would probably put paid to any play in the Test. On another day I might have worried about that: as it was I had other things to think about.

-7-

I don't know whether I was suddenly very tired or if there was a lot of dreaming that needed doing. It could have been both. When I finally woke up it was a long way into Saturday morning and my head was stuffed full with things that didn't make any sense at all.

There was a lot of talking going on in a big room, high ceilings and candelabras and all that jazz. Women in low-cut evening gowns and men in dinner jackets and tuxedos; everyone getting high and the conversation ringing through my head like knives being tapped against expensive wine glasses. There were quite a few people there including Marcia Pollard and Caroline Murdoch. Marcia was wearing a flame-coloured dress that hollowed out into a circle at the front and showed enormous areas of her breasts, the edges of the material cutting across the darker flesh around her nipples. Caroline Murdoch was in a tight black creation that went all the way from the floor to a high collar round her neck. Only there was a diamond-shaped section missing that left her navel exposed.

They were standing close to each other and smiling. It was a smile that suggested a lot of things. Things like sex and conspiracy and secrets well hidden.

The next thing that happened in my dream was that I was there in person. But not exactly as a guest; more as an offering. I was lying on a table in the centre of the room, surrounded by all kinds of food and, beyond that, leering faces. A hand hovered over me. It held a knife tightly and determinedly between its fingers. I recognised the knife: it was the one Charlie had cut me with in my office. Only it wasn't Charlie's hand. I was sure of that. I looked up and followed the fingers along the arm and over the shoulder: Frances McGaven's face stared back at me and the hatred that I'd always suspected was etched on it in lines that were inches deep.

The knife came down towards me and I wanted to shut my eyes but couldn't. I tried to turn my head away but I couldn't do that either. Hands were holding it. I didn't need to look to know that they belonged to Marcia and Caroline.

Just as the blade was about to enter my flesh everything went silent; and out of that silence rose the weird animal laugh of one-eyed Charlie. A laugh that was filled with madness and delight in pain. It rose and rose as the knife fell, fell . . . fingers that were long and smooth and cool slid down over my eyes and pushed the lids shut.

I lay there for a long while, the pain of my dream reverberating from a place a little to the left of my heart. I knew that I was awake and that the dream had broken. I looked at the time and knew that I should get up. Yet I lay there, still, thinking and waiting for the feel, of those fingers to disappear from my skin.

I was still there when the phone rang. I considered ignoring it but it rang on with the kind of persistence that suggests it would go on for ever unless I went over there and lifted up the receiver.

I recognised Patrick's voice immediately. What was less familiar was the tone of both anxiety and uncertainty that came with it

'Scott. Are you all right?'

'Sure. Nothing that several cups of coffee won't cure. Why do you ask?'

'It doesn't matter. I had a strange sort of feeling, a premonition. But it probably doesn't mean anything.'

I didn't say anything straightaway. I was thinking about what he had said. I felt like asking him the nature of his premonition but I didn't really want to know. If he started talking about expensive-looking dinner parties that might be more than I could handle.

Instead I asked him what information he had been able to find.

'Well, Scott, I went over and saw the man I know early. It may have been that he isn't better than a lot of other people in the mornings, but it's a sore point right enough. At first I got the impression that he wasn't going to say anything.'

'But . . . ?'

'But I spent ten minutes reminding him of the various favours I had done for him in the past and suggesting that I might be able to do likewise in the future. He finally gave me the names.'

'Go on.'

'There was a detective sergeant called Thomas and a detective constable called Botterill.'

'Good. Would he say anything about them?'

Patrick paused and coughed. He seemed to be having difficulties. 'This is where it began to look rather suspicious. My contact didn't say so himself, but I got the impression that he agreed with me. A month after the enquiry was over and Mancor Holdings had been found not guilty of any irregularities, Thomas resigned from the force. A couple of weeks after that Botterill was the subject of an A.10 internal police investigation. Not about Mancor, apparently, but something unconnected. He was suspended from duties and in the middle of that investigation, he resigned too.'

'And they allowed him to do so?'

'Apparently. I don't know whether the enquiry was carried through or not, but either way no prosecution was brought against him.'

'Your friend didn't know what had happened to him since.'

'No. Nothing at all. He seems to have disappeared from sight.'

'Which might mean a lot in itself.'

'Exactly. But, Scott, I do know what happened to the other man, Thomas, and that's even more interesting.'

'Let's have it.'

'Right. Here you are: he's working for a London security firm. Mancor Security.'

It was my turn to stop in my tracks. It hardly seemed believable yet there was nothing else to do but believe it. One thing was certain: there was no way in which it had been coincidence. It looked as though they had both accepted bribes to let the Mancor books go clean. The fact that Botterill was under investigation on another matter made it more than probable that they were both on the take. Then Thomas gets a nice convenient job with one of the Mancor set-ups. Very nice indeed. They could keep an eye on him and he could keep an eye on them.

'Scott. Are you still there?'

'Yes, sorry, Patrick, I was thinking.'

'I'm glad to hear it, Scott. What are you going to do now?'

'I'm not sure. I might use some contacts of my own and try to find out what happened to Botterill.'

'Scott.'

'Yes.'

'The Fraud Squad man I spoke to. He gave me the impression that it was a pretty dangerous business even to talk about. Can't you leave things alone?'

I didn't bother answering and he didn't waste our time asking a second time. I thanked him for his help and gave my best wishes to his wife. He accepted them but I doubt if he would pass them on.

I put the phone down and started my morning ritual several hours later than usual. The only thing that happened in the middle of it that was in any way disturbing was a call from Inspector Jones finding out if I was still coming down to the station to make a statement. I assured him I was on my way. He offered to send a car round but I declined. I wasn't at my happiest riding in police cars. I hadn't spent some of the best hours of my life in them.

Moving uncertainly between one cup of coffee and another I

switched on the radio to listen to the Test Match Commentary. All I got was music. It was raining at Lords. I checked the window. It was raining here too. That didn't stop it getting hot—and I felt it was going to get hotter.

Nothing exciting happened at the police station. They seemed happy with me and I was happy with them. What a friendly way to be! Jones seemed so benign I asked him how Marcia Pollard had taken the news of her husband's death. He said she might have reacted more violently if he had told her that she had a hole in her tights.

I thanked him and walked out of the station and headed back towards my office. The fact that Pollard's wife hadn't started wailing and weeping didn't necessarily mean that she didn't care. But I was willing to take bets.

Back in the office I put through a call to Tom Gilmour. Someone said that he was busy but would ask him to call me back, I said it was urgent and put my feet up on the desk. There was still music on the radio instead of the cricket commentary and when I looked out of the window the sky looked increasingly overcast.

I passed the time trying to make some definite connection between Marcia Pollard and Caroline Murdoch. Apart from the fact that they had shared the same man—if you can call a couple of hours a week sharing—there didn't appear to be any. I couldn't see that they would have been colluding about that.

When Tom came on the line he sounded busy and bad-tempered. It was good to know that things were much as usual. He had a few choice things to say about the heat and the drizzling rain and I listened while he worked his way through the accessary preliminaries. Then I asked him if he knew anything about a man called Franco Tabor, who headed a group of companies most of which used the name Mancor. It didn't seem to improve his mood.

'Tabor's a mothering son of a bastard who thinks he's a seventies Capone—or at least George Raft. Smooth as dog shit on the surface and just like that all the way through to the heart. He'd gamble away his mother's life if he thought there was a chance of winning and if he thought it would help he'd put the knife in himself. He likes to be seen in a lot of smart places round the West End and Soho and never moves far without a couple of hoods a yard behind his padded shoulders.'

'One of them a West Indian who's built like a small house?'

'That's him. How do you know?'

'We had a little, er, meeting.'

'Like hell! And you're still on your feet and talking about it?'

'It was a matter of touch and go. What about a character with a white stripe in his hair and one glass eye?'

'That's Charlie. Tabor doesn't like to be seen with that specimen hanging around him. But he uses him all right. Nasty bastard. The day he gets put away the safer it'll be for everyone. One day he's going to go berserk and then there's going to be a hell of a lot of blood letting before he's stopped.'

'You haven't got anything on them that would put them away for a few days, Tom?'

'I wish I had. But if I pick them up for no real reason, Tabor's lawyer will have them out again before they get their arses down on the station seats.'

I thought I'd try another direction.

'What about an ex-Fraud Squad copper called Botterill? He seems to have gone underground a few months back after they opened an A.10 investigation on him. He might have had some association with the Mancor people.'

Tom thought about it for a while and behind him I could hear men moving about and talking. Finally he said, 'There is something, and I should know what it is but my mind's gone blank. Let me have five minutes and I'll get back to you.'

I agreed and listened for the click of the phone going down. I wasn't sure if he meant what he said or whether he wanted to be sure I could have the information I wanted.

I figured I would have time to get the office coffee-making equipment working. I did, but only just.

Tom Gilmour's tone was quieter and more urgent. 'Okay,

Scott, I'll let you have what we know but I'm going to make a condition. I know it's no use asking you what you're working on, because you'll either refuse to tell me or lie. So if I give you the information, you've got to promise that you'll let me know if anything important gets turned up that we might be more than a little interested in. You got that?'

I crossed my fingers and held them behind my back, then gave my word.

'A week ago there was a fire in Soho. Two people were trapped in it; one was badly burned and shocked, the other died. It didn't get much coverage in the press because it happened at the same time as the first Asian stabbing occurred in Southall.

'The two were a prostitute and her client. They were in the top room of a three-storey building and the whole place went up like a sheet of brightly coloured paper. The fire brigade got there pretty quickly, but there was still nothing they could do to stop it spreading to the other buildings. The woman managed to get out on to the fire escape but not before she was badly injured. She was a Frenchwoman who came over here in the war and stayed. She wasn't young. She made a specialty of wearing high boots and wielding a whip. The client was tied down when the fire broke out. Not tightly, but enough to hamper his movements. He was twenty-seven and an ex-copper. His name was Botterill.'

I whistled and a cold chill went through my stomach and round to my kidneys.

Gilmour went on. 'The place went up so fast that we were very suspicious, but there was nothing we could pin on anyone. It wasn't possible to find any positive signs of arson, even though the building went up like a tinder box. The only line we had was that it was part of an underground gang war. Someone moving in on someone else's territory and applying pressure through the girls they had on the game.'

'Had there been other signs of that?'

'Well, there's always a lot of nasty niggling going on and now the Chinese are trying to move out from Gerrard Street and get a bit more of that action for themselves.'

'But you didn't prove anything definite?'

'No,' Gilmour said, 'though that didn't surprise us, nor does it prove we were wrong.'

I agree but without any sense of conviction in my voice.

'Come on then, Scott, what do you know that the police don't? We haven't got your talents so you may have to lead us by the hand.'

I grinned to myself. The thought of anyone leading Tom Gilmour by the hand didn't seem very likely.

'You did go into Botterill's police record, of course?'

'Yes. We looked at the case A.10 were investigating to find out if there was any possible connection. Nothing doing.'

'And nothing else caught your eye?'

'Will you stop mothering around and come out with it?'

He was getting exasperated, but I was enjoying it. It wasn't too often that I was in the position of knowing more than he did.

'One thing, Tom. The building the fire was in. What other people used it?'

He thought for a few minutes, then shuffled round a few pieces of paper on his desk. I could hear the rustling down the line.

'It's a betting shop. Run by Mancor Amusements.'

I nodded to myself and although I was pleased my hunch had been right, the wave of coldness had returned to my insides and was chilling me through and through.

'What significance has that?' Tom Gilmour asked.

'If you check back through Botterill's file you'll see that one of the cases he worked on was a fraud investigation of Mancor Holdings.'

There was a silence, which Gilmour hastily filled to overflowing with every familiar swear word in the language and several very rare ones.

'Why the fuck didn't we turn that up?' he demanded angrily.

'Because you were sold on the other angle, that of the woman. And because there are only so many hours in the day.'

'What else have you got?' He still didn't sound any happier.

'The Mancor group were certain to go down under the investigation and then they didn't. Botterill and the detective sergeant working with him, a guy called Thomas, gave them a clean bill of health. My bet is that they were on the take and big.'

'But you can't prove it?'

'No. But it's interesting that Thomas is now working for a firm called Mancor Security.'

Gilmour repeated a few of the words he'd used before but managed to find some new ones. Ever since the year he'd spent in New York his language—not to mention his ties—had been the most colourful in the London force. 'So why treat Thomas one way and Botterill another?'

'Could be a lot of reasons. The pressure Botterill was under from A.10. The fact that he was trying to up the ante for himself. Maybe someone else associated with Mancor was trying to do a deal with him.'

'You know someone who might have been doing just that?'

'Not really. It's a guess like any other. For the moment they're all guesses. But it does look as though Tabor or someone at the top is panicking. I ran across them quite by chance and they started leaning on me right away. They're as jumpy as a pack of acrobats with St. Vitus dance.'

'All right. I'll have words in the right places, Scott. We'll see if there's anything going on that we can pull someone in for questioning about. And we'll go over the fire reports again to see what we can turn up there.'

'Okay, Tom. Look, thanks and I'll let you know if anything comes up that I think you could use. Only you do the same for me. I don't have too good a feeling about this one.'

'Right.'

I waited because I thought he was going to tell me to take care, but he wasn't. I said goodbye and put down the phone. It had been a pretty long call but it had given me some useful information and had helped me to get a few things clear in my head. Talking to people did that sometimes. Maybe I should try it more often. There was always the speaking clock or Dial-a-Poem.

*   *   *

I sat in the easy chair for a while and tried my ideas on myself. That way they didn't sound so good, sort of hollow. There were things that I couldn't hope to understand, such as why Tabor had let Murdoch go as easily as presumably he had. But I was warming to one thing.

If Murdoch or, more likely, someone representing him, had tried to get to Botterill and had offered enough to blow the Mancor caper, including the bribing of the Fraud Squad, sky high, that might be enough to scare the shit out of Tabor and friends. But why would Murdoch, who wanted to keep his name out of everything six months before, try to get it all out in the open now? There was no way in which he could hope to stay out of the limelight.

Unless . . .

Unless . . .

I counted to five slowly and silently under my breath, then I went back to the phone. Patrick was out in the garden, turning the earth over. It had stopped raining in his part of London and the ground was movable for the first time in a long while.

He sounded rather short of breath.

'Everyman Insurance. Are they sound?'

'As a bell, as far as I know. Why?'

'You're sure of that?' I asked, disappointed and ignoring his question.

'Yes. Their motor division has lost some money lately, but that's fairly normal. Their overseas business is flourishing apparently.'

'Overseas, where?'

'Central America. The Middle East. The Arab areas mostly. South Africa.'

'Okay. What about Murdoch's own position as chairman?'

'That's sound too—again as far as I know. I keep telling you, I do try not to be a gossip columnist.'

'Sorry, Patrick. Only a few hare-brained ideas chasing each other round my head.'

'I don't imagine that I was any use then.'

'Not really. But thanks anyway. If you hear anything . . .'

'Of course. I'll let you know right away. Is there anything else? I should get back to the garden before the kids drag me off to the park.'

'No, Patrick. And thanks.' I lifted the phone away from my ear and then pulled it back again fast. 'Patrick.'

'Hello.'

'There hasn't been anyone hanging around your place, has there?'

'What on earth do you mean, hanging around?'

'Anyone unusual, not local. Watching the place or anything?'

'I haven't noticed anyone. Why should I? Is this something to do with what you're involved in?' He didn't exactly sound alarmed, but for a chess player he wasn't exhibiting an awful lot of cool.

'Scott, if you've put my family in any kind of difficult position, I shall . . .'

'No, Patrick. I'm sure it won't come to that. I was simply asking. Only . . .'

'Only what?'

'If you did notice anyone suspicious, would you promise to phone the police?'

'Scott, I'd do that anyway.'

'Yes, sure. I'll be seeing you Patrick. Give my best to Frances.'

I put down the phone and went over to the kitchen and poured myself a glass of cold beer. There had been other people who had trusted me and who had asked questions on my account and they had ended up on the receiving end of some very nasty business indeed. I didn't want anything to happen to Patrick, any more than I had wanted anything to happen to anyone else. Yet there were times when I needed information, and unlike the police, who generally used professional stoolies, I asked the people I knew. Which usually meant that to some degree they were my friends.

I got them to step out on the line for me without thinking

twice about it and usually when I did think it was too late. A face had been disfigured with acid or a beautiful body slashed with a razor. And all because I leaned on them for some information and they gave it. Or tried to.

It didn't make me feel any better, but I wasn't about to chuck up my job so there wasn't anything I could do. And I had warned him to be wary.

Christ! I thought as I put down the empty beer can, the ease with which we salve our consciences!

I broke some eggs into a basin and started to whisk them up with a fork. For a few minutes I forgot about Patrick and Mancor and where Murdoch might be hiding out and concentrated on filling my stomach. I hoped that when this omelette was ready there wouldn't be a phone call to interrupt the eating of it.

For a change I got my wish. The call came before I had poured the mixture into the pan. I swore and headed for the phone. As soon as I picked it up I started listening and listened good. It was a short call and as soon as it was over I went back to the kitchen and turned out the flame under the pan. I put the basin with the omelette mixture in the fridge and went out of the flat.

Fast.

-8-

The house was darker than I remembered it. It could have been the change in the weather. Or it could have been something more than that. I looked up at the windows. Although it was still the middle of the day, the curtains were mostly pulled to. As though whoever was inside wanted to cut out the rest of the world altogether. To hide from it.

I locked the car door and flipped the keys down and into my pocket. Then I walked towards the front door. I rang the bell. It sounded distant and hollow, as though it was ringing a hundred miles away.

As I stood there the rain began to fall again: a slow, low drizzle that touched my face like damp, rotting lace.

I leaned on the bell harder; it didn't make any difference to the tone, but it did bring the Chinese houseboy to the door. He opened it as though he was opening Pandora's Box and seemed disappointed to find that it was only me out there on the step . . .

Set yourself up to find the world's troubles and all you get is Mitchell. Some might say it was a more than fair swap.

He edged the door open far enough for me to slide in and proceeded to lock and bolt it behind me. It was more gloomy in the house than it should have been. The little feller looked up at me and for a moment I thought he was going to speak. But no, it was just a trial run. He was working up to it. Later.

He closed his tight little mouth again and nodded in the direction of the stairs. Then he padded off in his cotton shoes; down to the cellar to dream dreams of the Yangtse.

I watched him go, then moved towards the foot of the stairs. There were going to be a lot of rooms.

As it was I made it on first go. With instincts like mine how could I fail? I could sniff out fear at fifty feet. Finding it was never the problem: dispelling it didn't come so easy.

She was lying on the bed with a cover of white satin pulled over her. Her hair was splayed wide across the pillow and her head was facing away from the door. I saw her body convulse underneath the satin when I entered the room. After that she didn't move; didn't turn her head to see who had come in. It might have been because she knew it was me. More likely she was too frightened to find out.

I walked over to the bed and lowered myself down so that I was sitting close to her. Not too close. I didn't think she'd be able to handle that right now. Still she refused to turn her face round and look at me.

I stayed where I was for a while, waiting until her breathing had eased. I leaned over her and saw that her eyes were closed, but not naturally: they were clenched tight shut, the lids wrinkled with the pressure.

I sat back and waited some more. All the time the room seemed to be getting lighter, warmer. It wasn't good heat. It was heavy, sticky, clinging like fear or guilt. I wanted to wipe away the lines of sweat that were starting to run down my face but I didn't. I remained quite still.

Outside the slight sound of rain still falling. Downstairs nothing. In the room two people breathing. Through it all I imagined that I could hear my pulse beat as it ebbed and flowed against her.

When I looked at her face again, the lids of her eyes had relaxed and her skin seemed smoother. I spoke her name inside my head. It sounded okay. I tried it out loud and it came out all wrong: harsh, loud, jarring.

She didn't react. I eased my fingers along the pillow as far as her hair. It was damp and tacky with sweat. I didn't like it against my fingers. I moved them away and let it fall back on to the pillow.

Then I leaned over her and saw that her eyes were open: staring at the far wall: making pictures on it with her mind; I wondered what they were images of. I thought I knew and understood why she was unable to stop herself recreating them, like an old movie that you keep rerunning inside your head.

I tried again: 'Caroline.'

The eyes flickered. Her shoulder moved beneath the cover.

'Caroline.'

She turned her head and saw me. She didn't see me. She looked right through me. There was a glass on the little table beside the bed. I sniffed at it. Brandy. I moved a hand towards her and she flinched as if I had struck her across the mouth.

I stood up with the glass in my hand.

'I'll be back.'

I went out of the room, leaving the door wide open, and went downstairs. I checked my little red book and dialled a number.

'Hello, who is this?'

'Dr Laurence. This is Scott Mitchell.'

'Okay. What is it now?'

I hadn't called the man for several months and the last time had been for him to come and take a slug out of the arm of a feller who'd come into my office with the express purpose of shooting me and had shot himself instead. It wasn't as if I was overusing his services. Occasionally I even paid for them. Mostly we'd just meet a few times a year and listen to some old Mulligan and Parker records and get falling-down drunk. He was a good guy. Anyone who chose to fall down drunk with me was a good guy in my book.

'There's a woman . . .'

'There usually is,' he interrupted.

'That's your life, doc. Right now, this is mine.'

'Come off it, Scott, you have women like most of my patients have boils.'

It was a pretty thought.

'She's had a nasty scare and appears to be in a bad state of shock. I'm not sure what caused it exactly, but I've got a pretty good idea. D'you think you can get over here and take a look at her? It's probably best if it's kept pretty quiet for the time being.'

'That's what you always say and for the time being usually means forever. Where are you anyway?'

I gave him the address and he said he'd be there as soon as he could.

'Should I bring someone to stay with her or are you going after that role?'

'I guess not. Only make sure . . .'

'I know,' he interrupted me again, 'make sure she's discreet. And if she's under twenty-five and pretty that would be nice as well.'

Okay. So we'd done business together before. Only they were usually twice that age and had faces like the kind that used to get carved on church pews. They were discreet, though. Discreet as an old maiden aunt who starts her first affair when her nieces are into having babies.

I gave him my thanks in advance and went in search of the rest of the brandy. When I'd found it I put the bottle in the opposite hand to the still empty glass and went back up the stairs.

Caroline Murdoch hadn't moved. Her eyes focused on me when I appeared in the doorway and held me as I walked across the room. I sat back down on the bed and poured her a good shot of brandy.

'Here,' I said, 'drink this.'

At first she just lay there, but then she pushed herself up on one arm. I noticed for the first time that underneath the white cover she was still dressed.

She took the glass from me and her hand shook so much that I thought she was going to spill it. I reached out my own hand and steadied her grip, putting my fingers around her wrist.

Her eyes flashed on to mine and the look of fear showed clearly in them once again.

'Caroline?'

The eyes softened, then looked questioningly.

'Drink some of the brandy.'

She did as she was told. When I thought she'd had enough I lifted the glass away from her and put it to one side. I got up off the bed and went over to the window. I pulled back the curtains half-way.

When I sat back next to her, she pushed herself up further, until she, too, was sitting. Her hand was alongside my arm on top of the satin cover. I moved it very slowly so that it rested against her fingers. I watched as the fingers moved gradually on to my arm, circled it, holding it tight, tight, tighter.

I thought the doctor would put her under sedation as soon as he arrived. And there were things I wanted to know.

'Caroline. Do you want some more brandy?'

The head moved from side to side slowly, carefully. She was looking right through me again.

I put a hand on top of the one of hers that was still gripping my arm.

'What time did they come?' I asked.

For a moment it was as if she didn't know what I was talking about, but then the fear rose in her face again and the fingers dug into the skin of my arm with a force that made me wince.

'When did they come?'

She spoke so softly I could barely hear the words. 'Early. This morning early. I didn't know they were in the house and then, suddenly, they were standing in front of me.'

'Two of them?'

The head nodded as slowly as before, but in a different direction.

'A large black guy and a little thin one with a white stripe through his h . . .'

She wrenched her hand away from my grip and hurled herself down on to the pillow. She clung to it as though it was her own life she was hanging on to. I could see how wet her hair was now; in places it was starting to get stuck to her scalp in matted clumps. I went back over to the window and opened it as wide as I could. I didn't seem to matter if the rain came in.

Once again she hadn't moved; once again she went tight when I touched her; once again I managed to get her sitting up and went through the routine with the brandy.

Dr Laurence would arrive soon. I held her by the shoulders and got her to look at me.

'What did they want to know?'

She still wasn't going to say anything. Her eyes were becoming glazed over. I put the remains of the brandy that was in the glass to her lips and tried to get it down her. Most of it ran down her chin on to her neck and then her blouse. I put down the glass and sighed. Then I slapped her twice across the face. Once in each direction. Not hard, but hard enough.

'What did they want to know?'

'Where . . . where James was.'

'And did you tell them?'

'How could I?' She looked at me in astonishment. 'I don't know.'

I let her slump backwards on to the pillows and took hold of her hand. It should have been hot but it wasn't. It was as cold as alabaster.

She began talking in a voice that seemed to be coming from somebody other than her own. It was as though she was no longer there herself. Just the white body on the wide, white bed.

'The thin one, he didn't believe me. He told me that if I didn't tell him where James was he would kill me. Not quickly. He said it would take a long time. He said that by the time it was over I would be praying to die.

'They made me take off my clothes and sit on a chair. They did . . . they did things to my body. I kept trying to get them to believe me but the thin one only laughed. Then he took out a knife. He said that he was going to cut little pieces off me until I talked. I think I must have fainted because the big one threw water in my face and then started questioning me.

'It went on for a long time. It seemed a long time. All the while the thin man was getting more and more excited. He . . . he did horrible things with his eye. He took . . . took . . .'

I poured some more brandy in the glass and handed it to her. She sipped at it and coughed.

'When I still wouldn't tell them what they wanted to know I thought that he was going to kill me. The one with the knife. I'm sure he would have only . . . only the other one pulled him away. They argued. I thought they might fight between themselves. Finally the man put the knife away and they went out of the room. I stayed where I was, waiting to . . . then the door opened and he came back into the room. The one with the funny eye. He took out the knife again and held it in front of my face. He said that he was going to come back and kill me. He was going to . . . to . . . to carve me up. That was what he said, carve me . . .'

She stopped again and I knew that it was enough. For her and for me. They had got rid of Botterill and had been getting ready to get rid of Murdoch and now he'd disappeared from sight. I didn't know for sure what their motives were but there wasn't any doubting their methods. They would get to Murdoch if it meant tracking down anyone who had had contact with him and might be expected to know where he was. And the more frustrated they became in their search, the nastier they were going to get.

In the heaviness of the room there was only the sound of Caroline sobbing. Then from below I heard the bell. I went to the top of the stairs and saw Dr Laurence along with a young woman wearing a white blouse and a pair of blue denim jeans. The doctor was holding a brown leather bag and the girl was carrying a dark blue suitcase. I waited for them to come up.

The doctor went right in and started to examine Caroline, with the nurse helping him to undress her. I watched for a while, but I couldn't take too much of it. Why should I? I didn't have to.

I pinched the brandy bottle and went downstairs and waited until they were through. It seemed to take a long while. There wasn't much brandy left in the bottle by the time they both came into the room.

'Where's the coffee?' he asked.

I went off to find the kitchen and see. Ten minutes later we were sitting down and drinking coffee as if nothing had happened and there wasn't a sick, frightened woman lying in the bed upstairs.

'She'll pull through all right,' Laurence said, 'and surprisingly quickly on the surface. What it might do to her underneath, what the long term effects might be I wouldn't like to hazard a guess. I'll get Sandy here to stay over night and probably Sunday as well. I'll drop by in the morning to see how she's getting on.'

I gathered that the fair-haired girl who looked all of four days older than eighteen was Sandy. She also looked as though she knew what she was doing. I tried a quick smile out on her but she didn't seem impressed. When it came to nurses, perhaps I should stick to fifty-year-olds. Or break a leg fast.

Sandy finished her coffee and went upstairs to sit with her patient. Laurence looked levelly at me. 'There's no chance of them coming back? Whoever it was that did this?'

'No. I don't think so. They'll have moved on somewhere else by now. She couldn't tell them anything they wanted to know.'

Dr Laurence stood up. 'Poor lass. It would have been better for her if she could have done.'

I nodded and shook his hand. There wasn't anything else I could do there. I went out and walked over towards my car. The rain had stopped but the sky was still overcast and it looked as if it might start again at any moment.

I got into the car and sat behind the wheel, trying to sort out the ideas that were taking off inside my mind. Not that I thought it would do much good. There probably wasn't a lot of point in trying to work out logical explanations.

Life didn't work according to any logic that I knew. If it did, philosophers wouldn't still be arguing about things they'd been chewing over since the Greeks and all private investigators would be like Sherlock Holmes.

Only Holmes wasn't a real detective, whatever they get up to in Baker Street. He wasn't real but I was and I didn't need to pinch myself to make sure. So he could carry on using logic and scientific deduction and I'd muddle on the way I always did.

If I kept walking down enough dark streets and through enough doorways, something was sure to happen. One time it would be the wrong street or the wrong door and that would be the end. But that hadn't happened yet.

I switched on the engine and slipped the motor into gear.

−9−

I only knew of one other person who might know of the where-abouts of James P. Murdoch. I knew of her and Tabor's boys knew of her, too. They knew about her because when I was watching her, they were watching him. Which was the point where our lines became crossed and our interests began to get entangled.

One more case of adultery and suddenly, before you could say the word orgasm, never mind experience one, there was Mitchell up to his arse in murder and near-murder, in all the niceties of crooked business and high finance.

But, as the man said when he was preparing to push the sword down his throat for the third time that day, it's a way of making a living.

Not only living.

I sat at the red light, starting to feel impatient and tapping with my fingers against the top of the dashboard. Not that I really thought minutes were going to matter. Not for me. And not for Marcia Pol-lard. They had either visited her or they hadn't: she was either playing the part of a rather bored but statuesque widow or she wasn't.

I moved away to the news over the car radio that the weather prospects should allow play to be resumed in the Test on Monday. Well, good, a little reassurance was all I was looking for.

No Rover in the drive and the open garage door showed that it wasn't there either. The police would be hanging on to it until the inquest. I got out of my car and stood for a few moments in the drive, listening. I don't know what I was listening for, but it seemed important that I do it anyway.

It's times like that which enable me to live with the illusion that I am, in fact, some kind of detective.

Not that I detected much of apparent significance: the people on the right were either out or asleep; on the left someone—and it could be Marcia's neighbour—was listening to pop music on the radio and occasionally singing along; behind me the sounds of hammering—improbably a father and son building what looked, when I turned, to be a sledge.

And from the Pollard house?

Silence. Not the heavy brooding silence that had greeted me earlier at the Murdoch place. This was lighter, almost inviting. Asking me to fill it with sound, with activity.

The bell push was diamond shaped and dull orange in colour. I touched my thumb and forefinger to the woodwork and moved the next finger over the diamond. The bell wasn't going to be necessary: the door swung open several inches under my touch.

I felt as if someone was tapping me on the shoulder. Of course, they weren't, but if they had been I know what they would have said. They would have told me to turn around and go away. To get the hell out of there before I put my big feet in another mess it was getting increasingly difficult to extricate myself from. Turn round and get into your car and drive away. Don't make a fuss; don't cause the couple with the wood and nails to notice you. There's something about men with wood and nails that's always disconcerting.

I shrugged the imaginary hand off my shoulder. Marcia Pollard could leave the door open as force of habit. She could have slipped out for a loan of some sugar from the neighbour with the radio—even a little cuddle for consolation.

Hell! I wasn't going back to the car, and standing there like a novice encyclopaedia salesman wasn't going to get me anywhere.

I pushed open the door further, feeling the same fears that always shot through me whenever I did that same thing. The fears as to who or what would be waiting on the other side.

A carpeted hall that somehow should have had a fluffy white cat sitting on it, but didn't. Half-way down on the left a small table holding a green trimphone and a dark blue vase out of which stuck a bunch of cornflowers. They were past their best and turning white around the edges. The heads were drooping forwards, their weight causing several of the stems to break. A thin scattering of white lay over the table's surface. The only other thing there was a white note pad for taking telephone messages.

Immediately to the right of the front door were the stairs, which doubled back on themselves at the landing. These were carpeted in the same thick material, but the colour now was dark brown. There was a bright yellow vase on the landing floor. It was made from some acrylic substance. There were no flowers.

Back down the hall and opposite the telephone table there was an open door. I moved forwards so that I could see inside: it was the kitchen. Black and white alternating tiles; fitted cupboards and shelves; a stainless steel double sink. Washing machine. Fridge. Freezer. Mixer. Blender. A pin board with recipes and a postcard from someone who had gone to Portugal.

Alongside the sink there was a door which seemed to lead out into a back passage. On the other side of it something moved. A small movement, small but insistent. I slipped back two bolts, top and bottom, and turned the handle. A grey and white cat ran in, circled my feet twice, put his front paws up to the level of the sink, finally stood beside an empty saucer with traces of cat food still remaining.

I could have taken a tin from one of the cupboards and fed it. I didn't. I hoped it wouldn't be too long before someone else fed it.

At the end of the kitchen there were two wooden doors which made a hatch through into what I guessed would be the dining room. It was. A table in what might have been oak but probably wasn't. Four dining chairs. A metal and wood shelving system with some expensive looking books and enough bottles of booze to make them apply for a liquor licence.

Them. Her. Whoever.

I knew from my previous visit that the other downstairs room was the living room; the one with French windows that led out into the garden.

There was no one there this time. No love. A three-piece suite symmetrically arranged and looking so clean that it might have been delivered from the shop that morning. A fireplace that had never known a fire. A glass-topped table with the usual magazines on it. They hadn't been read; magazines that are arranged that precisely and artistically are never actually read. It only showed that the local Women's Institute gave classes on magazine arranging.

Alongside the fireplace was several hundred pounds of stereo; all carefully assembled for the purpose of playing James Last versions of the classics and 'Bridge Over Troubled Waters.'

I shut the door behind me and stood in the hall once more. Every minute I spent in the house I cared less and less about the people who lived in it—had lived in it. Whichever tense was appropriate.

Everything so ordered and right: a veneer to hide the fact that he was fucked up by her and she was fucked by someone else.

I know that my life isn't anything to write home about when it comes to coping with relationships, but at least I don't hide my failures behind an expensive, wall-to-wall carpeted and centrally heated façade of normal married life.

How the hell did I know? Perhaps that's what married life was. A detached furniture store within easy reach of the shops; an old man who takes an overdose in his last year's Rover and a woman who opens her legs the way most people breathe.

Perhaps that's what's meant by the nuclear family: get two people together, give them a ring to exchange and a vow that says till death us do part, then put a fucking great bomb beneath them.

Well, death had parted the Pollards, sure enough. One down and . . .

It had to be the stairs. After going through doors that were already just that little bit open, the thing I hated most was walking up flights of stairs in houses I didn't know. I did know the kind of things private investigators were liable to find—I'd read the books, I'd seen all those movies. Thank Christ there wasn't a cellar in this place!

The carpet was soft under my feet and it carried on across the space at the top of the stairs. Three doors and one open. Every visit was getting to be like roulette and I didn't feel I could carry on winning.

The open door was the bathroom. I took two steps along the carpet and from there I could see into the mirror that ran down past the frosted glass window. I stopped walking and drew in a little more oxygen. I'd found the right room: won and lost on the first turn of the wheel.

I could see the reflection of the side of the bath. Cold, white, smooth-looking; like the hands that had closed my eyes in my dream. Only no hands were closing my eyes now: least of all Marcia's.

Two things disturbed the clean line of the bath edge. A leg, bent across it at the knee. Higher up, lower in the mirror, an arm and head, the one lolling over the other. The hair was falling away from face and neck. I wished it hadn't been. It might have covered the gash that began immediately below the ear and curved round sharply to a point underneath the jaw. The flesh hung open, like an obscene mouth widened through the shouting of obscene words. A mouth heavily smeared with lipstick. Except that it wasn't lipstick.

The blood had caked and congealed; it ran around the gash in thick corrugations—and around that a sated bluebottle made its noisy way.

As I walked forwards it buzzed loudly as if to show its annoyance and flew up from the opening in the throat; down again to land upon one of her closed eyelids, its colour blending with the dark eye shadow. I raised a hand at it and it moved across the room and proceeded to knock itself silly against the closed window. I wondered where and when it had got into the room. Wondered how long she had been there like that I touched her skin. In the heavy, sticky heat of the room it was cold. Cold and stiffening fast.

I went round and looked at the body from the end of the bath. One leg over the edge, the other jammed up against the tiles at the other side. Her pubic hair was short, as though she was in the habit of keeping it trimmed. Short and tightly curled. Dark. Three spots of blood had fallen on to it and hardened there like paint.

The rest of her lay towards the side of the bath; the position in which her head had fallen dictating the angle at which it lay. Her breasts swung to the same side, the nipple of the left one squashing against the porcelain. The right breast was badly bruised and there was a tight grouping of reddish-purple marks around that nipple, as though she had been bitten. I tried to guess whether in love or in anger but I gave it up. I didn't think it made any difference.

High on her right arm there was a mark which could well have been a burn. The more I looked the more I saw: more bruising above her stomach; a cut along the sole of her right foot; an arrested swelling over the nose.

A solid trail of blood traced its way down the side of the bath and over the tiled floor. But there was very little blood. Not enough blood; not enough for what they had done to have happened in the bathroom. She had been carried there afterwards. Carried and dumped: dead weight.

One more thing: around the ankle of the left leg, tightly around the ankle then dangling towards the floor, a piece of red flex.

I wondered whether she too had known nothing to tell them, known nothing to appease Charlie's anger.

And this time the big West Indian had not been able to hold him back.

The bluebottle was still hammering its fat body against the window. I turned around and pushed the top of the window open. The insect flew up towards the opening, but fell down the pane away from it. It tried again, tried again, fell again, fell again. I clenched my fist and brought the side of it down upon the bluebottle. Not hard; I didn't want to crack the glass.

I felt the thing squash and rubbed my hand a few inches either way. When I lifted the hand away it was speckled with black and tiny spots of blood. I wiped the mess off on a piece of toilet paper and dropped that into the toilet. I flushed the chain and waited until the water had swirled through and the noise had died away. Then I walked out of the bathroom. At the door I turned back and looked once more in the mirror. This time I hardly noticed the gash: all I could see was the length of red flex.

I tried the bedrooms. In one of them the top cover had been thrown carelessly across. I went forwards and pulled it part way back. The bottom sheet was dyed red with Marcia Pollard's blood.

I threw back the cover and went downstairs. I went into the dining room and poured myself a brandy. Then I poured myself another brandy. I didn't bother to make them small ones. The executors were unlikely to measure the amounts left in the various bottles.

I was more careful with my fingers. There was no point in leaving a lot of prints around which would confuse the men from the Yard.

I went back into the kitchen and opened some cupboards. I found a tin of cat food and used the tin opener on the wall. I'd once met a girl and known her for four days. She'd been young and pretty and her breasts had been firm and full underneath the see-through material of her blouse. We'd drunk coffee together and talked about things that had nothing to do with being a private detective. Four days and at no time had I even wanted to touch her. Four days and somewhere in that time she'd shown me how to use a wall-mounted can opener. I'd never used one before.

I remembered her now as I put the cat's food into its saucer. I tried to remember her name and I couldn't. I tried to recall what had happened to the photograph I'd taken of her but I couldn't do that either.

I watched the cat eating and was bothered about the photograph. It bothered me more than the dead body of the woman upstairs in her own bath. But before the cat was half-way finished I stopped worrying: neither of them mattered one goddam scrap.

What did matter was that I was going to call the police. There was no point in sneaking away. If I did that someone would have seen me; would have made a note of the number of my car. Only if I sneaked away. If I stayed there and the cops went around the neighbours asking if they had seen me and when, nobody would have seen me at all.

I picked up the phone and began dialling. I didn't dial the police straight away. There were a couple of other things and if I didn't get them seen to now, my time alone with the telephone might be restricted.

I called Patrick and dragged him away from the sink. Made sure everything was still all right and scared the shit put of him by telling him to keep himself and his family indoors. I was so convincing he said all right and sounded as if he meant it.

Next I called Tom Gilmour and he was out. I tried his home number and he was still out. I swore and tried the Murdoch house. A voice answered the phone which definitely didn't belong to the Chinese houseboy so I guessed that it was Sandy. It was and she said her charge was starting to sit up and take notice and was threatening to teach her to play gin rummy before the day was out. I gave them both my love and put down the phone before they could give it back.

I tried Tom again at home just for luck and he was there. I didn't say too much but I did tell him that I had good reason to believe a friend of mine and his family were in danger of being attacked and that if he could arrange to put a man watching the house he might find someone looking remarkably like Charlie about to do someone some very nasty mischief.

Tom said he would do his best on the condition that I filled him in with the details. I said I would as soon as I could but right now I had another dead body to declare. Then I got the receiver down again fast.

It was one thing I was good at.

Inspector Jones wasn't as easy to find and in the end I had to leave a number and a message that he should ring me about the Pollard case.

I went back into the kitchen and fooled around with a cona coffee-maker for about a quarter of an hour. Finally I got it to work and while I was waiting for it all to drip through I gave the cat some milk. He started purring as though he wanted to adopt me, which in the circumstances wasn't as dumb a move as it might have been. He was going to need somebody to look after him and I thought I had a lot of time for cats. I'd owned cats before. They'd all got run over, one after another, just when I'd got to really like them. So I'd stopped having cats: it wasn't good for them.

I sat on a stool and drank the coffee and for the umpteenth time asked myself why the Mancor crowd had known where Murdoch was on the Thursday and had been happy to do nothing about him, while on the next day they were apparently anxious to put him away. Right now they were so anxious to catch up with him that it was okay if they terrorised one woman and killed another.

I choked on my coffee. Closed my eyes and started to run it over again inside my head. They didn't have to have seen him at the hotel. All they knew was that I was snooping around and showing an interest in him. Which they could have got from the little old lady who ran the place and who was so insistent about Murdoch's initial. Just like I always did I'd left her one of my little cards in case she thought of anything else she wanted to tell me about or in case she ever wanted some business of her own handled.

So Big G could have heard Murdoch might be there, could have missed him, but in checking with the manageress picked up on both Marcia Pollard and me. And look what had happened to Marcia.

I went back to the coffee and tried to pursue the line of thought a little further. It wasn't easy: I didn't have the brain for it. It came as considerable relief when the phone went and it was Inspector Jones at the other end.

'Hello, Inspector, this is Scott Mitchell. You remember me, I'm the guy whose clients kill themselves on his doorstep.'

'All right, Mitchell. I remember you all right. What is it now?'

'Well, I'm going in for a subtle change of line.'

'Stop playing around and get on with it.'

'I'm moving into the family business. I'm thinking about going into it in a big way with a firm of tombstone-makers—cheaper to have all the names on the one stone.'

'What the hell are you on about? Have you been drinking?'

'You bet I have. I've had two very large brandies and one cup of coffee. It's not everyday you call round to console a new widow and find she's taken her mourning a little too seriously.'

'Where are you?'

'Didn't you recognise the number? I'm at the Pollard house and Marcia Pollard is upstairs taking a bath with no water and a five-inch hole in her throat.'

He swore and slammed down the phone and I went across the hall into the kitchen and poured myself another cup of coffee.

-10-

Sunday morning. Only it wasn't looking peaceful or lazy or any of the other things that Sundays are supposed to be like. From where I was sitting it wasn't looking anything. All I could see were four walls, a scratched wooden table and two chairs, a metal ashtray that was full to overflowing with butts and ash, a dark green filing cabinet that didn't look as if it was used any more.

Police interrogation rooms were no respecters of days: they looked the same seven days a week, twenty-four hours a day. The same sounds came out of them if you were walking by. The same monotonous drone of voices; one voice punctuated by long silences; a voice raised in anger; other sounds—dull, thudding sounds, high-pitched, sharp sounds. The door would swing open and a man would storm out, slamming the door so hard behind him that it vibrated inside the frame. Ten minutes later he would have washed his hands, wiping his sweating face, had a couple of cigarettes and maybe some bitter coffee or a quick pull at the bottle he kept in his desk. Then he would yank the door open just as hard and shut it just as hard. Back in the room with the fresh conviction that he was going to make the lying bastard talk this time.

The next time he came out, another man would take his place. Taller, heavier, the expression in his eyes leaden, shirt sleeves rolled up high around the muscles of the upper arm.

After that they would take it in turns, never working together. One building up the confidence of the man at the other side of the table, the other knocking it down hard. Let him have a cigarette and a cup of tea and let him know that really you're on his side. Take out a single strong-smelling Galoise and enjoy it, blowing the smoke full in his face with a sneer, then refuse to let him go outside to the stinking gents.

Teamwork.

Jones had begun by himself and after several hours he'd brought in my friend Tom Gilmour. Except that he wasn't behaving much like a friend. Not any more. He thought I'd been holding out on him and, of course, I had. Jones thought I'd been holding out on him and I had been doing that as well.

Sunday morning early when you've spent the night in the alternating company of two cops who didn't like you wasn't at all the way Sundays were meant to be.

Not that I had anyone but myself to blame. Like they said, I'd withhold vital evidence. I had denied that the other case. I was on had had any connection with the Pollard case. I'd even started off by trying to deny it again.

Said that I went over to Marcia Pollard's to find out if she was okay. I'd been feeling sympathetic all of a sudden. For a time they bought it. It was one great stinking coincidence and they didn't like that but right then they didn't have any reason not to believe my story.

It still looked too fishy. Too odd that I should be around at the right time to find both of them dead. It wasn't a coincidence that either man liked.

But after several hours it seemed that they were getting prepared to live with it. Then Tom Gilmour came in with a particularly nasty look on his face and an envelope in his right hand.

He sat down on the chair so hard that I thought the legs must give way. He held the envelope out in front of my face for several moments as thought it was meant to mean something to me. It didn't. After all, it was only a plain brown envelope. Nothing written on it and I couldn't see what was inside it. There had to be millions of envelopes like that so why should I get excited about it?

Why was Gilmour excited about it?

I was going to find out. He dropped it down on to the surface of the table and a cloud of ash lifted up into the heavy air. By the time it had settled again I thought I might have reason to know that particular envelope.

I prayed I wasn't right and if I was I didn't like the fact that Gilmour had got hold of it. I didn't like how he must have got hold of it.

Only I wasn't in a position to plead ethics.

'Well?' he shouted in my face.

I tried staring back at him but it didn't do me any good. He simply yelled the same question again and this time when I just carried on looking at him he hit me.

I'd seen Tom Gilmour hit people before; he'd taken a poke at me more than twice. He seemed to be putting something special into this. Possibly he'd been getting in a lot of practice.

His open hand had caught me at the side of the face, between the cheekbone and the chin. I gulped in some of the heavy air and then wished that I hadn't. I moved my head back round to the front and looked at him some more. Then I looked down at the envelope. I wanted to rub my face but I wasn't going to let him have that satisfaction.

Not yet.

One of his fingers tapped down on the still unopened envelope. 'Well?'

The voice was quieter this time. The blow that followed it was harder. The fist was closed instead of open. I toppled backwards far enough for the chair to go over with a sudden cracking sound. My hands went out to break my fall and I found myself on all fours, staring at a piece of broken chair leg and a pair of shoes. Black shoes. Gilmour's shoes. Dark grey trousers. Two clenched fists. A face I didn't want to look at.

'Get up!'

I got up. I still didn't want to look at his face. But there wasn't anywhere else to look. I didn't like what I saw. Nor did he. He stared at me as though I was already dead, then wheeled around and went back to the other side of the desk.

'Get him a chair,' he snapped to the uniformed man who was still standing against the back wall.

The cop left the room and Gilmour started to come back around to my side of the desk. He kept coming until he was standing less than a foot away from me. I looked at his eyes and could read nothing in them. I knew that behind one of my own eyes a nerve was twitching away like some berserk metronome.

I was still trying to read something in those eyes when his right arm went back then forwards. My mouth opened as the fist rammed into the pit of my stomach. My right hand went forwards and grabbed at his shoulder. It was either that or fall down.

He looked at my hand as though someone had thrown up all over his best suit. He took half a pace backwards, knocked the arm up into the air with his left and punched me again with his right in the same place as before.

I did it: I fell down.

I don't know at what point the uniformed cop came back into the room but he must have done because when I next looked round there was a different chair standing behind me. Gilmour was back in his seat and the other guy was back in his place by the wall doing a pretty useful impression of all the three wise monkeys rolled into one.

I got up slowly and eased myself on to the chair. I pulled myself round to the table and rested my arms against it. The envelope was still there; still unopened.

'Open it!'

I wasn't going to argue any more. By now there was only one thing that could be in it. One set of things. My ringers fumbled with the flap and I was right: the pictures of Murdoch and Marcia Pollard at the hotel by the river. The ones showing Murdoch's face. Three days ago. A lot had happened in those three days. At least two people had died. There'd been some very nasty business with knives and a hell of a lot of lying. There was always a lot of lying.

'You know who that is with the Pollard woman?'

'James P. Murdoch. Missing as from the time those pictures were taken at lunchtime Thursday.'

He looked at me in amazement. 'You just said it. You said it, you dumb motherfucker! Two simple fucking sentences that you could have said as easily when you were talking to Jones on Friday. Of all the stupid, blind, thoughtless . . .'

He looked up at the grey ceiling and then past me at the wall. Then he stood up and picked up the photos.

'You took these out of the envelope you gave to Pollard. When and why?'

I blinked and cursed the nerve behind my eye which had started up again. 'When is easy. After I found his body and before the cops got there. Why is more difficult.'

'With you it always is,' Gilmour interrupted.

I shrugged my shoulders and carried on. 'I knew that Murdoch was important and that it wasn't only his wife who wanted to find him. I told you I'd had a visit from Charlie and Big G. They were interested in Murdoch, too. Somehow I figured that if I could keep the connection between Marcia Pollard and Murdoch clear from your boys that might make it easier for me to operate. I might be able to trace the line from her to Murdoch sooner. As it was . . .'

He came round the table again. 'As it was you left the lines clear between those hoods and the Pollard woman too. If we'd known about it we could have picked her up for her own safety or put a guard on the place. Which would have meant she would be alive now.'

'That's not necessarily so. It's possible and nothing more, you know that as well as I do.'

'Possible, as far as Marcia Pollard's concerned, is at least something. Since yesterday morning, possibilities are the one thing she hasn't got.'

He stood over me and I closed my eyes and waited to get slugged again or for him to walk away. He walked away: as far as the door.

'Mitchell! I've gone out to bat for you time after fucking time. You use me like paper to wipe your arse on and you keep on doing it and think it's all right. Well, I'm telling you this. It's not going to happen again. Not ever.'

The door opened and then slammed behind him.

I looked at the guy in uniform. He looked back at me and still he didn't alter his expression one inch.

I studied the photographs that Gilmour had left on the table. Looked hard at the man's face, her face, the man's face again. Maybe I should have looked at them before. Maybe before would have been too early.

There was a shot of her looking up into his eyes. He was looking away, not noticing her at all: It was her expression that kept me returning to it. It was nothing like the way she had looked at any of the others. What could you call it? Admiration? Pride? Excitement? Maybe even love?

And in his face there were other things: determination, strength, the will to win—more than that, the knowledge that to win was his right.

He was not noticing her at all; looking out in front, forwards, looking into a future in which he felt perfectly safe and secure.

The door opened and I dropped the photo down on to the desk. Jones came towards me with a half-smile on his face.

'Interesting, aren't they?'

I nodded. They were interesting all right. But that wasn't what he was feeling so happy about.

'I've been talking to a man called Allen. Don Allen. Name mean anything to you?'

It did. He was the chief accountant for the Mancor group. He had been at the time of the Fraud Squad enquiry.

'Yes,' I said, 'it means something.'

'He's down the corridor singing like a bird. He's coughing the lot. The dirty side of Mancor's business. Murdoch's involvement.

The bribing of the Fraud Squad men. There's enough there for half a dozen trials, never mind one. We've already picked up Thomas and that bloody great West Indian. Tabor's made a run for it but he's not going to get very far.'

'And Charlie?' I asked.

He sat back on the chair and crossed his legs. 'Not yet.'

I started talking. I told them all about the visit the two heavies had made to my office and about the red flex. I gave them everything else they wanted to know. Everything that was definite.

'And Murdoch?' I asked later. 'You haven't picked up a trace of him?'

'One or two strong leads, you know. We'll get our hands on him soon. We've got questions to ask him. A lot of questions.'

I nodded and walked towards the door. My statement had been typed up and signed. There was nothing else for me to do. If they tried a charge of withholding evidence they'd either have to admit they got the photos by breaking into my flat without a warrant or prepare to commit perjury on a pretty bare-faced scale.

As I was opening the door Tom Gilmour walked through, heading the other way. He looked at me but he didn't see me, just pushed past and on into the station. I stepped out onto the pavement and let the door swing shut behind my back.

I looked up and down the street: it was still Sunday.

-11-

I was sitting with nothing on but a pair of shorts. I was hot and tired. Very tired. The cops had kept me awake and talking for the best part of a night and a day. My stomach had a couple of bruises that looked like a Mark Rothko original and the split alongside my lower lip reopened every time I used my mouth.

The temperature had climbed into the nineties. London wasn't used to it. Everything happened in slow motion and what I'd bothered to watch of the Test on TV was the slowest of all.

I'd slept for a long time. The windows had been open and the covers had been on the floor. Anything that faintly resembled a clock had been turned around to face the wall. I just hadn't wanted to know.

Now I had nothing better to do than wait until the jug of coffee I'd made and put in the fridge was cold enough to be drunk as iced. I didn't care how long it took. From where I was sitting there didn't seem to be any place to go or anything to do.

I'd already made a couple of phone calls. Patrick said that the neighbours had started asking why there was a police car driving past every half an hour and what did he know about the young man in cavalry twill trousers and a blue open-neck shirt who kept taking slow walks round the block. Apparently, Frances had really got annoyed when she heard that they needed protection and had told him that if I came to the house again, she was leaving inside the same minute.

Okay, I could understand her annoyance but it was better to complain about being protected than not.

Sandy sounded wide awake and pretty. She said that Caroline Murdoch was looking much better and that she was wanting to drive down to the shops later in the day. I asked if there'd been any phone calls to speak of. She told me that she didn't see how that could be my business but anyway there hadn't been anything special as far as she knew.

She did tell me that there had been some police hanging around from time to time and that one of them had stopped Dr Laurence on his way in and asked him who he was and what he was going to the house for.

No, she didn't think they were there all the time. Just at fairly frequent intervals.

She asked me if I wanted to speak to Mrs Murdoch. Said that she thought she was strong enough. I told her that her patient might be feeling strong enough, but I certainly wasn't.

I got up and switched on the set. It wasn't cricket any longer but tennis. I waited long enough to be told that the temperature on the centre court was nearing the hundred. Then I turned it off. I didn't think I could look at all that energy being expended. Not even for the sake of a glimpse of Chris Evert's frilly knickers.

I walked out to the kitchen and checked the coffee. It would be a long wait yet. I contented myself with a glass of milk; lay down on the settee and shut my eyes. I thought that with a little effort I could get to sleep again.

I did: and it turned out not to be any effort at all.

When I woke up the heat had faded a little and I guessed that it was evening. I spent about quarter of an hour scraping my skin off the surface of the settee and made it out to the kitchen once more. By now the coffee was good and ready for me and I was good and ready for it.

That's what they call compatibility.

Don't knock it. There isn't much of it around.

I divided the remainder of the evening between not answering a batch of letters I'd been successfully not answering for quite a while now, not reading a book and not getting too drunk. When I was drunk just the right amount I went to bed.

And slept.

The telephone woke me. At first it seemed to be ringing in some far away country to which I was only an occasional visitor. Then it became clearer, louder: it was ringing in the next room.

I slid off the bed and pulled on a pair of briefs. You never knew who it was going to be.

I was glad I had. It was Caroline Murdoch. She still didn't sound the way she had the first time we had spoken, but a lot of the backbone had returned, a lot of the coolness along with it.

Her husband had phoned her and given her an address to take his passport and money to. Only she wanted me to take it. For one thing she was too frightened and for another the police were likely to follow her. I didn't say that they might be likely to follow me as well.

Apart from anything else, it probably wouldn't have been true. If they wanted to get to Murdoch I was the last person they were going to waste their time following. I was the guy who'd been paid to find him.

The meeting was arranged for that evening. He was going to phone again an hour before time and let her know the exact place, but it would probably be somewhere in central London.

I said that was okay and asked her if she wanted me to come over beforehand. She said that it was better if I didn't and while I was still trying to figure out how to take that, she hung up.

It was a long day. I made a trip in to the office and tore up a few circulars that some optimist had pushed through the letter box. I sat there and waited for someone to use the phone or walk through the door with a job that was going to send me for a month to Corfu. If you were going to have all that heat then you might as well have the scenery to go with it.

No one came. I might as well have had the first private investigator's office on the moon.

I shut the door in disgust and went down to the coffee shop. Tricia was back and she was serving iced coffee that managed to taste better than mine and didn't come with a three-hour wait. I stood there like an idiot and smiled at her until she asked me if I was all right.

She sounded as though she thought that the heat might have been getting at me, what with my advancing age and everything.

I told her I was fine and that it was just nice to see her back again after her day off. She still looked at me as if I wasn't quite right in the head, so I paid for the drink and took it over into the corner where I could sit and look at her in comparative safety.

What the hell! I didn't think they could lock you up for it. Not yet anyhow, though someone, somewhere was probably working on it.

Three iced coffees later I went back to the office, wasted some more time, then drove back home. The car radio filled me in on what wasn't happening in the Test. It sounded as though both sides had blown it. I thought to myself that didn't make it a blow job, it just made it a wank.

Christ! Tricia was right. The sun was affecting me.

I headed north as fast as I could.

The phone was ringing when I walked across the space between the car and the front door. It was still ringing when I got to it. I picked it up and heard Dr Laurence's voice.

'I thought you might like to know that your patient has dispensed with our services.'

'Since when?'

'Since lunchtime today. She told Sandy, who phoned me. I drove out there and tried to reason with her, but she was firm. Polite, a trifle cold, but firm. There was nothing we could do but leave.'

'Do you think she needs to be under care still?'

'It's difficult to say. She should be. She was evidencing strong symptoms of shock three days ago. Today she seemed to be pretty well back in control.'

'Do you think the shock reaction was a true one?'

'Certainly. Even a professional actress couldn't fake that much for that long. Maybe she really is all right, but it seemed to me that there was something she wasn't going to talk about that was driving her on. I wouldn't be surprised if when that drive is satisfied, she has a bad relapse.'

'Okay, doc. Thanks anyway. And say thank you to Sandy for me.'

He grunted and said goodbye.

I sat down and tried to think. I wasn't sure whether I should ring Caroline Murdoch now or whether I should wait for her to call me as arranged. I considered phoning the police. As far as they were concerned I was a loser who only needed to lose once more for them to cash in my licence for Green Shield stamps and put me out of business for a long time.

Then it would be either working for some security firm taking bank money around dressed up like a superannuated Hell's Angel or standing guard in gallery thirteen at the Tate.

I got as far as half-way through the number before one of the bruises on my stomach had a little word with me. I put the phone back down and decided to wait for Caroline.

She took her time. It was well into the evening and a slight breeze had come up and was moving the curtains away from the windows for seconds at a time. I was back in my shorts and trying to work out why South had replied three Spades. For the life of me, I couldn't see it. Even when the guy in the book told me why, I still couldn't see it. That was the trouble with those intellectual games. Maybe I should stick to the more basic sports like all-in wrestling.

I'd just thrown the book across the room in a vain attempt to knock some sense into it when the phone went again. It was her.

'Scott?'

'Yes.'

'James phoned. I've got the address.'

'Okay. What is it?'

'You'll have to come to the house.'

'Why?'

'Scott, what's the matter? You've got to come here to collect the things you're to deliver, after all.'

'And you won't tell me because you don't trust me to keep it to myself. Maybe you think I'd hand the information over to the cops or whoever else might be interested and leave it at that.'

Her voice was softer, as though she was coaxing a child. Or a husband. 'Now, Scott, did I say that? Of course I trust you. Please come.'

'All right. And listen, why did you get rid of the nurse?'

'Because I'm feeling fine.'

'So you say. Look, are there any police around watching the house?'

'I don't think so. I haven't seen anyone for a long time.'

'I'll be there as soon as I can.'

'Good, Scott. I shall be waiting for you.'

She was waiting right enough. She was wearing the same outfit as she had on the first time I saw her. Her hair looked its beautiful self and her face was as flawless as before. There was nothing to show that she had recently been threatened to the point of her life or that her husband was hiding both from the police and from a one-eyed lunatic who wanted nothing more than to kill him.

Nothing except for the packet she handed to me with a passport and a large sum of money neatly tied up inside it. She told me where to take it. It was a flat in Frith Street, on the first floor above a restaurant.

I took the package from her and looked for something in her eyes. Whatever it was, I didn't find it. She kept hold of my hand and her fingers were as cold as ever, despite the heat. She murmured thank you and leaned up her head and kissed me quickly on the side of the face.

'When it's over,' she said, 'will you come back here?'

'I'll see,' I said.

'But you will let me know if it went off all right?'

'I'll do that.'

I went to the front door and hesitated a moment. She wasn't going to wish me good luck or tell me to take care either. I went on out.

I had to park the car on the south side of Piccadilly and walk the rest of the way. I had the packet in my left hand and all the while I was conscious of the absence of weight in my right hand pocket. I hadn't seen my Smith and Wesson .38 since Charlie had been scratching himself with it back in my office. And that seemed a hell of a long time ago.

I walked along a fairly roundabout route, checking out whether I was being followed or not. I couldn't spot anyone so I made it into Frith Street.

The restaurant was the usual kind of Italian job; chianti bottles arranged in a cute pattern so that they hung from the ceiling at just the right height to sock you on the head at least half a dozen times before you found your table. On one wall there was a fishing net that they used to throw over customers who tried to get out without paying their bills.

The waiters tended to burst into song between tables and were experienced at avoiding your eye when you wanted an extra cup of coffee.

I checked it out from the other side of the street a couple of times, before going over to take a closer look. I made a big show of going through the menu, all the time running my eye over the customers. There weren't that many of them and none of them looked like hoods or plain-clothes cops.

I went back across the road and stood a while outside a dirty book shop looking at the first floor above the restaurant through reflections of things like 'Flasher', 'Mother and Daughter', and 'Schoolgirl Frolics'.

There were two windows, small squared glass and tatty lace curtains pulled half-way across. The windows were shut and it had to be as hot as all hell in there. Especially with the trattoria downstairs. There was a doorway between the restaurant and the place next door, which was a strip club with a bright red sign above the door flashing 'Sexy Show.'

The door itself was a scuffed and dirty green and was two-thirds open. Alongside were three bell-pushes; I bet none of them worked.

I kept looking at the doorway, the stairs. It was the way Caroline had said her husband had said I should go in.

I guessed there was another way up through the restaurant. I thought I'd try that.

I went in and sat for a few minutes at one of the tables, playing with the menu, conscious of the packet on the table beside me. Then I looked round and found what I was looking for—a sign that said 'Toilets.' I got up slowly and headed towards the bead curtain towards the back. I grinned at the nearest waiter and pointed at the sign, then parted the curtains.

The toilets were side by side on the first landing. I gave them a quick glance and went on up. The dirty lino that had been on the first section of stairs disappeared and I was walking on bare boards. I went carefully, hoping they wouldn't creak too much, yet knowing that to be too slow was as little use.

What was I worried about anyway? All I was doing was delivering this nice rich guy a passport and some cash that would ensure that he could stay nice and rich.

Mitchell the delivery boy.

The door at the top of the flight of stairs was shut. I stood beside it and listened. Nothing. If Murdoch was in there he was being very patient, very still. I drew a breath and did what every good delivery boy should do. I knocked. Once.

Knocked and waited. Still nothing. I had a quick look back down the stairs. At the landing they divided, the main flight carrying on down to the street, the other turning right down to the restaurant.

There was no sign of anyone about to come up. I turned the brass handle on the door and it moved with my hand. The door eased open. I let go and allowed it to swing. I could see a single bed with a gaudy red and gold cover draped across it, an easy chair with frayed upholstery, a wooden table marked with cigarette burns. I put my hand on the door and pushed it right back as far as the hinges would take it. They took it back to the wall. There was nothing to prevent it. No one.

I went in fast and pulled the door to behind me. I put the packet down on the table and looked round the room. There was little to add to my first impression. A further door led off from the back of the first room. I went through that one with all of the precautions I had used the first time. The result was the same. More drab, over-used furniture, and no Murdoch. Nobody at all. Two empty rooms.

I searched for a sign that someone had been there recently but there wasn't any. Just the emptiness and the heat.

If James P. Murdoch had ever been here it hadn't been for very long and it hadn't been very recently. Which meant . . . ? Which meant . . . ?

I remembered the look of assured determination on his face in the photograph. Remembered Marcia looking up at him adoringly. Remembered the touch of Caroline's fingers as she handed me the packet that lay on the table.

Remembered all those things and came close to realising how stupid I had been. Only close. I'd probably never realise it all.

I picked up the packet and walked out of the flat. I was three paces from the landing when one of the toilet doors sprang open and the hot evening air was filled with that high animal laugh. The laugh of an animal on the hunt; one that has cornered its prey.

I stared at Charlie's face, the one eye that flickered haphazardly, the other which glared glassily back at me. I stared too long. His right hand streaked towards my body and the block I dropped on it was purely, instinctive. It knocked the knife down, but not away. I felt the blade dig into the top of my thigh, before his arm pulled it away.

I wasn't about to let him get a second try. My left hand opened towards where the knife was waiting, my arm half stretched outwards. At the same time I threw a punch with my right that he tried to avoid but it still caught him close to the edge of his chin. He stumbled back against the open door and I saw the knife hand dip.

That was enough. Both hands dived towards it, gripping the wrist and twisting hard. He moved back into me and rammed his knee up into my groin. It made my eyes shut for a couple of seconds and when they opened again they were watering. But I still had tight hold of his right arm.

He tried to bring his knee up into me again but I blocked it with my own, then lifted the arm high and hammered it against the wall. I got my fingers out of the way as much as I could, but even then it hurt like hell. It must have hurt him more. Especially when I did it a second time, then a third.

He wasn't laughing now. I looked at his face and the one good eye was working overtime and there was a gurgle of foam around the edges of his mouth. He was making a noise all right, but it wasn't one I'd heard before. It was a cross between a growl and a hissing of breath and it was a sound no human should make.

I did it to his arm a fourth time. The strange noise became a scream and the fingers opened. I watched the knife fall to the floor and kicked it away.

There was a moment's stillness when we both listened to it bouncing down the steps.

He launched himself at me, the white streak of hair jutting hard into my face. I fell back on to the stairs and sensed his fingers going for my throat. I pulled them away and his head came up in front of mine. I butted it. Hard. There was a sharp splintering sound and he staggered backwards both hands now to his own face trying to stop the flow of blood. I lay back and swung both feet upwards, levering myself against the stair edge.

His body went several inches off the floor as my feet struck home between his legs. He smashed back against the still open toilet door, flattening it against the wall. I pushed myself up and dived at him head first. The impact sent him along the landing and down on to the flight of stairs that led to the street.

Hands reached out for the bannister rail that ran down at one side. Hands found it. His hand. My hands. His face looking up at me again. His nose a mass of split skin and gristle, pumping blood. His eye looked at me unbelievingly. Charlie's face. I didn't like it. Didn't want to see it again. Ever.

I kicked out with my right foot and the toecap snapped his head back hard. Arms flailed wildly, even as he fell. There was nothing for him to hold on to. Not any more. And he wasn't about to fly. Not Charlie.

I stood there for several minutes leaning against the wall, recovering my breath. Voices behind me made me turn around. Four Italian waiters were gazing down in disbelief. I pushed my way back through them and picked up the packet I had been entrusted with. Then I walked down to where Charlie's body was jammed across the bottom of the stairs. He could have been trying to stand on his head . . . and had not quite made it.

Something glittered up at me from the pavement. Charlie's glass eye stared back up at me blindly; the neon lights from the strip club reflected in it, flashing off and on, off and on incessantly. I stepped over Charlie's body and brought my foot down on the eye, enjoying the crunching feeling beneath my foot.

Good night, Charlie!

Back at the Murdoch place everything seemed pretty much back to normal. I rang the doorbell and the little Chinese answered the door. He was in as talkative a mood as usual. He nodded towards the stairs this time, then made his normal graceless exit.

So what could I do? I climbed up the stairs and what do you know? She was in the bedroom. The white satin cover was in use again only this time she didn't look as though anything in the whole wide world would ever shock her again.

'Scott,' she said with a sort of husky eagerness, 'did you give James the . . .'

I pulled the packet from behind my back and tossed it on to the bed. I thought it would be a shame not to let her go through her piece. I watched it with more than a little admiration. She was good. She was very good. On another night she could have convinced me that she was as surprised as she was making out. But this wasn't another night.

I stood there unmoved and unmoving and eventually even Caroline Murdoch realised that it wasn't working. She stopped talking and let the cover fall a few more inches down her body. This time she certainly wasn't dressed underneath it.

'Scott,' she said, in a way that meant everything and nothing.

I looked at that perfect face and then I talked to it as though it wasn't there. 'All right, Caroline, I don't pretend to understand everything. But one thing I do know. Your husband was never going to be at that place tonight. It was part of a pretence that was probably going to end with a statement about his disappearance and the supposition that he'd been killed. He wasn't going to be there because he hasn't been in this country since Thursday, after he said his goodbyes to Marcia Pollard. He's abroad somewhere under an assumed name and with a fake passport. I reckon he's also got enough with him to put all the Mancor people down for a long time if necessary.

'I haven't any good ideas why he did it, but if Everyman Insurance goes bust in a month or so I won't be surprised in the least. I do know that both you and Marcia knew where he was yet you allowed your lives to be put at risk rather than tell a lunatic with a knife. I don't know why you did that and I don't want to so don't waste your breath telling me.'

She looked up at me as though I'd been reading her the weather report.

Then she smiled and said, 'Scott, you won't tell your suspicions to anyone else, will you?' She paused and gave a half smile. 'You know how much money there is in there.' Her eyes flicked to the packet at the bottom of the bed. 'You can keep it.' She looked at me and her eyes dilated. 'You can . . .'

The voice disappeared and the white satin cover slipped down further until all of her breasts were exposed. She was very beautiful. I walked over to her and reached down with my hand. I pulled the cover right back and gazed at her totally naked body.

I gazed at it for a long time. I didn't want to forget it. Then I turned around and walked out of the room, shutting the door firmly behind me.

Outside, I sat in the car and looked back at the house. What was it that made a woman die for a man, a man for a woman? Whatever it was there was one thing I was sure of: I didn't want it.

I put the car into gear and pressed the button on the car radio. A friendly guy with a nice friendly voice told me it was going to be hotter than ever tomorrow. I thanked him and drove on home.

ABOUT THE AUTHOR

John Harvey (b. 1938) is an incredibly prolific British mystery writer. The author of more than one hundred books, as well as poetry and scripts for television and radio, Harvey did not begin writing professionally until 1975. Until then, he was a teacher, educated at Goldsmiths College, London, who taught literature, drama, and film at colleges across England. After cutting his teeth on paperback fiction, Harvey debuted his most famous character, Charlie Resnick, in 1989's *Lonely Hearts*, which the English *Times* called one of the finest crime novels of the century.

A police inspector noted for his love of both sandwiches and jazz, Resnick has starred in eleven novels and one volume of short stories. The BBC has adapted two of the Resnick novels, *Lonely Hearts* and *Rough Treatment* (1990), for television movies. Both starred Academy Award–nominated actor Tom Wilkinson and had screenplays written by Harvey. Besides writing fiction, Harvey spent over twenty years as the head of Slow Dancer Press. He continues to live and write in London.

THE SCOTT MITCHELL MYSTERIES

FROM MYSTERIOUSPRESS.COM
AND OPEN ROAD MEDIA

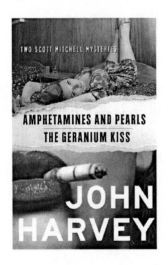

MYSTERIOUSPRESS.COM

OPEN ROAD
INTEGRATED MEDIA

MYSTERIOUSPRESS.COM

Otto Penzler, owner of the Mysterious Bookshop in Manhattan, founded the Mysterious Press in 1975. Penzler quickly became known for his outstanding selection of mystery, crime, and suspense books, both from his imprint and in his store. The imprint was devoted to printing the best books in these genres, using fine paper and top dust-jacket artists, as well as offering many limited, signed editions.

Now the Mysterious Press has gone digital, publishing ebooks through **MysteriousPress.com**.

MysteriousPress.com offers readers essential noir and suspense fiction, hard-boiled crime novels, and the latest thrillers from both debut authors and mystery masters. Discover classics and new voices, all from one legendary source.

FIND OUT MORE AT

WWW.MYSTERIOUSPRESS.COM

FOLLOW US:

@emysteries and Facebook.com/MysteriousPressCom

MysteriousPress.com is one of a select group of publishing partners of Open Road Integrated Media, Inc.

THE MYSTERIOUS BOOKSHOP, founded in 1979, is located in Manhattan's Tribeca neighborhood. It is the oldest and largest mystery-specialty bookstore in America.

The shop stocks the finest selection of new mystery hardcovers, paperbacks, and periodicals. It also features a superb collection of signed modern first editions, rare and collectable works, and Sherlock Holmes titles. The bookshop issues a free monthly newsletter highlighting its book clubs, new releases, events, and recently acquired books.

58 Warren Street
info@mysteriousbookshop.com
(212) 587-1011
Monday through Saturday
11:00 a.m. to 7:00 p.m.

FIND OUT MORE AT:

www.mysteriousbookshop.com

FOLLOW US:

@TheMysterious and Facebook.com/MysteriousBookshop

OPEN ROAD

INTEGRATED MEDIA

Find a full list of our authors and
titles at www.openroadmedia.com

FOLLOW US
@OpenRoadMedia